B

Murder in School

A detective novel

LUCiUS

Kindle edition first published by Lucius 2014
Paperback edition first published by Lucius 2014
For more details and Rights enquiries contact:
Lucius-ebooks@live.com

Cover design by Moira Kay Nicol

EDITOR'S NOTE

This novel, *Murder in School,* is a stand-alone whodunit, the second in the series 'Detective Inspector Skelgill Investigates.'

BY THE SAME AUTHOR

Murder in Adland
Murder in School
Murder on the Edge
Murder on the Lake
Murder by Magic
Murder in the Mind
Murder at the Wake
Murder in the Woods
Murder at the Flood
Murder at Dead Crags
Murder Mystery Weekend
Murder on the Run
Murder at Shake Holes
Murder at the Meet
Murder on the Moor
Murder Unseen
(Above: Detective Inspector Skelgill Investigates)
Murder, Mystery Collection
The Dune
The Sexopaths

1. THE TAJ MAHAL

'Guv, how can you do that? Three *naan* breads in one sitting must be a Cumbrian record.'

Skelgill grins sheepishly. 'I ate four after my last *Bob Graham*. And you did take a chunk.'

'About two square inches, Guv.'

'Got to keep your figure, I suppose.'

DS Jones approximates the area with right-angled fingers and thumbs, and then playfully raises the little rectangular window to her twinkling right eye. She frames Skelgill and says, 'You might be on telly tomorrow morning, Guv.'

Skelgill rocks back in his chair. There's a worrying creak and he jolts forward with a thump that draws anxious glances from fellow diners. In a lowered voice he hisses, 'What? You must be joking. When the Chief can steal the show? I'll be ordered to attention in the background – which I don't need. Let's just remind the local crooks what the plain-clothes cops look like. Smart can go instead and take the credit.'

'But, Guv – it was your case. You cracked it. Why should DI Smart appear at the press conference?'

'He's good-looking, isn't he? Photogenic...'

'He's a slimeball, Guv.'

Skelgill raises an eyebrow, perhaps betraying a hint of approval. DI Smart fancies himself around the station, and always casts a smooth line of patter in the path of DS Jones. Whether out of good nature or political expediency, she appears to bite on these little morsels, much to Skelgill's chagrin.

'You're not jealous of Smart, Guv?'

There's a *bing* from Skelgill's mobile, which lies on the tablecloth between them. He opts for the distraction it provides.

'Sorry – I'll switch it off in a sec.'

Still he checks the message, a frown methodically carving its furrows across his brow as he reads.

'What is it, Guv? Work?'

He reaches for his glass and drains the last few dregs of Indian lager, taking his time to swallow.

DS Jones inserts a prompt. 'Good news or bad news?'

Skelgill can't conceal a momentary flushing across his high cheekbones. After a pause he says, flatly, 'Both, I guess.'

'Well – what's the good news?'

'If you'd call it that. I'm excused from the press conference. The Chief wants me at Oakthwaite first thing.'

'The school?'

'Aye.'

'I remember when I was about fifteen some of the Oakthwaite sixth-formers used to drink in Penrith.'

Skelgill's gaze rests thoughtfully on DS Jones. At twenty-six she's not long out of teenage, at least from his late-thirties perspective; while his own memories of that era are a distant haze of pub-smoke and rock music.

'There's been a suicide.'

'Wow. A boy?'

'Nope. One of the masters.'

'Ah.' DS Jones ponders for a moment. 'That's almost as bad in the publicity stakes. Gruesome?'

'She doesn't say – except that he drowned.' Skelgill sounds a touch exasperated. 'Why the heck does she want me to follow up a suicide? Either it is or it isn't.'

'Her son's a pupil there, you know?'

Skelgill sits upright, more circumspectly now. This piece of news might in part explain his summons. 'I didn't. How come you do?'

'My Aunt Emily – she works there in the personnel department.'

Skelgill looks thoughtful. 'Do they have *them* at schools – personnel departments, I mean?'

'It's private, Guv. They can have anything they like.'

He nods. 'I suppose so. Not my strong suit. When I was a kid we played football, they played rugby. They didn't mix with the local comp.'

'They only compete against the other private boarding schools.'

'You're a mine of information, DS Jones.'

'I could certainly get us an inside track, Guv. There's no great love lost between the ancillary staff and the rest.'

'What do you mean?'

'*Upstairs, Downstairs* kind of thing. The common room is ninety percent Oxbridge, and half the boys are minor royalty or the sons of international billionaires. They've got Mexicans, Russians, Chinese.'

Skelgill grins ruefully. 'Could get interesting on parents' evening. The cartels meet the mafia meet the triads, eh?'

'I don't think it's quite reached those proportions, Guv. The new head's apparently a throwback to the days of the Empire – a stickler for all things pukka. Cold showers and stiff upper lip. You'd better wear a tie, Guv.'

Skelgill seems lost in momentary reverie. 'Sorry?'

'When we go down to the school in the morning – you ought to wear a tie. I take it we're meeting the Head?'

A pained expression takes hold of Skelgill's features, their creases made more sinister by the dim lights and shadowy deep crimson velvet backdrop of the restaurant.

'That's the bad news, Jones.'

'You don't have a tie?' DS Jones sounds unsurprised.

Skelgill licks his lips as if his mouth has suddenly become dry. 'No, it's not that – I'm talking about the Chief's email. DS Leyton's back from leave. Appears he's done the initial groundwork. I'm to meet him at Keswick and go on to the school. You're to report at county HQ for your next assignment.'

2. BASSENTHWAITE LAKE

It is raining steadily as Skelgill rows with deceptive economy in a southerly direction, some thirty yards out from the leafy osiers lining the east bank of Bassenthwaite Lake. At just before six a.m. he's the only soul on the water, though its protected conservation status and secluded character ensure a minimum of human interference at most times of day. The Lake District's only 'lake' (as Skelgill is wont to point out to bemused visitors) lies in quiet contrast to the likes of Windermere and Derwentwater, which on Bank Holidays boil with the flailing oars and over-revved outboards of an unseaworthy fleet of day-trippers.

Skelgill, however, holds the requisite fishing and boat permits: those in authority are content to have him prowling on their behalf, albeit at the hidden price of the odd salmon or sea trout that finds its way into his freezer. Not that Skelgill is a game fisher. His obsession is the pike: a catch-and-return species. He holds the unofficial top weight for the water and is convinced a monster British record not only haunts its depths, but on three occasions has 'snapped him up'; fishing parlance for one that gets away, tackle and all.

Today, however, pike are not the target. Instead a whippy twelve-foot perch rod trails prominently from the stern. This would tell the seasoned Skelgill-watcher that, while he's clad for the occasion in a weather-beaten *Barbour* outfit, he's not fishing seriously – at best he's stalking bait. In fact, the rod is strictly for appearances, and his mission is one of reconnaissance.

His boat slides near-silently across the silvery mere. The faint swish and splash of his oars harmonises with the pervasive sibilance that is the hiss of millions of raindrops entering the water, pitting its surface with an ever-changing yet homogenous tessellation. He rests mid-stroke, pausing to shake off beads of sweat mingled with rain that drip from his eyebrows and nose. The heatwave might have ended, but the relative humidity must be close on a hundred. High above, to his left, Skiddaw's vast grey-green bulk may no longer exist; even its little outrider,

Dodd, is blanketed in mist, signalling to Skelgill that the cloud base is well below fifteen-hundred feet; a thousand, at best. Only the whitewashed *Bishop of Barf*, a pale smudge over on the afforested western flanks, is visible of the customary landmarks. Typical Lakeland summer weather has returned.

Skelgill espies the first neatly painted sign that proclaims, beneath a crest in the shape of an acorn, 'Private Property – Keep Out'. There's smaller lettering beyond the limits of his vision – no doubt it warns, 'Trespassers will be prosecuted'. He stares intensely, as though he objects to the concept: they've effectively abolished private land up in Scotland, and such egalitarian rights of access appeal to his fierce sense of fairness. It's the source of long-running beer-fuelled dispute with one of his gamekeeper pals, though in a more reflective moment Skelgill would be forced to concede there's a flipside in the exclusion of the ignorant excesses that some townsfolk persist in bringing to England's green and pleasant land.

Now he hauls in the oars, glancing shoreward as their hollow dunk against the hull threatens to announce his presence. But there's no one abroad at this hour, never mind in this weather. He straightens out the creases in an ancient stained bush hat and improves his disguise substantially. Without bothering to bait the hook, he deftly flicks out the line from his perch rod, engages the bale arm, and assumes the position of an angler concentrating upon his float. The boat drifts slowly, parallel to the bank, its residual momentum conveniently assisted by the faintest of northerly breezes. The air movement is insufficient, however, to disperse the midges that have been trailing him, and which now move in for a feed. He rummages for repellent in a rusty tin of miscellaneous tackle, but to no avail; he must resign himself to an uncomfortable vigil.

What he can learn, however, is a matter for conjecture. Oakthwaite School stands on a blunt peninsula of gradually rising ground half a mile from Bassenthwaite Lake. Its watery margins are defended by a rocky shoreline bordered by marshy scrub, and are not a place to make landfall. The main edifice is invisible from the lake, being set in heavily wooded parkland;

only the white tips of rugby posts and match-day hoorays give a clue to what goes on within.

3. DS LEYTON

'Alright, Guv? Got one over on DI Smart, I hear.'

'Leyton, your whining Cockney accent's annoying me already.'

'That's great, that is. I come back from Majorca singing your praises and I don't even get a 'How's your holiday?' or 'How's the Missus?' – never mind a 'Morning Sergeant.''

'Aye – okay, okay. I've had an early start. On top of a late night.'

'I shan't ask. If you tell, I shall keep shtoom.'

Skelgill pulls open the door of DS Leyton's unmarked car and slides into the passenger seat. 'Stick to the school business, eh?'

'Your call, Guv. But first things first. I passed a new burger van in the layby just after the Crossthwaite roundabout. I reckon there's time for a bacon roll if we get our skates on. What do you say?'

'Leyton – I'd forgotten you had your uses.'

*

DS Leyton, having been delegated to queue in what has become light drizzle, delivers his purchases to Skelgill through the open window and scuttles as fast as his bulk will allow around to the driver's side. The small car lurches mildly as he settles behind the wheel.

'Blimey, Guv – they tell me I've missed a heatwave. But actually it's decent British grub I miss.' He takes a gulp from the plastic cup handed to him by Skelgill, then recoils. 'Ah! And good old scalding Rosy Lea.'

Skelgill checks his watch and takes back the cup. 'Leyton, you'd better drive, else we're going to be late. Remember, Big Brother's watching us. I'll have your bacon roll if necessary.'

DS Leyton shakes his head ruefully, as if to say, 'Same old Guvnor'. Nevertheless he turns the ignition key and checks his mirrors.

'Anyway,' Skelgill continues, more brightly, 'You can't eat and talk. I need to know the story, top-line.'

DS Leyton spins the car into a tight U-turn and guns its modest engine, to limited avail. Fumbling for his seat belt, he peers determinedly into a cloud of spray as he sets about tailgating the juggernaut ahead, despite the fact that in fewer than two hundred yards he will exit the main A66 trunk road to head through the lanes for Oakthwaite School. It is a constant source of disagreement between the colleagues: Skelgill insists that DS Leyton is a typical 'London driver' (more haste, less speed), while the latter's counter argument goes that when they need to battle through traffic, he's their man.

'All I know, Guv, is limited to what I've gleaned from reading the statements. It was DI Smart who filed the reports. They've moved him onto some big drugs case and left this one to us mugginses.'

Skelgill is glowering, and now DS Leyton swings off at a roundabout, just as he attempts to take a mouthful of tea.

'Oi! Where's the fire?'

'Guv – I thought we were in a hurry.'

'Okay – well, from now on take it steady. We're not the North Lakes Sweeney.'

'Despite what they call us at the station?'

Skelgill shoots a questioning glance at DS Leyton, as if this is new information. After a moment he says, 'Leyton, the suicide?'

'Sure, Guv. The autopsy report says it's categorically death by drowning. No signs of injury or struggle, no trace of drugs or even medication, nothing untoward in the stomach. No indication of illness or disease. He just drowned.'

'In Bass Lake?'

'Yeah. They've got a little wooden rowing boat. He went overboard. It was found anchored about thirty feet out.'

Skelgill frowns. Just a few hours earlier he had inspected the rickety landing stage and small, dilapidated row-in boathouse. The craft itself was in equally poor repair, possibly shipping water. Held fast by a rusty chain and padlock, it didn't look like it was a facility of which the school made much use.

'How come we're so sure it was suicide? He could have fallen in.'

'Velcro weights, Guv.'

'Come again?'

'You go to the health club don't you, Guv?'

'Leyton, I wouldn't know the inside of a health club from the inside of your sweaty underpants. Why would I spend a packet to run about indoors when for free I'm surrounded by four hundred fells and the finest countryside in England?'

'Oh – thought you did, Guv. I'm with you though – for the same cash you get far better value from a satellite subscription.'

Skelgill grins. For different reasons, DS Leyton, too, is almost certainly unfamiliar with the inside of a health club. 'Velcro weights, then?'

'Yeah, Guv. Apparently you strap 'em on your wrists and ankles to make training more difficult.'

'Or sinking more easy.'

'You got it, Guv.'

'Where did the weights come from?'

'The school gym. They're big on sports, by all accounts.'

Skelgill nods. 'What do we know about the victim?'

'Name of Querrell, Edmund Donald. Sixty-eight. Fit and healthy. Longest-serving member of staff. Mainly spent his time running their outward-bound trips, and that Duke of Edinburgh malarkey. Sports coach for one of the year-groups, but not an official PE master. No disciplinary issues, no criminal record.'

'I take it there was no suicide note?'

'Not a sausage, Guv. He lived in the converted gatehouse – it was all totally shipshape.'

'Was he married?'

'Bachelor. Apparently no next of kin.'

'Will?'

Leyton shakes his head. 'Don't suppose he'd need one, Guv. Admin are still working on it.'

'When did the death occur?'

'Pathologist reckons he went into the water between ten p.m. and two a.m. last Wednesday/Thursday. He'd not turned up for assembly, and mid-morning the Head sent the groundsman to scout for him. He spotted the boat. Querrell kept the keys – so they suspected an accident and called 999.'

If Skelgill hadn't returned so sleep-deprived from his trip to London, he might well have been out on the lake at the very time. One of his piking strategies was dead baiting in the small hours. It's a couple of moments before he asks, 'Did they find the keys?'

'On a nail in the boathouse. Usual place if the boat was taken out, apparently.'

'What was this guy Querrell wearing?'

'Regular attire: tracksuit, trainers, underwear.'

'Socks?'

'No – but apparently he didn't generally wear socks. Usually trainers or open-toed sandals.'

'So he went out normally dressed?'

'Looks like it, Guv.'

'State of mind?'

'Nothing in the reports, Guv. I'm sure we asked the question, though.'

'Aye.' Skelgill sounds like he wouldn't be surprised if 'we' didn't.

'Thing is, Guv, seeing as it's cut and dried – why are we doing this?'

'Leyton, that's what I'd like to know.'

'So what are we going to say, Guv?'

'Search me, mate.'

4. OAKTHWAITE SCHOOL

In all his thirty-seven years as a Cumbrian resident, Skelgill has never had cause to set foot inside the territory of Oakthwaite School. As he discussed with DS Jones, private and state schools exist in orbits that rarely intersect, and their product tends to settle in mutually exclusive echelons of the great British socio-economic firmament. Indeed, in common with most of the indigenous North Lakes youth Skelgill was blissfully unaware of the school's presence until advanced teenage, when he detected competition for the favours of desirable local lasses in the form of sports car driving incomers, flashing banknotes with denominations the likes of which he had never seen. Not surprisingly, there were occasional rumpuses of a town-and-gown nature, though these days it seems that Penrith and surrounding villages are off limits to Oakthwaite pupils.

After a couple of wrong turns, for which Skelgill unfairly blames DS Leyton, and thus a formidable demonstration of both officers' proficiency in Anglo-Saxon terminology, Skelgill determines that the high wall bordering the lane to their left marks the perimeter of the school. While he finishes DS Leyton's bacon roll, Leyton eventually navigates their way to the entrance, which is marked by a stone archway bearing the school crest. There is little else to give away its presence; to all intents and purposes unsignposted, such casual anonymity exudes a quiet confidence: those who need to know will find us.

This isolated setting is typical of many of northern Britain's great public schools. Whether by coincidence or design, such unanimity of location certainly must have secured for the privileged classes an education– both academic and social – conducted in an environment unpolluted by the undesirable mores of the great unwashed (these schools' founding fathers unable to foresee the advent of social networking.) Either way, the legacy is a cohort of highly regarded institutions that attract applicants from all corners of the globe.

Oakthwaite is no exception to this rule. Founded in 1866 by an enterprising locally born industrialist who made his fortune in the Satanic textile mills of Lancashire, the school was named after the eponymous hamlet that was flattened to make way for it, and from where he hailed.

As they enter the property, Skelgill would like to pry about the gatehouse, but they are already ten minutes late and obliged to press on. The main building is a further quarter-mile, within an estate of some six hundred and fifty acres. Constructed in neoclassical style from imported buff-coloured sandstone, its first impression is of the Cotswolds, making it doubly incongruous in a region famed for its vernacular application of the ubiquitous locally hewn slate.

As DS Leyton slews their car to an undisciplined halt, spitting gravel and carving tracks in the neatly manicured turning crescent before the grand frontage, they inhale in silent unison: the place looks more like an imposing stately home, a far cry from their own educational experiences. After a short pause, Skelgill, not overly tall at five-eleven, but lanky enough, spills out of the small vehicle as if he has been cramped in for a much longer journey. He brushes flakes of crust from his person and straightens his jacket. Ignoring DS Leyton, who comes shambling after him, he pulls back his shoulders and trots up the five steps to haul on the large iron ring that serves as a bell-pull.

5. JAMES GOODMAN, OBE

'Sorry to keep you, sir – we had to deal with a minor incident en route.'

Mr Goodman, a small neat man in his late fifties, with thinning oiled hair and thick round-lensed spectacles (a combination that, among successive generations of schoolboys, has consistently earned him the nickname *Himmler*), rises from behind an expansive oak desk as the detectives are ushered into his airy study. It's a large room, and he does not come forward to greet them, instead choosing to stand his ground and check his wristwatch. He indicates somewhat unsmilingly that they should be seated before him.

Mr Goodman's office shows signs that status is important to him. There are trophies and prizes, and his qualifications are prominently displayed. One wall is almost entirely given over to a collection of professionally produced photographs that can only be classified as self-aggrandisement: in which the Headmaster is seen meeting minor royalty, accepting awards, and giving speeches. He wears an expensive-looking tailored suit, and highly polished brogues.

DS Leyton straightens his tie – an act perhaps borne out of habitually being hauled before the Head in his own schooldays – while a twitch from Skelgill reveals he almost succumbs to the same reflex. However, Skelgill – as predicted by DS Jones – sports no tie. Earlier he had searched about, and located two – but they were already pressed into use in suspending a clutch of fishing rods from a beam in his garage, and he was not about to disturb the equilibrium of this important practical arrangement.

'How may I help you, gentlemen?'

In phonological terms, the Head's accent falls somewhere between BBC Bush House and Buckingham Palace.

As Skelgill might have anticipated, he's calling their bluff. It's a natural question, but surely disingenuous? And unfortunate for Skelgill, since the Chief's instructions state that he is on no account to mention that this appointment came about at her behest – indeed her name is entirely off limits. That the Head and she are likely to be on hobnobbing terms would be a handy calling card. Instead, Skelgill is left to come up with something of his own invention. He gives a little cough.

'DI Skelgill, sir. And this is DS Leyton. Naturally, sir, it's in connection with the death of your schoolmaster.'

Barely perceptibly Mr Goodman cocks his head, as if he's expecting Skelgill to elaborate. There's a small battle of wills, during which the perspiring DS Leyton squirms uncomfortably in his leather seat, making a sound close to that of breaking wind. After what seems like an age, the Head 'blinks' first.

'Officer, I understood your investigation is complete. I trust there's not some frivolous reason for extending matters beyond their natural conclusion?'

While the Head's tone is not offensive, his choice of words could be interpreted as somewhat patronising. In which case Skelgill exhibits considerable self-restraint in replying, 'Certainly not, sir – we entirely understand the sensitivity of this issue.'

'Do you, Inspector? What did you have in mind?' Behind the spectacles, the pale blue eyes seem to narrow.

'Your school's reputation, sir – as a beacon of excellence and an important contributor to the local economy – we don't want an unfortunate event like this to get blown out of proportion.'

The tension evident in the Head's angular shoulders might now fractionally diminish. Perhaps Skelgill is talking his language. However, there's scant indication in his inscrutable features to indicate any corresponding softening of his attitude towards the detectives.

'You're quite right, Inspector. But why should that be?' We might be a 'live-in' institution, so to speak, but we can't be held responsible for the private act of an individual. Therefore I don't see any reason for this matter to become 'blown out of proportion', as you put it.'

Skelgill nods sympathetically. Then he turns to stare encouragingly at Leyton, who starts in surprise and then begins to look panicky, eyes widening. Is Skelgill expecting him to come up with the 'bogus' reason for their visit? He shuffles again in his seat, with accompanying sound effects.

'Well, Inspector... is there something I ought to know?' It's the Head that speaks. His tone is one of impatience.

To Leyton's evident relief, Skelgill turns back to face Mr Goodman.

'Sir – you'll appreciate I'm not at liberty to divulge precise details, but I realise we can fully rely upon your confidence.'

His inflexion suggests a question, to which Mr Goodman responds with the merest inclination of his head.

'If I were to put it hypothetically, sir – let's say somebody dies – and then a second person comes forward claiming to be an heir...'

'Querrell has no heir. He lived here as a bachelor throughout his entire adulthood. The school was his life.'

'So we understand, sir. In which case the scenario I'm describing would be a criminal offence and we would be obliged to investigate the imposter.'

Slowly, and with evident reluctance, the Head nods his affirmation.

'On the other hand, sir, if by some small quirk of fate they turned out to be genuine, and we were – how can I put it? – *heavy handed* – they could kick up quite a stink – at the inquest, for example. The school might come in for some collateral damage. You know what the press can be like, these days, sir.'

The Head twists his lips like someone who has bitten into a lime. After a moment's silence he intones, 'So, Inspector – I return to my original question: how may I help you?'

'Well, sir – you said it yourself. The school was Mr Querrell's life. If we're to nip this in the bud as quickly and quietly as possible, we have to start here. Of course we have your own statement. Perhaps if we could speak with those other members of your staff that were closest to him?'

'And no requirement to interrogate any of the boys? You appreciate we're right in the midst of exams?'

'We'd be discretion personified, Mr Goodman.'

The Head rises and steps out from behind his desk. He crosses to the large sash window that gives on to the front of the school and looks out, rocking from his heels to the balls of his feet. Then he turns, revealing the remnants of a disapproving scowl. He says, 'You could begin, Inspector, by parking less conspicuously. There's a tradesman's area at the rear.'

Skelgill bows in a deferential manner, then points a reprimanding finger at Leyton, as if passing the blame in clumsy schoolboy fashion. The Head returns to his desk and leans over an intercom. His call is immediately answered by a well-spoken female voice.

'Yes, Headmaster?'

'Miss Brown, please spend a few moments assisting these officers with the arrangement of some interview times. I would suggest it might be most tactful to begin at first sports period this afternoon, when certain masters are free.'

'Of course, Headmaster.'

6. THE BURGER VAN

'He bought it, Guv. Nice one. I'd never have thought of that. For a moment there you had me filling my pants.'

'It sounded like you were, Leyton.'

'It was the chair, Guv. I was boiling in that office. Brushes with authority always bring me out in a sweat.'

Skelgill munches into his third bacon roll of the morning and shakes his head. 'Leyton, you crack me up. And of course he didn't buy it.'

'What do you mean, Guv?' DS Leyton sounds nonplussed.

'What he bought was that if we need to invent a reason to poke about, we would – I just gave him one that saved him losing face.'

DS Leyton looks bewildered, and consoles himself by tucking into his overdue breakfast. They both chew in thoughtful silence for a few moments, until DS Leyton remarks, 'Decent rolls these, Guv.'

Skelgill nods. 'We'd better not make a habit of parking here – the Chief comes this way to work. We'd be sitting ducks.'

'She can't get too shirty yet, Guv – we've only just started on this one.'

'Maybe – but there's not much window of opportunity – unless we can quickly find some grounds for suspicion Goodman will turf us out on our ear.'

'It'd be nice to know what the Chief's got up her sleeve, Guv. It's not right sending us out in the dark like this.'

Skelgill nods resignedly. 'She can't chance it going public.'

'If it were a murder, Guv, I don't see how she could have any inkling.'

'If it were a murder, it was a bloody clever one.'

'What else then, Guv?'

'Search me. Some bigger picture that the school doesn't want us to see?'

DS Leyton nods reflectively, but doesn't offer any suggestion.

Skelgill continues, 'At first I wondered if it were the school calling us in on the QT – via the Chief. She must be acquainted with this Goodman character – you know how all the local bigwigs and the county set knock about together. But Goodman's reaction seems to dispel that theory. We're definitely undesirables in his book.'

'What about her son, Guv – she might have heard something from him? It would explain why she can't risk getting involved.'

'I expect the social networks have been buzzing – did you notice that honours board in the entrance hall? It lists the families and the number of generations they've sent to Oakthwaite. It included the name Querrell. That's why I figured I was on safe ground hinting an heir had come forward.'

Leyton crams the remainder of his bacon roll into his mouth and gives a wide-eyed nod of affirmation. It doesn't look very convincing. He washes down his food with the remnants of his beaker of tea. 'So, Guv – what have we got? The perfect murder? Or Querrell driven to suicide by forces unknown? Or nothing sinister whatsoever?'

'Or something else.'

DS Leyton sighs quietly. This is a familiar situation: if DI Skelgill gets the merest hint of some irregularity, an errant piece of the jigsaw that doesn't fit – that might have found its way in by accident from another puzzle altogether – he'll refuse to be drawn towards what might seem the obvious, convenient and perfectly adequate conclusion. Instead he'll pursue any number of unpromising leads, explore blind avenues, and concoct improbable theories, giving the impression that the investigation is going nowhere fast, and everywhere else slowly. Then, suddenly, early one morning, he'll come back from a fishing trip on Bassenthwaite Lake and move in for the kill with all the devastating speed and single-minded ruthlessness of the pike.

Another of Skelgill's traits – *techniques*, even – is one for which DS Leyton plays a natural if sometimes unwitting foil. As in the case of their interview with Mr Goodman, the Head of Oakthwaite, as Skelgill will happily admit after a few pints of local ale, he likes his opponent to think he's stupider than he really is.

Now Skelgill uncharacteristically collects together the debris of their second breakfast, and to DS Leyton's obvious surprise climbs out of the car and heads for the litter bin at the far end of the layby. En route, it appears that his mobile phone rings, for Skelgill extracts it from his pocket, peers at the screen for a moment, and then puts it to his ear, lingering beside the waste depository. Leyton can see what's going on, but can't hear the conversation.

'Jones.'

'Guv?'

'Why are you whispering?'

'Hold on a sec.' There's a pause and, after a couple of moments, Skelgill hears the sound of a door closing. 'Guv – it's a kind of stakeout.'

'Where are you?'

'In a bar in Carlisle. In the Ladies' – now.'

'A drug deal about to go down?'

'Supposedly, according to...'

'Smart? You're not with DI Smart?'

'Fraid so, Guv.' Jones must sense Skelgill's irritation. 'Look, Guv – he's okay – I can handle him.'

'So what are you two – playing the courting couple, smooching in the corner?'

'Look, Guv – you know how these things work. Don't let Alec get under your skin.'

'Alec?'

'Give us a break, Guv – it's just another job.'

'Aye, but...'

Skelgill's voice tails off. Perhaps the significance of her words sinks in.

'Guv – I'd better get back. Can I call you later?'

'I need your help – PDQ.'

'The school?'

'Aye. I've got a list of masters and staff as long as my arm. The Head's put up a few for interviews, but they'll be his stooges. I want someone who's been there a long time and might know something about the guy, Querrell. If your family mole could suggest a name?'

'Sure, Guv – I'll text her right now. I called her this morning to say we may need a favour.'

Skelgill allows himself a small grin. She's ahead of the game as ever. 'Great – just drop me the details as soon as you get them. I'll be at Oakthwaite from about one.'

'Will do.'

'Send my regards to Smart.'

'Naturally, Guv.'

Skelgill walks back to the car, shaking his head. As he does so, a shapely blonde woman in a close-fitting miniskirt alights revealingly from a small scarlet convertible that has pulled up between the burger van and the unmarked police car. Evidently consumed in thought, Skelgill doesn't seem to notice her passing. He clambers back in beside Leyton, who quips, 'Guv – get an eyeful of that.'

'What?'

'The skirt – she slipped right under your nose. Not like you to be so unobservant, Guv.'

'Behave, Leyton.'

'Behave?'

'For a change, eh?'

'Blimey, Guv – a fortnight with Fast-track and you've come over all PC.'

'That's what you'll be Sergeant, if you don't watch your lip. Leave DS Jones out of it.'

DS Leyton shrugs resignedly. There's no accounting for DS Skelgill's capricious mores. And he knows better than to ask about the telephone call his superior has just taken. Instead he grins good naturedly, and says, 'DC, Guv.'

'What?'

'DC – not PC. If I were demoted, they wouldn't want me as an advert for uniform, would they?'

Skelgill is forced to chuckle. There is something Chaplinesque about the clumsy, self-deprecating but stoic DS Leyton. It's an endearing combination.

'Well, pull out the stops and see if you can find the way to Oakthwaite without getting lost. But, first, drop me off at my car in Keswick.'

'Hold your horses, Guv. Why am I going back to the school?'

'To interview the groundsman who found the boat.'

'Is he on our list?' DS Leyton sounds surprised. 'I thought it was just teachers.'

'Have you got the list?'

'But you've got it, Guv.'

Skelgill nods. 'So it would be easy for you to make a mistake?'

'But, Guv...' Then Skelgill's intention dawns on DS Leyton and a philosophical expression washes across his features. 'Ah... a mistake.'

'Just get the exact detail of what happened, and anything he noticed out of the ordinary. I'll catch up with you in time for the one o'clock appointment.'

'Right, Guv.'

'And remember to park less conspicuously.'

DS Leyton grimaces. 'I bet Mr Goodman wouldn't tell the Chief where to stick her Seven Series Beamer.'

'Not many would, Leyton.'

7. THE PROFESSOR

Skelgill noses his car into a tight space in the busy supermarket parking lot. He squeezes out sideways and heads for the store, sniffing the air and casting about for views of his beloved fells. But, while the rain has abated – temporarily, at least – the cloud base clings stubbornly to its early morning level, thwarting his ambitions. A couple of minutes later he strides from the automatic doors clutching a carrier bag, gripping its evidently weighty contents through the flimsy plastic material.

Instead of returning to his car he makes a left and walks briskly in the direction of Keswick's unimaginatively named Main Street. Despite the gloomy weather the grey stone nineteenth century thoroughfare is thronged with a colourful cagoule-clad procession of trippers and walkers – the former distinguished from the latter by their ill-fitting waterproofs and inappropriate footwear. Still, they mingle amicably, bearing the phlegmatic demeanour of English holidaymakers who today can neither see nor explore the hills they have come to admire.

Skelgill prefers the less-touristy Penrith for shopping: his staples being fishing tackle and outdoor equipment. But Keswick, though its main drag is ornamented with a rather disappointing necklace of retail fare, nonetheless hosts the odd specialist gem that might ordinarily challenge his bank balance. Today, however, he merely pauses for thought at the occasional intriguingly stocked window, before finally succumbing to a different impulse: the enticing aroma of hot sausage rolls that emanates from a bustling baker's.

Munching on the move, he ducks into a narrow paved ginnel and follows its course with the gentle trickle of rainwater it carries in the direction of Derwentwater. In just a short distance he draws to a halt beside a rather Heath Robinson assemblage of angular modern buildings, and turns into a doorway beneath large white lettering that proclaims this is *Keswick Library*.

The female receptionist stares at him quizzically. Skelgill raises a Bond-like eyebrow, perhaps mistaking her interest – for there is a prominent flake of pastry attached to the tip of his nose.

He leans forward and in hushed tones asks, 'Is Professor Hartley in today?'

The woman can't help brushing her own nose, as if it will cause Skelgill to mirror her and remove the offending morsel. But he stands unmoving and holds her gaze. After a moment she nods and mouths, 'History section.' She points to an archway that leads into another room.

Skelgill affects a suave bow and sets off gingerly in the direction indicated, though his wet soles squeak a protest with each step across the parquet surface, raising disapproving glances from several elderly readers.

As he enters he spies his quarry, the sole occupant of the area, a bespectacled man in his mid-sixties, notable for his shock of white hair, poring over a yellowing tome that looks to have been retrieved from some dusty archive.

'Jim.'

The man glances up, surprised for a moment, seeming severe as he squints over the half-moon reading glasses. Then his expression softens into a smile as he recognises Skelgill.

'Ah, Daniel.' He lowers his voice, 'Let me guess – you've been eating pastries.'

'What?' Skelgill whispers. He looks down at his jacket for the evidence.

'Told you I'd have made a good detective.' Professor Hartley taps his nose.

'Oh.' Skelgill gets it and wipes away the crumb, and with it the fleeting realisation that it was present during his interaction a few moments earlier. He reaches out and offers the supermarket bag to the older man. 'Lagavulin – for that case of flies you tied for me.'

'Daniel, they were a gift. I enjoy doing them.'

'Jim, they're worth five times what this Scotch cost – and they've already paid for it in trout alone. A dozen two-pound Brownies.'

'Ah – excellent, lad. Glad to hear that. Whereabouts?'

'Just below Little Crossthwaite, where the Derwent flows into Bass Lake.'

'I know it. Beautiful spot.'

'Come with me some time.'

'That would be an honour – though the hours you keep send a shiver down my spine.'

Skelgill grins. 'A policeman's lot.'

'On which note – there must be something I can do: for you to have run me to ground in my lair here.'

'I did want to pick your brains. It's about Oakthwaite School.'

'Be my guest.'

The Professor indicates a chair opposite, but as he does so the shadow of the librarian darkens the doorway beyond, her posture communicating a hint of disapproval.

'We're making too much racket, Daniel. Shall we retreat for a cappuccino? Let me just tidy this lot up. I'm giving a talk to the Borrowdale History Society next month: *The Flight of Mary, Queen of Scots*. She came this way, you know, when she was driven from Scotland?'

'She got around a bit, I know that.'

'She was an extraordinary girl – she would have been a media sensation if she'd lived four hundred years later. Not least because she was six foot two in her party shoes.'

Skelgill watches as he neatly stacks and files his meticulous notes and coloured pens: no sign of any new technology. Jim Hartley, now retired, was for many years Professor of Medieval History over at Durham University, some eighty miles due east across the Pennines. A native of Keswick, and an ardent angler, he'd kept on a house in the small Lakeland town, and had come to know the spotty teenage Daniel Skelgill when the latter had attended one of his 'summer schools' on fly-casting. He'd identified Skelgill's natural talent at once, and 'young Daniel' became something of a protégé in the absence of children of his own.

They make their way through to the little cafeteria attached to the library. As the Professor takes his seat he says, 'Oakthwaite – now there's a curious coincidence, Daniel.'

'Oh?'

'Yes. I came across a reference to the place only this morning. Not the school, you understand? There has been a stronghold on the site since the Dark Ages – probably earlier.'

'What – like a castle?'

'Yes. Perhaps some kind of broch originally, but certainly a substantial fortress in late medieval times.'

'What became of it?'

'It may be that Mary proved its undoing. In 1568, aged just twenty-five, she'd escaped from confinement in Loch Leven Castle, and rallied an army that was on its way to take up position at Dumbarton Castle. Their defences would have been impregnable. But they were intercepted and routed at the Battle of Langside, south of Glasgow, by forces under the Earl of Moray – her half-brother, no less.'

'Sounds like my family.'

The Professor grins. 'Then she fled south, misguidedly hoping Elizabeth would help her. From Dundrennan Abbey she was smuggled across the Solway disguised as a fisherwoman, and rumour has it she was given refuge at Oakthwaite. She was a staunch Roman Catholic, naturally, and this part of Cumberland was a clandestine stronghold. It may be that in time the local lords suffered for providing assistance to the pretender.'

'So the castle at Oakthwaite was destroyed?'

'If it wasn't one catastrophic event, certainly the barony was strangled into decline over the course of a couple of generations, the estate with it. I expect half the farms in the vicinity have pieces of the castle stone in their walls. The foundations will still be intact, though, somewhere beneath the school. There would have been extensive vaults, wells, dungeons, and a crypt under the chapel. I've read of a tunnel that led away to safety in case the priest ever needed to evade capture. But of course it's never been excavated: the school was built before they thought of *Time Team*.'

'Quite a history, buried away.'

'But it's the present you're interested in, Daniel. I should cut to the chase rather than try out my lecture on you.'

Skelgill grins ruefully. 'That depends where history ends and the present begins.'

'Ever the philosopher, Daniel.'

'I doubt that's the term my Sergeant would use for me, Jim.'

'I'm sure you're secretly admired.'

Skelgill's cheeks colour a little. He retreats to the invitation to discuss the present. 'Do you know much about the school today?'

The Professor shakes his head apologetically. 'I'm afraid not Daniel. It wasn't ever my remit – admissions – so I didn't have any direct association. Of course, we had a few Oakthwaite freshers coming up each year into our faculty. Always well presented, diligent, solid performers. The ones that just missed out on Oxbridge, I imagine.'

'Did you ever visit the place?'

'Sadly, no. What I've assimilated down the years is from local hearsay – folk who've worked there. I've always had the impression that they operate in a rather cult-like manner. Most of the masters live on site, I believe, and they like to keep their own company. I suppose when you have several hundred charges to occupy round-the-clock during term times, you must run a pretty tight ship. Being a closed community facilitates that.'

'Ever heard of a family named Querrell? The last one spent his life there, man and boy.'

The Professor stirs the residue of milky froth and chocolate flakes into the last dregs of his coffee. 'It rings a very faint bell, Daniel. Of course, it's an unusual name. Was there one at Bosworth, now? I'd have to look that up. Querrell's your man?'

'Was. Drowned last week in what appears to be a suicide.'

'Appears?'

Skelgill nods slowly.

'I'll put my thinking cap on. You know how these things can come back to you when you're least expecting it.'

'That's my system, too. At least, it's my excuse to go fishing.'

'Quite reasonable, Daniel. Complex problems can't be solved by rational thought.'

'Just as well, in my case. However, if it's any help he was born in nineteen forty-six. Christian names Edmund Donald.'

'So the parents had a classical education. And a sense of humour.'

'Come again?'

'Querrell, Edmund Donald: initials QED. *Quod erat demonstrandum.* That which is proven.'

Skelgill grins sheepishly. 'Over my head, Jim. My Latin starts and finishes at *Esox lucius.*'

'And no better place to begin and end.'

Skelgill smiles. 'I'd better let you get back to finding out something about Mary.'

As they rise the Professor asks, 'How's your mother keeping these days?'

'Ah – slowing down at bit. But still cycles over Honister every morning.'

'I wish I could decline to such heights, Daniel. And I read about your latest fell-running exploits in *The Westmorland Gazette.* Like mother, like son.'

'What – mad as hatters?'

8. THE GROUNDSMAN

'Can you believe it, Guv – they've even got a shooting academy!'

'That would have been popular where you went to school, eh Leyton?'

'Too right, Guv. It ran in a few families round about our gaff.' He scratches his head absently. 'They're all bang to rights now, of course.'

'What is it, air rifles?'

'No – clays, Guv. Twelve-bore, and four-tens for the juniors.'

'They obviously blood them young, the gentry.'

'You're spot on there, Guv. Apparently some of the sixth-formers are expert shots, national competition standard. Half a dozen of them stand to inherit shooting estates, mainly up in Scotland – though there's one beyond Brough. They do gundog training as well. The groundsman's got a couple of labs in a kennels round the back of the school – says he used to be a keeper over Cockermouth way. Seemed a bit wide to me, though. Couldn't be certain, but I think he might have smelled of drink.'

'Name of?'

'Royston Hodgson, Guv. Ring any bells?'

Skelgill looks pensive. 'Maybe. Does he run the shooting club?'

'He says he just helps out, setting up the clay traps. Apparently it's all above board. Our licensing boys inspected back in March and renewed their certificate. They've got a gun room in the cellars of the main school building.'

Skelgill nods. 'Be interesting to know who keeps the keys.'

'A master called Snyder is in charge.'

'He's first on our list.'

'Bit of a red herring though – shotguns – eh, Guv?'

Skelgill shrugs. 'I guess I just like to know the lie of the land if I'm within a quarter of a mile of a twelve-bore. I developed a dislike of them early in my career.'

'So you've mentioned, Guv.'

Skelgill flashes DS Leyton a disapproving glance. 'What's Hodgson's story, then?'

DS Leyton consults a small black notebook. He flips it open where the elastic band marks a page. Considering his somewhat shambolic deportment, his printing is surprisingly small and neat, if a little elementary.

'He said the Head called him to ask if he'd seen Querrell – and he replied not since the previous afternoon when he was taking a cricket practice. So Goodman asked him to have a look round and check Querrell's cottage in case he was ill.'

'What time was that?'

'He reckons about eleven. He drove to the gatehouse – he's got a quad bike that he uses for the mowers and whatnot. It was unlocked and empty – the key was on the inside of the door.'

'Was that unusual?'

'He's not sure. He said he wouldn't be surprised if Querrell didn't lock up, the generation he was, though the lodge is near the road and an easy target. He says they've lost quite a bit of sports equipment in the past couple of years.'

'Probably the PE staff from my old comp.'

'Ha-ha, Guv.'

'Go on.'

'Querrell owned a motorbike. That was still in its shed, so Hodgson figured he must be somewhere on the property. They've got a jogging track that more or less follows the perimeter of the grounds. He didn't see anything until he passed the boathouse and noticed the boat anchored out on the lake.'

'What made him stop there, do you think? The water's shielded by all the vegetation?'

DS Leyton looks quizzically at his superior, as if wondering how he knows this. 'Dunno, Guv – he didn't say. Just that he went down onto the landing stage – climbed onto the railing in case Querrell was asleep in the boat. But he couldn't see anything, and since Querrell apparently wasn't much of a swimmer that was enough for him to raise the alarm. Obviously it was our search team that found the body.'

Skelgill nods pensively. After a minute's silence he says, 'What did they use the boat for?'

'He said Querrell kept the only key – at least that he knows of. And the boat's not generally used any more. They don't let the pupils out on the water – there was some accident years ago. And now there's all this Health and Safety palaver.'

'And Querrell didn't fish.' Skelgill says this as a statement – it's something he would know.

'That's right, Guv. I asked about that. It's not proper angling here, apparently.'

'What's that supposed to mean?' Skelgill's hackles rise.

'It's all coarse fishing on Bassenthwaite Lake – you'd know this, Guv? For the young gentleman fly-casting's the thing.' DS Leyton must notice Skelgill's black expression, for he quickly adds, 'According to Hodgson, anyway.'

'I've caught plenty of big pike out there on a fly.' Skelgill tuts. 'I'd like to see them try that.'

'Definitely, Guv. You're the expert.'

Skelgill nods, apparently feeling vindicated. 'And what did he say about Querrell?'

'Nothing untoward, Guv. No indication he was about to top himself. He'd asked Hodgson to use the heavy roller on the juniors' wicket for the match at the weekend – which he never made, of course.'

'Who did they play?'

'School from Edinburgh, Guv.' DS Leyton checks his notebook. 'Merchiston Castle.'

Skelgill shows no indication that the name has any significance to him. 'How did Hodgson get on with Querrell?'

'Alright, he reckons. He says Querrell was a bit of a loner, but didn't look down his nose on the ancillary staff like some of the masters do.'

Now Skelgill's features involuntarily flicker with the recollection of DS Jones's remark.

DS Leyton continues, 'Called him cantankerous, though. And that's me missing out the two expletives, Guv. Says he took the hump whenever the school brought in new equipment or started chopping down trees to make room for car parking spaces.'

'What about Hodgson himself, think he was hiding anything?'

'Not especially, Guv.' DS Leyton pauses, and jolts mildly, as though he's just received a small electric shock. 'One thing he did say, though – just as I was leaving.'

'Go on.'

'Well – you know how I was supposed to ask about Querrell having any relatives – to fit in with our excuse for investigating?'

'Aha.'

'Well – I nearly forgot. But I think I pulled it off – like as a casual afterthought, Guv.'

Skelgill raises his eyebrows reproachfully.

'He said as far as he knows Querrell had no living relatives – but only because that's the story that does the rounds.'

'So – what's the big deal?'

'Well – he said a few weeks ago he got a surprise – could have sworn Querrell had an identical twin.'

'What made him say that?'

'One evening he'd seen Querrell going into the school, then a few minutes later he went down to mark out some lines on the athletics track, and there was Querrell walking up the field from the direction of the lake. He couldn't figure out how he could have been in the two places almost at once.'

'But both sightings were Querrell?

'So he says, Guv.'

'Maybe he mistook the person going into the school for Querrell. You know how bad eyewitness testimony can be. More likely Hodgson had his lunch in the Blacksmith's Arms.'

DS Leyton nods ruefully.

'Thing is, Guv – I put in a call to the station to get him checked out. The reason he stopped being a gamekeeper was because he had his shotgun licence revoked. He put the wind up a couple of walkers who'd strayed off a public footpath. Claimed he thought they were poachers.'

'No excuse.'

'He only got a caution but it was enough for the Chief at the time. What do you reckon, Guv?'

Skelgill screws up his face and shakes his head. 'I don't reckon the Chief is going to be reaching for the cigars just yet.'

DS Leyton looks slightly crestfallen. Skelgill reaches across and pats him on the shoulder. 'Come on, Leyton – cheer up. Let's go see what else we can turn up. And, remember – we act like we're daft local coppers.'

'I'll give it my best shot, Guv.'

9. DR SNYDER

'So, I'm sure you'll understand, Inspector, we don't indulge in what you might call parochial advertising. In this era of the global village, Oakthwaite positions itself firmly on the international stage. And indeed we attract applicants from all four corners of the earth.'

Skelgill nods politely, despite the somewhat oblique reply to his observation that the school keeps the surrounding community at arm's length. Dr Snyder, a tall stooping long-headed man in his mid-forties, is reminiscent of a character from a gothic horror movie, with jet-black swept-back hair, contrasting pale skin, dark sunken eyes wide set astride an aquiline nose, prominent jaw and brows – overall a caricature underscored by the fact of him wearing his academic gown, an elaborate hooded affair of charcoal and deep purple. He sits watchfully still, and when he speaks, which he does slowly, he embellishes his words with paddling gestures of large hands that articulate at the wrist.

'Certainly, sir – and there's no law against that. On this occasion, the school and Mr Querrell being something of unknown quantities – it means we have no real alternative but to begin here in order to establish whether there are any surviving relatives.'

Dr Snyder blinks slowly, perhaps in lieu of a nod of acceptance. He says, 'Well I'm sure you are aware that as far as we know Mr Querrell was the last of his line.'

'So I gather, sir. And do you have any reason to doubt that?'

Dr Snyder flaps his flipper-like palms. 'I have seen no evidence to the contrary. The school's historical personnel records were destroyed in a fire in the early nineties, so there is no file on him, either as a master, or earlier as a pupil.'

'How long had you known Mr Querrell?'

'This is just my second year at Oakthwaite.'

Dr Snyder rubs his nose between his two forefingers. He shows no sign that he will elaborate, so Skelgill asks, 'Where were you before that, sir?'

'At an international school... in Singapore.'

'Is that why you came – because of your experience abroad?'

'It probably did no harm to my *curriculum vitae*, Inspector.

'And is that your remit here, sir – the foreign students?'

Dr Snyder sits back and folds his arms, as though he's bored with the direction the questions are taking. 'My role is largely administrative. Admissions, examinations, timetables, university entrance, IT policy, discipline. I take the occasional class in the event of illness. The usual stuff of the Deputy Head.'

'It sounds like Mr Goodman gets off lightly.'

'Oh, I think you'll find he's kept adequately busy, Inspector. What with corporate strategy and our gamut of outward facing matters.'

'So, like the Head's, your acquaintance with Mr Querrell has been relatively short-lived.'

Dr Snyder seems to approve of this statement. He leans forward and places his large hands flat on the desktop, extending their long fingers as though he is in the habit of playing piano. 'Quite, Inspector. I honestly hardly knew the man. He kept very much to himself.'

'Presumably you had some interaction with him over routine work matters? As you said, timetables and so on.'

Dr Snyder shrugs languidly. He casts a glance across the two detectives. 'Rather curiously, gentlemen, Querrell operated in his own little anachronistic bubble. He managed our programme of outdoor activities – something that has evidently been running like clockwork in the same way for many years, decades I believe. And by tradition he looked after the first-form for team sports – that's the eleven-year-olds, our intake group – nothing much required in the way of technical expertise.'

'But he reported to you?'

'I think, Inspector, if you had asked Querrell, he would have asserted he reported to nobody.'

Again Dr Snyder leaves any further explanation hanging in the ether. He bridges his chin on the back of his intertwined fingers.

Skelgill says, 'Sir, you say his activities ran like clockwork. So there was nothing troubling in his job that might have prompted him to take his own life?'

Dr Snyder shakes his head. 'Apparently not, Inspector.'

Skelgill persists, 'Is it possible he owed money?'

'I doubt very much he had any debts. He spent most of his time here at the school, and there's little to lavish one's salary upon in the tuck shop.'

'These days there's online gambling, that sort of thing?'

'I have no reason to suspect that, Inspector. It would have been entirely out of character. Besides, our security settings prevent access to undesirable websites. Though of course you're welcome to examine his computer.'

'Well, that might be helpful, sir.'

'I shouldn't hold your breath, Inspector. It was a devil of a job even to induce him to reply to an email. If you wanted an immediate response it was better to send a small boy with a handwritten note. He preferred what he referred to as the foolproof methods.'

Skelgill raises his eyebrows empathetically. 'If nothing else, sir, we might find some contact details of friends who could assist us.'

'I'm sure your fellow officers would have looked last week.' Ostentatiously he consults his wristwatch. 'However, I could meet you down at the gatehouse in exactly one hour. I have an appointment imminently.'

'That's fine, sir – we have another of your colleagues scheduled to see next.'

Dr Snyder rises, perhaps with a triumphant glint in the shadows of his hooded eyes. His willingness to provide access to Querrell's computer could be interpreted as an unexpected demonstration of openness. He takes long loping strides to the door, and holds it sufficiently ajar for Skelgill and DS Leyton to exit. Just as they are doing so, Skelgill pauses and points to his temple as though he's just remembered something.

'Oh, one other thing, Dr Snyder.'

'Aha?'

'The Sergeant in our licensing section asked me to double-check a point concerning the recent shotgun re-certification – to save a trip out here from Penrith, you understand?'

'Certainly, Inspector.' Dr Snyder's sombre features darken once again.

'There's a box on our computer form for nominated key-holders – in the event of an emergency. We just have you listed at the moment – but there's a query marked against it. I think the visiting officer may have omitted to note down whether there is anyone else.'

'Well, Inspector, I can confirm that I am the sole key-holder.' He jangles a pocket concealed somewhere beneath the extensive folds of his academic gown. 'The key and others of similar importance are kept on or very near my person at all times.'

'Excellent, sir. That sounds very sensible. I'll report that back and there'll be no need to trouble you further about it.'

10. DR JACOBSON

'Guv – how come they're all called 'doctor'?'

'Leyton – shush – he's coming.'

'Well it gives me the willies – I feel like I'm inside a mental institution.'

'Maybe you should be, Leyton.'

'Guv, an ordinary bloke could get a complex around here. All these posh folk with qualifications coming out of their ears.'

'Forget it, Leyton. Until they invent a PhD in nicking villains you've got nothing to worry about.'

'Fair point, Guv.'

There's a prolonged scrabbling noise beyond the varnished wooden door at which they've been waiting. It bears an unevenly polished brass plaque with the words *Dr G W Jacobson, Head of History, Housemaster – Blencathra.'* Suddenly it swings open and a small red-haired boy in Oakthwaite uniform tumbles down the two internal steps, apologising and bowing subserviently. He scuttles away, leaving them facing an empty carpeted hallway. Then a piebald dog appears – it looks like a large Staffie – and silently rushes them.

'Blimey, Guv – it's a Pit Bull!'

DS Leyton backs away, but Skelgill stands his ground, and in a moment the hound is rolling over in front of him on the top step, seemingly wanting its stomach tickled.

'Hello, girl.' Skelgill stoops and obliges. 'She's friendly, Leyton.'

But DS Leyton keeps his distance, eyeing the dog suspiciously.

'Ah, gentlemen – you've met Cleopatra, I see.'

The detectives look up. In the light cast at the far end of the corridor stands a small crooked man wearing a decorative waistcoat and matching bow tie over a white shirt, his lower half clad in what look like striped pyjama trousers finished off with carpet slippers.

'Come in, come in – this way please.'

Skelgill stands upright and Cleopatra – evidently not yet satisfied with the level of attention she has received – launches herself at the unsuspecting DS Leyton and catches him full in the groin, producing a pained gasp.

Grinning unsympathetically, Dr Jacobson calls out over his shoulder, 'She obviously likes you – the boys call her the *Canine Cannonball* – that's her sign of affection.'

DS Leyton makes to reply, but powers of speech have temporarily deserted him. Wheezily, he follows Skelgill through into a parlour-like room of floral patterns, where tea things and cakes are laid out on a low table amidst two easy chairs and a settee. Behind upon a dresser there's a crystal sherry decanter and half a dozen inverted glasses arranged on a round silver tray, and various bottles of the commoner spirits.

'Be seated, gentlemen, won't you?' Dr Jacobson makes a sweeping gesture of the arm, as a seventeenth century cavalier might have extravagantly doffed his plumed hat. 'Please accept my apologies that I can't offer you much in the way of refreshment – I wasn't expecting you until the call was put through from reception just a few minutes ago.'

'Must have been an oversight, sir – but if it's inconvenient we can come back another time.' Skelgill affects to rise.

'No, no – not at all. Do stay. I'm free right the way through until prep. There isn't a full timetable at the moment because of the examinations. And this is far more exciting. Fancy them letting me loose on you. Have a fruit scone, please.'

'Don't mind if I do, sir.'

Skelgill takes the proffered tea plate and helps himself to a scone. He makes their introductions and purpose of visit known whilst spooning liberal dollops of strawberry jam and clotted cream for himself and DS Leyton.

Dr Jacobson assumes responsibility for the teapot, quipping, 'I'll be Mother, ha-ha.'

In his mid fifties, he has a somewhat clownish appearance as a consequence of a bald pate partly ringed by a crescent of mousy hair that sticks up in prominent tufts above the ears, as though he's just been roused from slumber. His round face bears a fixed simper and his small pale blue eyes exude a natural sparkle. It's hard to judge whether he is on edge, or if his continual restless movements and fidgeting are the norm.

Skelgill makes a little cough and says, 'Dr Jacobson, as you'll have guessed we'd like to talk to you about Mr Querrell.'

'A dreadful tragedy – we're all devastated – the boys especially. They're still in mourning for him.'

'Oh?' Skelgill sounds a little surprised.

'Querrell was a living legend. Taught many of their paters, of course. Must have marched half the serving British Establishment up and down the hills of northern England in his time.'

'Apologies if I've misjudged the mood, Dr Jacobson, but I rather got the impression that he won't be missed in certain quarters?'

Skelgill glances at DS Leyton; otherwise occupied with his scone, he nods enthusiastically in confirmation.

'Gentlemen, you know how it is.'

The detectives look like they don't. But Dr Jacobson, unlike his more senior colleagues, needs no encouragement in order to elaborate.

'There can be a competitive jealousy among schoolmasters. Deep in our hearts we all yearn to be popular: most of all to be respected by the boys. And when that respect stems not from fear – of the rod, or detention, or an everlasting – but from admiration, well that is a very precious commodity, indeed.'

'And that was Mr Querrell?'

'Quite right, Inspector. I marvel at his secret, because he was as much a disciplinarian as anybody in the school – with the exception of Snyder, naturally – but the boys would always go that extra mile for him. He'd have the timidest first-formers tackling like tigers within three weeks of the start of Michaelmas term.'

At this point DS Leyton, who has been looking a little agitated, swallows and asks, 'Excuse me, sir – what exactly is an *everlasting?*'

'Ah, Sergeant – one of our peculiar anachronisms. It must make us sound like Hogwarts. It's simply a cunning variation on the old punishment of giving out lines. Almost impossible to finish in under an hour. Funnily enough, Querrell was credited with devising it, though he always denied it.'

Skelgill shows signs of being irked that DS Leyton has wandered off track. He places his cup and saucer crudely on the coffee table, attracting the attention of Dr Jacobson. He says, 'The thing is, sir, we're at a bit of a loss regarding Mr Querrell – life history, interests, out-of-school acquaintances, that kind of thing.'

Dr Jacobson shakes his head and inhales in the manner of one who is about to disappoint. 'I quite understand. Although the short answer is there weren't any. At most he took the occasional spin on that infernal old motorcycle of his.' He reaches for the teapot. 'A top up, Inspector? And have another scone, please – I have no more tutorials this afternoon, so everything must go, as they say. You too, Sergeant, tuck in.'

Skelgill obliges, gesturing to DS Leyton that he should follow suit. Plate replenished, he turns to Dr Jacobson and says, 'I understand, sir, that you've been here a good many years?'

Dr Jacobson feeds a last morsel of cake to his dog and absently wipes his fingers upon his flannel trousers. 'Not by Querrell's standards, of course. He must have come as a pupil in the late 'fifties, then returned to teach from nineteen seventy onward. I arrived in ninety-one. A mere whipper-snapper.'

'But Mr Querrell's death makes you the longest-serving master, by some distance?'

'Well, I suppose it does; now you mention it. We've had a bit of a reshuffle of the old pack in the past couple of years, what with the last Head and his Deputy stepping down at the same time.'

'And Mr Goodman – he made further changes?'

'You know, Inspector – new broom and all that? Every regime likes to get its hands upon the levers of power.'

'That's more along the lines of what I meant when I said perhaps Mr Querrell wasn't going to be missed.'

'Well – I understand what you suggest, Inspector. Not mentioning any names, of course. But let's say the *modernisers* would see his passing as the removal of one small obstacle to progress.'

Skelgill pats the dog, which has moved to beg beside him now that its master has no food left. He says, 'Though it's hard to see how he could have got in the way – it sounds like he was sidelined long ago.'

'Well, you're quite right in that regard, Inspector.' Dr Jacobson leans forward conspiratorially. 'To be frank we've been carrying Querrell for years. He originally taught Classics, but it has withered on the vine in the majority of public schools. And his extra-curricular duties could easily have been shared among the other staff. I'd even suggested to him that Greig – he's head of sport – should take over his more arduous Duke of Edinburgh trips – he wasn't getting any younger, you see – but Querrell wouldn't hear a word of it.'

Skelgill nods sympathetically. 'I'd probably feel the same, in his shoes.'

Dr Jacobson agrees, 'Of course, Inspector – turkeys don't generally vote for Christmas. But I was rather surprised the new Head didn't retire him when he arrived. I assume he decided that only so many feathers could be ruffled in one fell swoop. There were one or two casualties who struck me as more valuable to the school. However, what with these tribunals they have these days – perhaps if it looks like you'll go down kicking and screaming it might be easier simply to let nature take its course.'

Skelgill raises his eyebrows. 'You might say it did, sir.'

Dr Jacobson is suddenly flustered, sitting back and flapping his hands with dismay. 'My apologies, Inspector – such an unfortunate turn of phrase.'

Skelgill grins ruefully. 'Do you think there was any pressure lately on Mr Querrell – to leave the school?'

Now Dr Jacobson ducks as though a schoolboy has just flung a paper dart in his direction. He purses his lips and holds open his palms. He rather looks like he's trying to tell them something but is worried about eavesdroppers. Then he says, 'I really couldn't say if there were anything through the official channels – you'd have to ask Goodman or Snyder. I suppose since we're heading towards the end of Trinity – that's our summer term – if they were thinking about changes, now would be the time.'

'What about Mr Querrell? How had he seemed lately?'

'Not so different from usual, Inspector – perhaps a tad more grouchy. But I simply put that down to advancing age and its accompanying recalcitrance. He was our very own *Victor Meldrew*, so you could never read too much into his black moods.'

'Where would he have gone – if he'd left the school, that is?'

Dr Jacobson absently scratches the tufts of hair above his ears. 'That's the sixty-four thousand dollar question, Inspector. It's not like he had a home town or favourite holiday location to retire to. He spent his whole time here. And, of course, there are no relatives – at least not that we know of. That *would* be a tabloid sensation if some long-lost offspring turned up.'

'It was more in the way of a cousin that we had in mind, sir.'

'Then you may well have an imposter on your hands. My understanding is that the last three generations of Querrells have been only-children. You can see their names on our honours board.'

Skelgill nods. 'Yes, I've noticed that – you have some long-standing family associations.'

'We're very strong on tradition. Fathers like to know their sons are in safe hands. The boy who left just as you arrived – Cholmondeley – he's sixth generation Oakthwaite, all Blencathra House.'

'Of which you're housemaster?'

'That's correct. The other three are Helvellyn, Scafell and Skiddaw.'

Skelgill grins. 'Yours is the only one under three thousand feet, sir.'

'I see you know your mountains, Inspector.'

'I guess Scafell and Sca Fell would be too confusing?'

'I believe that was the thinking behind it, quite so.'

'Was Querrell a housemaster?'

Dr Jacobson shakes his head and grimaces. 'Oh no, Inspector. He thought the house system was divisive. Never would admit what house he'd been in when he boarded here – claimed he didn't want to be accused of favouritism.'

'Yet he was all for competition?'

'Perfectly happy for us to knock seven bells out of other schools, especially Sedbergh, naturally.'

Skelgill nods, but there is an insistent rapping on the outer door. The dog bounds away, barking fiercely. Dr Jacobson pulls a reluctant face, but then with surprising alacrity springs to his feet.

'Apologies, Inspector, Cleopatra informs me that I have an unwelcome visitor. Unfortunately one I cannot ignore. Uncanny how she can detect the presence of certain people.'

'No worries, sir. We'll be getting along right now. We're on quite a tight schedule. Thanks for your help, so far.'

Dr Jacobson momentarily glances back at Skelgill, and takes a small breath as if he is about to speak. Then he obviously thinks the better of it and continues into the hallway. Cleopatra is now sniffing under the front door, a low growl rumbling in her throat.

'Come away, girl – there we go. Good girl – now pipe down.' Dr Jacobson opens a side door and bundles the dog into what must be his study. Skelgill is afforded a brief glimpse of a disorderly desk, a computer screen adorned with yellow butterfly-like *Post-it* notes, and an ornately papered wall hung with certificates.

Dr Jacobson pulls open the front door to reveal the stern personage of Dr Snyder – no longer wearing his gown, but still looking rather like he has just returned from a wake, his dark suit draped loosely over his long sparse frame.

'Your internal telephone is off the hook, Jacobson.' His gaze flickers disapprovingly over the detectives as they sidle past Dr Jacobson and step down into the school corridor beside him. 'There's a matter about which I must speak with you.'

Dr Jacobson bows his head, and makes a motion with his left hand as if he's about to touch his absent forelock. 'Why certainly, Dr Snyder. I can't think what happened to the telephone. I'm perfectly free – do come in, please.'

Dr Snyder turns to Skelgill. 'I shall meet you gentlemen as arranged.' He nods unsmilingly, and ponderously mounts the steps into Dr Jacobson's quarters. The detectives' last view is of the latter's face as he carefully closes the door: an expression of resignation, and perhaps not intended for them.

'No love lost there, Leyton.'

'It's a doggy dog world, Guv.'

11. THE GATEHOUSE

The lodge of Oakthwaite School bears scant resemblance to the grand edifice that is the educational establishment itself. Constructed from rough-hewn grey stone with a steeply sloping slate roof and overhanging eaves, it is little more than a one-up one-down cottage, and surely could not have been intended for permanent living. Neither is it an object of which the school makes a feature, and indeed is largely – perhaps intentionally – sheltered from the entrance by a small stand of ornamental conifers, nestling within the greater woodland fringe of the land itself. However, it has a side window that gives on to the driveway, and is undoubtedly a convenient lookout for anyone who would wish to observe whatever comings and goings take place.

Skelgill and DS Leyton arrive on foot – the former having opined that one never knows what one might miss in the car, the latter having complained at regular intervals about the unnecessary quarter-mile walk, and his superior's brisk and somewhat challenging pace. There is no sign of life – no car outside, for instance – but the simple white-painted front door is ajar. Skelgill pushes it open.

'Hello. Anyone home?'

'Inspector, come in.' The voice belongs to Dr Snyder; its tone is perhaps less hostile than they have encountered thus far.

A cramped vestibule leads into the room that occupies almost the entire ground floor. There's a faint musty hint of damp, and the shimmering light that slants in through the surrounding trees unevenly pierces the gloom. A bespectacled Dr Snyder sits on a stool to the right of the entrance, at a narrow computer desk crammed into the darkest corner; there's no sign of a printer. He swivels around, planting his large feet one after the other.

'Blimey.' DS Leyton can't contain his surprise.

'Yes, Sergeant – he was something of an ascetic.' Dr Snyder incorrectly interprets DS Leyton's reaction, though the room, which has a far exit door, is indeed coarsely furnished. The floor is stone flagged; a worn upright armchair rests upon a threadbare rug before an open hearth – the grey ashes in the grate perhaps accentuating the air of austerity; a precipitous open flight of stairs – more of a ladder, really – climbs against the distempered left-hand wall into the attic bedroom above; beneath it there is a modest kitchenette – a sink and a butane gas ring; an old-fashioned typewriter is set proud upon an oak writing desk before the window that looks out over the driveway.

'How could you live here?' DS Leyton's tone still verges on the incredulous. 'I mean – there's no telly.'

'I don't think television numbered among Querrell's interests.' Dr Snyder flaps a long hand at the wall to his left. It is lined floor-to-ceiling with bookcases, crammed with mostly old-looking books. 'As for facilities, there is a toilet through there – a more recent extension.' He indicates in the direction of the far door. 'Otherwise, the school provided for all his requirements. The staff take their meals in the refectory, and we have a laundry, drying room, showers – remember we cater for four hundred boarders. Even during the long vacation we retain a skeleton staff for maintenance purposes, and we run a programme of summer schools. The majority of our more junior masters have a study bedroom in one of the house wings.'

Now Dr Snyder rises and gestures at the computer screen. 'I have opened the email system for you. I think everything else is pretty standard.'

He looks at Skelgill, who in turn nods to DS Leyton. 'I'm not a great one for technology myself, sir – Sergeant Leyton will have a go.'

DS Leyton glances down at his feet and shuffles towards the computer. 'I'm not much better – our kids run rings round me.'

Dr Snyder removes his reading glasses takes half a pace backwards, but seems intent on watching as DS Leyton settles down with a grunt and gets to grips with the mouse. Skelgill is drawn towards a traditional split-cane fishing rod that stands in one corner; the line is threaded though there's no hook or tackle attached. Then he wanders over towards the window, and experimentally taps out a random word or two on the typewriter; the keys are well oiled, and return satisfyingly into place. He drifts back to examine the wall of books, and begins taking down individual volumes and examining the flyleaf of each.

'Seems like they're all textbooks.'

'I believe, Inspector, that Querrell's motto was why read fiction when there are so many facts to know?' He says this rather disdainfully, and without taking his eyes away from DS Leyton's progress on the computer screen.

Skelgill nods to himself, pursing his lips as he peruses one dusty tome after another. After a minute he says, 'I had the idea that maybe one or two of these would be gifts – from relatives. You know how people write their message inside the cover?'

'I think you'll be disappointed, Inspector, though I admire your detective skills.'

Skelgill raises an eyebrow – Dr Snyder's compliment was negated by its dismissive quality.

'Whoa!' Suddenly Skelgill cries out, his intonation suggestive of an imminent physical threat.

Dr Snyder turns to see him about to be engulfed by a landslide of books: perhaps one has been so tightly jammed in that, in trying to extract it, Skelgill has pulled the entire vertical section of bookcase towards himself. Now he stands fighting against its weight as individual books begin to spill onto the flagstones.

'Hold on, Inspector.'

Dr Snyder strides across in his undulating gait and joins with Skelgill in wrestling the bookcase back against the uneven wall surface. Together they manage to right it, and press and pat the books back into some semblance of regimented order to further restore its balance. Skelgill kneels and collects those scattered on the floor, and hands them up to Dr Snyder for replacement.

'Better watch that, sir – a bit of a hazard for anyone coming in here on their own.'

Dr Snyder grimaces. 'I shall instruct a tradesman to secure it. The cottage will be locked in the meantime.'

'Good idea, sir.'

Skelgill straightens his jacket and shakes his arms. Shadowed by Dr Snyder he moves across to DS Leyton, who has perhaps surprisingly stuck to his task on the computer during the temporary crisis.

'What do you reckon, Sergeant?'

DS Leyton shakes his head casually. 'Not a lot on here that I can see. The emails are all connected with the school – mostly received; hardly any sent. And the saved documents are just standard forms and itineraries for outward-bound courses – that sort of thing.'

Dr Snyder rubs his pterodactyl-like hands as if he's just devoured a small prey item. 'As I intimated, gentlemen, Querrell never really emerged from the Palaeolithic when it came to new technology. If you are satisfied, I shall lock up – the Headmaster will be collecting me outside in a minute or two: he's catching the 16:05 to Euston and I shall be bringing his car back from Penrith.'

Skelgill checks his wristwatch. 'Certainly, sir – time presses for us, too.'

He glances across at the typewriter sitting before the window. 'If you don't mind, sir – could I possibly just nip into the toilet? – I think I had one cup of tea too many with Dr Jacobson.'

With a hand movement Dr Snyder again indicates in the direction of the rear door. Skelgill nods and quicksteps across the room, as if to emphasise his pressing need. Meanwhile DS Leyton succeeds in closing down the computer, then stands to wait with Dr Snyder in a moment or two of uncomfortable silence until his partner reappears.

'Ready, Inspector?'

'All systems go, sir. Though there is just one other thing.' Skelgill reaches out and takes up a small book that is lying flat on top of a shelf of others. 'I noticed this earlier – would you mind if I borrowed it for a day or two?'

Dr Snyder frowns and then squints at the book. But he's no longer wearing his reading glasses. Skelgill has offered no explanation and Dr Snyder seems reluctant to ask why he wants it. Just then there is the sharp honk of a car horn, and Dr Snyder seems momentarily discomfited by the need to make a decision.

'Oh – fine, Inspector – if you must.'

'Thank you, sir – I'll drop it straight back.' Skelgill turns to leave.

Now for a second Dr Snyder seems distracted, and he delays for a moment to cast a last glance around the room before following the detectives through the vestibule, ducking stiffly to avoid the low lintel. He pulls the outer door shut and extracts a bunch of keys from his jacket pocket. Just across on the slick tarmac of the driveway a large gleaming silver Mercedes sits idling, the drip of condensation from its tailpipe revealing it has not long been running. The driver shows no inclination to wind down a window or come out to meet them. With the dappled woodland light reflecting off the tinted glass, it is impossible to tell if it is indeed the Head, and what attention he pays to them.

'Goodbye Gentleman, enjoy the stroll back up – the grounds are very pleasant at this time of year.'

Dr Snyder stalks silently away and circles the car in predatory fashion, disappearing like an octopus into a crevice as he folds his gangly limbs into the passenger side, before a soft clunk of the door announces the vehicle's departure. As the car passes from sight out of the gateway – turning in the correct direction for the road to Penrith – Skelgill raps a beat with his knuckles against the book and says, 'Well? What did you get?'

'Interesting Guv – and nice one with the bookshelf, by the way – though he must have wondered why I didn't come and help you.'

'I think we pulled it off, Leyton – daft coppers is our forte, remember. So?'

'History cleared. Recent items wiped. Trash emptied. Cookies removed.'

Skelgill folds his arms and glowers at DS Leyton. 'What are the odds of that being a normal thing on a computer – even the computer of someone who doesn't use it much?'

DS Leyton makes a bookmaker's tic-tac signal and says, 'Century, Guv?'

'That's a hundred to one against, I take it?'

DS Leyton nods, 'Snyder didn't want us to see something, Guv.'

Skelgill spins on his heel and sets off walking in the direction of the school, leaving DS Leyton to stumble after him in order to catch up.

'Not necessarily Snyder. Not necessarily *us*.'

'Suppose so, Guv. But, what with him getting there first – and he was watching me like a hawk until you pulled the bookcase stunt.'

'You could be right, Leyton – but it's not the only possible explanation.'

DS Leyton shakes his head, as if to say, 'Here we go again, let's make life difficult for ourselves'. Between breaths he gasps, 'And what was that business with the book, Guv – is there a name in it?'

'Use your loaf. I took it to unsettle him – he doesn't know why I want it. Plus it gives me an excuse to come back.'

'Good thinking, Guv.'

Skelgill shrugs. Then he holds up the small tome and scrutinises the worn dustcover. 'Mind you, it's a first edition *Wainwright* – they're like hen's teeth, these things. I shall enjoy reading it.'

'You're not half-inching it, Guv?'

'Leyton – behave.'

DS Leyton waggles his head from side to side, and the pair walks on in silence for a couple of minutes. Then Skelgill says, 'Over there – through the gap in the trees.' He points with the corner of the *Wainwright*. 'Reckon that's Goodman's house?'

DS Leyton squints in the direction indicated. There are glimpses of a substantial sandstone property, mirroring the fabric of the school itself.

'Look at the place, Guv. What with that and the Merc, he's onto a good number. My headmaster lived in a council flat and drove a maggoty Lada Riva.'

'Your education didn't cost twenty-five grand a year, Leyton.'

'Just as well, Guv – twenty-five quid would have been daylight robbery.'

12. THE PAVILION

'Leyton – I think I've just spotted our next pit stop.'

'What do you mean, Guv?'

'Look – a cricket match – there's always a tea – there might be some left over.'

'Blimey, Guv – my missus reckons I'm the only person who goes on holiday and actually loses weight.'

'Leyton, don't be a killjoy. Anyway – you've just walked half a mile, surely that deserves a cucumber sandwich.'

'What about the final interview, Guv?'

'We'll come back tomorrow – it's only going to be one of Goodman's cronies. Follow me, Sergeant. Remember, we're spectators. Walk this way.'

Intent on returning to the reception of the school via a circuitous route, Skelgill has led them seemingly randomly off the main driveway along a narrow woodland path, to emerge in their present location on the edge of the superbly manicured oval. In fact, his ears had twitched on detecting the distant thwack of leather on willow. Now he slips the *Wainwright* guide inside his jacket, slides his hands into his trouser pockets and begins casually to saunter towards the perimeter of the cricket field, where a white rope marks the boundary.

'I never got into cricket, Guv – too dangerous where I grew up.'

'What – the big West Indian kids bowling bumpers?'

'Nah, Guv – dogs. Feral dogs. If they didn't get you, their business would. It was like a minefield round our estate.'

Skelgill grimaces at the thought. It is one of the hazards of cricket played out on public open-spaces. You never quite know what kind of soft landing the ball is going to make. Now he inclines his head in the direction of the clubhouse, around which a small gathering of parents who have travelled with the visiting team recline in striped deck chairs swathed by matching tartan rugs in Oakthwaite colours provided by the home side.

'Look at that pavilion, Leyton. It must be brand new. And they've got a proper scoreboard and sightscreens – better than most clubs I've played at.'

'No expense spared, eh, Guv?'

'Shot!' Skelgill adds a few handclaps to the ripple of applause that greets the batsman's latest effort.

'Look out, Guv – duck!'

The ball has been hoisted high above square leg, and its trajectory, even to DS Leyton's untrained eye is unequivocally bringing it over the rope for six and down upon their heads. DS Leyton starts shifting from one foot to the other, as if he's uncertain about in which direction to take evasive action. Skelgill, in contrast, stands stock still and faces the oncoming missile. Then at the last split second he makes a small adjustment of his feet and neatly catches the ball baseball style over his left shoulder and, left handed, sends it zipping back without a bounce to smack firmly into the waiting wicketkeeper's red gloves. This exploit brings a small gasp of admiration and further applause from the crowd.

'Nice one, Guv – I heard you were a bit of an Ian Botham on the quiet.'

For a moment Skelgill looks like he's pleased with himself, but the impression quickly passes and he scowls in self-reprimand.

'How not to draw attention to yourself, Leyton.'

'I shouldn't worry, Guv – they'll have to give us a cuppa now.'

Skelgill nods. He says, 'If asked, let them think we're friends of the family of a pupil – it's more or less accurate.'

'Apart from the word *friends*, Guv.'

Skelgill laughs. 'It sounds better than servants, Leyton.'

'True, Guv – although I get the feeling if you said we were servants they wouldn't bat an eyelid round here.'

'You're probably right, Leyton – I think our accents are going to be a bit of a giveaway. I'd tell them we were farmers, but I've never heard of a Cockney shepherd.'

'Farmer Giles, Guv?'

'What?'

'Rhyming slang – piles.'

'I think you'd better let me do the talking, Leyton.'

'Quite right, Guv.'

By now they are approaching the pavilion. Skelgill attracts one or two approving glances and a quip of, 'Well held, that man,' that he affects modesty in order to shrug off. The building itself is indeed spanking brand new, and includes such professional facilities as a viewing balcony on its upper floor, and a well-stocked mini-cafeteria on the lower. As Skelgill predicted, there has been a cricket tea, the generous though slightly curling remnants of which are laid out upon a long trestle table manned by a young black-haired woman in a close-fitting catering outfit.

'Tea or coffee, sir?' Her proud pale blue eyes seem to defy her deferential manner. But her accent reveals she's a local – as much as Polish is local these days.

'Two teas please, love.' Skelgill leans in a little closer. 'It's okay – we're with the workers. Can we sample the buffet?'

'You are welcome – it is for guests.' The hard glaze over the eyes softens and she affords a little smile.

Skelgill looks like he's tempted to blow their cover, but a timely elbow from DS Leyton alerts him to the approach of someone from behind.

'You guys with the opposition?' Now the accent is decidedly South African.

The detectives turn to face a short fresh-faced man of about thirty, an athletic figure clad in cricket whites and boots. His close-cropped ginger hair and freckles speak of Celtic origins that belie the voice.

'You might say that.' Skelgill evidently decides to opt for the route of least resistance.

'Howzit? Mike Greig, Director of Sport – welcome to Oakthwaite.' He extends a small hand that delivers a surprisingly firm grip. Both detectives manage to return his greeting without revealing their names.

Greig gestures with a sharp gun-fingered jerk towards the buffet table. 'Don't let me keep you from filling your plates, gentlemen. You need to keep your strength up in this weather.'

'A bit different to where you hail from?' ventures Skelgill.

'Ja – you're not joking. They warned me it was changeable in Britain – what I didn't expect was that you have all four seasons every day.'

Skelgill nods. 'The Lakes gets the highest rainfall in England.'

'I suppose that's why there are lakes, nee?' Greig beams endearingly.

Skelgill grins in solidarity. 'So what brings you to the North?'

'Ja – I'm on a two-year exchange. Got a year to go. I coach cricket and rugby in a school in Joberg. On the Highveld. We're connected to The Wanderers.'

'The infamous *Bullring*.'

'You know your game.'

Skelgill shrugs. 'That sounds like a high standard you bring with you.'

'Well, your English boys are not so far behind – just lack a bit of the killer instinct that we tend to breed back home.'

'Is that why you're here – to toughen them up?'

Greig smiles apologetically. 'Don't get me wrong – we play fair. We don't generally walk, though.'

'Nothing wrong with that, eh Leyton?' Skelgill pops a whole quarter-sandwich into his mouth.

DS Leyton stutters, and then says, seemingly out of the blue, 'What does *Loong* mean?'

Skelgill does a kind of double-take, and for a moment must be wondering if DS Leyton has lapsed into Afrikaans. But Greig is unfazed by the Sergeant's seemingly peculiar question.

'I get asked that a lot.' Greig glances across to a point above the servery. There's a large brass nameplate bearing the words *The Loong Pavilion*, and this year's date. 'One of the boys who went up to university last year, Singaporean – nice little leg-spinner – his father, Mr Loong, evidently paid for this place to be built.'

'So you might call this the Loong Room?' DS Leyton grins.

Skelgill rounds on him. 'Very funny, Leyton – I thought you were a cricket ignoramus?'

DS Leyton shrugs, 'I've been known to stand in front of the Lord's Tavern with the lads of a Saturday afternoon.'

'I've heard not a lot of cricket gets watched from there.' Greig, too, knows his subject. 'Are you in the Barmy Army?'

Skelgill laughs out loud. 'He's barmy alright, but that's where it ends.'

Greig grins amicably. 'Well, gentlemen, it's been good speaking with you – but if you don't mind I promised I'd relieve the scorer so he can get some chow. He missed the tea interval.'

Skelgill puts up a palm to indicate they shouldn't detain him any longer.

'Nice speaking with you, er...' Greig realises he doesn't know Skelgill's name, but extends his hand all the same.

'Dan.'

'Yeah – nice speaking with you, Dan.' He turns to DS Leyton. 'And you too, Leighton – perhaps catch up after your boys have had a bat.'

DS Leyton, a little lost for words, shakes the offered hand and mumbles, 'Yeah – cheers, mate.'

Greig strides purposefully out of the cafeteria and skips lightly down the pavilion steps. Skelgill, still grinning, carefully reaches out and with a crablike pincer movement extracts a strip of sandwiches. 'Don't want to waste these on the scorer. Come on, Leyton – fill your boots and we'll head for your car.'

*

'Not bad sarnies, these, Guv.'

Skelgill, chewing, nods in agreement. He swallows and holds up the last of his supply for inspection. 'Takes a few to fill you up, though.'

'Wonder what they do with all the crusts?'

'They'd make decent ground-bait.'

'Perhaps they feed 'em to the ducks, Guv?'

'Leyton, this isn't Derwentwater – there's no ducks on Bass Lake.'

'Really? I thought all lakes had ducks.'

'There's *wild* ducks – but not the greedy fat tame lumps the tourists stuff with French fries.'

'Oh.' DS Leyton looks bewildered, as if these were the only kind of ducks. 'Mind you, Guv – it's good fun for the kids. Our little 'un still likes chasing 'em.'

'A bit like us, eh, Leyton?'

'How do you mean, Guv?'

'This.' Skelgill gestures with both hands in the direction of the rear of Oakthwaite School. 'The Chief's wild goose chase.'

DS Leyton, about to take a bite of his last remaining sandwich, looks rather forlornly at Skelgill. 'Do you still not reckon we've got anything, Guv?'

'Do you?' Skelgill sounds scathing. He brushes crumbs peremptorily from his lap.

'What about the computer, Guv? That's definitely odd.'

Skelgill purses his lips and shakes his head. 'Aye... but, we're looking for what? Signs of a possible murder? At the very least, malicious persecution that drove Querrell to drown himself. So, his computer may have been wiped – he could have done it himself – maybe that was his routine after each time he used it. On its own it doesn't mean a thing, Leyton.'

'Well, that Snyder gives me the creeps. Imagine being a little nipper and having to go to him for the cane. Strike the fear of God into you.'

'They don't cane, Leyton – corporal punishment was outlawed years ago.'

'Oh – I thought maybe the private schools still have it – Jacobson mentioned it, remember, Guv?'

'I assumed he was harking back to the good old days.'

'Not so old, Guv – I recall it well enough.' DS Leyton affects a pained shudder.

Skelgill stares through the windscreen as if mesmerized by a memory. A regular array of black-tarred toilet outflows emerge from the roughly harled wall of the building at second-floor level.

Diagonally, they join a horizontal that feeds into a downpipe. The corresponding washroom windows are frosted, while the smaller clear glass ones on the floor above look like they might be dormitories, sporting stickers, and the odd pile of books capped by a chewed soft toy. It's a contrasting image of the school to that portrayed by the immaculate neoclassical frontage. After a moment he says, 'You're right about one thing, Leyton – Jacobson was off message, as the spin doctors put it.'

'How do you mean, Guv?'

'Since he wasn't on our official list he hadn't been briefed on the party line. Snyder looked none too pleased when he discovered we'd been in there. I doubt he or Goodman would want us hearing gossip about them putting the squeeze on old Querrell.'

'I suppose Snyder being Querrell's direct boss – must be a pain if you've got an uncooperative subordinate you can't get of shot of.'

'Tell me about it, Leyton.'

'Ha-ha, Guv.' DS Leyton grins obediently. 'But, apart from the missing computer data, it's just about the only line we've got.'

'Hardly grounds for suspected murder.' Skelgill's tone is scornful.

DS Leyton shrugs resignedly. 'Thing is, Guv, if you ask me all three of them were acting a bit queer – cagey, like.'

'I wouldn't have called Jacobson cagey.'

'Well, no, Guv – but... he was like an old mother hen, clucking about in one corner of the yard so we didn't notice the nest over in the other.'

A semblance of a grin creases the corners of Skelgill's severely set mouth. 'Thing is, Leyton – who doesn't have a guilty secret? Coppers come poking around – you know how folks are? Think we've got x-ray specs and can read their mind. Might be nothing to do with why we're there, but they behave suspiciously when they hear the skeleton start rattling in the closet.'

DS Leyton is beginning to look exasperated. He throws his hands up in frustration. 'Well, I wish the Chief had given us more of a steer, Guv. How are we supposed to know why she's got her knickers in such a bleedin' twist over this one?'

Skelgill's phone rings – it's an unusual tone. As he reaches inside his jacket he smiles inanely at DS Leyton and says, 'Shall I ask her now?'

DS Leyton feigns injury as Skelgill answers the call.

'Yes, Ma'am?'

He casts an optimistic glance at DS Leyton.

'Yes, Ma'am – we're there now.'

There's a long silence as he listens. The subtle change in his features suggests the tenor of his superior's monologue is unfavourable.

'Well, Ma'am – we... er...'

Evidently he is interrupted.

'No, Ma'am it was...'

And again.

'I, er... think we got the names mixed up.'

Now follows a further soliloquy. DS Leyton shrinks supportively in his seat, pulling down an invisible tin hat over his ears.

'No, Ma'am – I mean yes, Ma'am – we'll do our best.'

This remark brings a stinging rebuke, if Skelgill's involuntary wince is anything to go by.

'Yes Ma'am, I...'

But the Chief has rung off.

DS Leyton slowly turns his head, his expression one of a person anticipating a cuff across the scalp. He knows better than to ask a dumb question at this particular juncture. Instead he just says, sympathetically, 'Ouch, Guv.'

Skelgill slides the handset inside his jacket and leans back in the passenger seat, folding his arms. After a moment he says, 'Goodman's phoned and given her a flea in her ear. "Why are coppers talking to my staff without permission?" He knows about Jacobson – obviously Snyder will have told him – and about Hodgson. Probably knows how many sandwiches we ate as well.'

'Does he know *she* put us up to it?'

Skelgill shakes his head slowly. 'That's the one small bit of credit we come out with, apparently.'

'So, what else could we have done, Guv?'

'Well, Leyton, we're supposed miraculously to discover something as yet unknown to man, in the dark, with both hands tied behind our backs.'

DS Leyton nods understandingly.

'Oh – and we've got until close of play tomorrow to do it, or else.'

DS Leyton's demeanour takes on a hint of the hunted animal. 'Or else what, Guv?'

'An *everlasting*, Leyton.'

13. THE GATEHOUSE

'Jones.'

'Yes, Guv.'

'Are you still on duty?'

'Till late, Guv.'

'Not the same stakeout, surely?'

'Well, we've moved to another bar – then it's a club tonight – we're not past the reconnaissance stage.'

Skelgill audibly grinds his teeth, though the sound probably doesn't transmit over the airwaves. But he evidently decides to concentrate upon police matters. 'I need your help, Jones.'

'Sure, Guv – whatever I can do.'

'Firstly, see if your aunt can find out where the Head and his Deputy came from. Mr Goodman and Dr Snyder.'

'Sounds like Dr Jekyll and Mr Hyde, Guv.'

'In this case I'm pretty certain there's two of them. Snyder mentioned he'd been at a school in Singapore. I didn't dare ask the Head, he was bristling as it was.'

'I'll pass on the request, Guv. It's going to be tomorrow, though, before we get an answer – she'll have finished at five today.'

'Just as early as possible – the Chief's on the warpath.'

'That didn't take long.'

'You know me, Jones.'

DS Jones inhales to reply, but then checks herself. After a second's pause she says, 'What else, Guv?'

'How do you mean?'

'You said *firstly* – I assume there's a secondly?'

'Ah – Miss Marple. What time do you knock off?'

'I think the club shuts at midnight weekdays.'

'Fine – then pick me up at one a.m. on the dot. I'll text you the directions. I may not be able to communicate with you until I see you, so keep your eyes peeled.'

'But... Guv, what exactly...?'

'Thanks, Jones. You know how the signal can be...'

Skelgill takes the handset down from his ear and ends the call.

Breathing heavily and dripping water from his hair, Skelgill gingerly wades barefoot through the rocky shallows on the osier-lined eastern shore of Bassenthwaite Lake. It's a clear night and behind him a waxing gibbous moon sails high over Thornthwaite Forest, illuminating his approach to Oakthwaite's landing stage and throwing inky shadows beneath its spindly form. He hauls himself with some care onto the splintering timbers and turns to sit in childlike fashion, legs dangling, the water droplets on his naked body glistening like beads of mercury. It might be a scene from a werewolf movie. He turns his head this way and that, and after a minute has satisfied himself that nobody is afoot. The distant engine-rumble of a late-night truck on the A66 reaches across the calm surface, easing up a gear as it leaves the s-bends after Peel Wyke, and fading Cockermouth way. He affects a shudder, perhaps as a reaction to the cold he must be feeling – even in late summer the water temperature rarely exceeds twenty degrees Celsius. He unclips what, apart from his wristwatch, is his only other item of apparel – a bloated waist pack – unzips it with trembling fingers and begins to extract the contents.

Now he curses under his breath – the rudimentary waterproofing system comprising three layers of dog-eared supermarket carrier bags has failed badly. A lightweight mountaineering vest and trousers emerge sodden, and a pair of well-worn slipper-like fell-running shoes are waterlogged to twice their normal density. Rain-soaked gear is an occupational hazard for a hardened amateur fellsman like Skelgill, though such discomfort when on duty (albeit unofficially) must be less familiar. So it's not without several additional hissed expletives that he contrives to struggle his way into the uncooperative outfit.

The final object in the waist pack is at least impermeable – a small black tubular torch. He presses the lens against his right palm and briefly depresses the on-off switch: a glowing blood-red ring confirms it has survived as advertised. Keeping the torch to hand he sets off, turning almost immediately southwards to follow the running track – little more than a narrow unmade footpath – which passes close by the boathouse as it traces the perimeter of the extensive school grounds. Initially it winds amongst willows and scattered alders – species that can tolerate the vagaries of fluctuating water levels – but as the boundary veers and rises eastwards from the lakeside, the woodland belt thickens with oak and beech and sycamore, robbing Skelgill of most of what little light there is by which to navigate.

Still he walks at a brisk pace, trusting to practised intuition the course of the path, silent upon the damp earth, compressed over decades by the thousands of *pad-pad-pad* footsteps of reluctant schoolboys, their ghosts perhaps still running. But, while the current crop of would-be harriers are safely tucked up in their dorms, more ancient forest inhabitants are abroad. In a glade, Skelgill pauses to watch a pair of *Natterer's* bats hawking acrobatically for moths, while the insistent *wick-wick-wick* of a tawny owl ahead tells him all is clear. He moves on, re-entering the musty, velvety void beneath the trees, for a moment more vivid until his senses readjust and he detects a low shape moving his way. A warning flash of his torch reveals two-tone headgear, and simultaneously sends its wearer scuttling noisily into the undergrowth.

Skelgill covers the mile and a half to the gatehouse inside fifteen minutes, though in the darkness time and direction can lose their linear quality. When it appears on his right, the shadow of the high wall that marks Oakthwaite's boundary with the winding lane he drove with DS Leyton must be a reassuring sight. He halts some twenty yards short of the unlit property and waits, breathing through his nose, listening intently. But the only sound is the lightest patter of leaves in the canopy, as irregular air currents disturb its minutely tiled surface. He checks his watch – it's already after twelve-thirty – perhaps he misjudged the swim; his rendezvous with DS Jones is impending.

The footpath passes the rear of the cottage and invisibly crosses the main driveway, reappearing as a vague smudge that divides the undergrowth beyond. Skelgill stalks towards the back door, but makes a right turn and skirts the building, taking care to tread on the soakaway gravel that expediently accepts no tracks. Rounding the corner that incorporates the jutting toilet extension, he stops and, facing the wall, pulls his sleeves over his hands as makeshift mittens, then reaches up and opens the small window he had unlatched on his unscheduled visit earlier. A hop-cum-heave sees him sliding snakelike over the sill and into the bijou cubicle.

Once within he pulls back his cuffs – his fingerprints are already in all the expected places, his presence thoroughly witnessed only hours earlier. Cautiously entering the main living space, he makes for the stair-ladder – it creaks alarmingly as he ascends – and raises his head into the attic space. A quick sweep of his torch confirms he's alone. A forsaken sleeping bag is cast roughly upon a single mattress that rests in turn on the bare boards and, beyond, cramped beneath the low eaves, a chest of drawers and wardrobe, of knotted wood, stand slightly askew on the uneven surface. Skelgill kills the torch beam; the aspect of the room changing as filtered moonlight diffuses in from the rear-facing of the two dormer windows that nestle within opposite sides of the roof.

He descends, bending at the knee with each step to cushion his weight. Regaining the unyielding stone floor he makes a beeline for the old typewriter. It sits in the gloom, a Dickensian presence; what forlorn beats have its keys tapped out, what expectations of hope and despair? Now Skelgill turns on the torch again and grips it between his teeth. He reaches out with both hands and experimentally fiddles with the knobs and levers on either side of the antique machine until he finds the combination to release the sprocket that restrains the ribbon. Carefully he winds it back a few inches, then takes the torch in hand and stoops to examine the exposed strip. For a moment he stiffens, as if disbelieving of what he sees: the tape is blank. Now he repeats the process, grimacing as he bites on the torch. He unwinds a few more inches – and again checks it minutely. He shakes his head, and then rewinds the ribbon in the forward direction. After a final inspection he switches off the torch and stands upright, staring out into the darkness of the school driveway.

After a minute he exhales a long breath and, as if rallying himself, turns briskly and strides across to the chimney breast. He stoops at the hearth and directs the torch upon the ashes in the grate. Taking a small iron poker from a stand he prods tentatively at what is an amorphous grey mass. It gives little clue to its original form, though it's certainly not coal. However, there is no fuel stacked nearby to help in its identification: perhaps not surprising at this time of year. He seems to pause for thought, then rises and, with an unexpected movement, hefts the armchair from its place before the fire. He lifts the mat: his torch reveals only undisturbed flagstones. Carefully, he replaces the chair. Next he performs a quick sweep of the remainder of the room, apparently testing that the rows of books are really what they seem; he inspects the cupboards in the kitchenette area; lastly he returns to the hearth and, on one knee, shines the torch up into the chimney.

He consults his wristwatch – it's now twelve forty-five. He returns to the stair and climbs, more swiftly than before. Gaining the bedroom he hauls up the mattress and shines the torch on the bare boards. He replaces the sleeping bag then repeats the search with the chest of drawers and wardrobe, heaving them aside and checking beneath, before returning them to their original positions. He takes a cursory look inside – together they hold a sparse ensemble that evokes stale sweat mingled with mothballs.

Again he checks the time. Now he prowls about the room, covering the remaining floor area with deliberate small steps, pressing down as if to detect a loose board. His methodical choreography brings him to the rear-facing dormer window, one side now brightly lit by moonlight that has found a clear channel between trunk and bough.

It must be a view taken in by Querrell on countless nights, peering perhaps short-sightedly, night-gowned, leaning out to sniff the cooling air and listen to the sounds of the woods. However, Skelgill cannot dwell. He turns to go. But he takes one step and is stopped dead in his tracks by a clank from below: like the crack of a pistol, a key is inserted into the mortise lock on the front door. In two seconds it opens, then closes, and heavy footsteps clump into the room. The person evidently checks the back door, for there's the rattle of a handle, then the light is switched on, sending a bright shaft of illumination up through the hatch into the attic.

At this, Skelgill makes an instinctive movement – but unavailingly it's for his inside pocket and his warrant card; neither of which are there. Swivelling slowly on the balls of his feet he faces the window. He reaches out and gently slips the catch. Perhaps unexpectedly it's well oiled – maybe Querrell did regularly avail himself of the view – and the sliding casement feels loose in the frame. From downstairs there comes the scrape of a chair, as if the person has seated themself either at the typewriter or the computer. Holding his breath, Skelgill takes a firm grip of the window-handles and begins to raise the casement – but, though it moves freely, it emits a tell-tale squeal to equal the warning cry of the Giant's golden harp in the arms of a fleeing Jack. Skelgill recoils. Immediately there's another scrape of the chair from below, and the sound of feet approaching, then stepping upon, the foot of the ladder.

Skelgill slides the torch from his pocket. Masking the beam against one palm, as before, he engages self-defence mode, a fearsomely dazzling flashing function guaranteed to repel even the most determined of assailants. Thus armed, he slips back into the alcove of the window.

A growing shadow begins to darken the bright rectangle of the attic hatch. Skelgill raises the shrouded torch, his body visibly coiling like a cat making ready to pounce. His best bet must be to temporarily blind his opponent, push him over if necessary, and make good his getaway.

Then comes heavenly intervention – or so it seems. A much greater light intercedes upon the scene. From somewhere a vehicle rapidly approaches and slews to a halt, its bright headlamps flooding the cottage with a powerful swinging beam.

Almost immediately the person on the staircase begins steadily to retreat. The creak of the ladder becomes footsteps upon the flagstones. The front door is opened, and then there's a crunch of pebbles on the path. Listening intently, Skelgill springs into action. In one smooth movement he pockets his torch, leaps to the hatch and launches himself into the void, breaking his fall by grabbing the cross-member in front of him, but he misjudges his forward motion and strikes his head as he descends through the small frame. He loses his grip and drops awkwardly to the ground, landing heavily upon one knee instead of the intended two feet. But without hesitation he lurches across the room and gains the relative sanctuary of the toilet. He makes to slide the bolt, but declines – perhaps he decides it would leave confirmation of his presence. In two or three more seconds his feet are disappearing through the small window and he tumbles onto the mixture of earth and gravel beneath.

He rolls onto his stomach, close against the wall, and raises himself like a sprinter poised in his blocks. He must be disoriented from the blow to the head, as he casts about for the best line of escape between the bright lights of the car beyond one corner of the cottage, and the indistinct sound of male voices around the other. For the present he is sheltered between the jutting extension of the toilet cubicle and the ramshackle lean-to that covers the late Querrell's motorbike. For a few seconds he stares at the old machine, its gleaming chrome exhausts and gloss black paintwork reflecting tiny twinkling moonbeams. As an occasional biker himself, a Steve McQueen moment could be on the cards, but instead he exits in less elegant fashion, staggering to his feet, almost toppling over, but just contriving to employ his momentum as a means of propulsion that sees him crash into the shadows of the undergrowth, unruly uninvited rhododendrons that patrol the perimeter and hug the boundary wall. He presses himself into their welcome cover, and clambers through to the brickwork. It rises to some eight feet, but poses no obstacle to his practised scrambling technique, and he's atop in a trice, tumbling over into the lesser undergrowth of springy bramble and brittle stinging nettle that inhabits the no-man's land lining the lane.

Recovering his breath he lies hidden from sight, gazing up at the glittering Great Bear. Then suddenly he freezes and listens again. There's the sound of an automobile, slowly approaching. He turns onto all fours, attracting the painful attention of the hostile herbage that seems designed both to repel and entrap. Squinting through the low foliage he sees the headlights only twenty feet away; then the hazard lights begin to flash. He leaps up and limps out into the road, flagging down the car with his torch.

The vehicle draws to a halt and he yanks open the passenger door and swings inside. 'Go! Go! Get us out of here! And switch off all your lights!'

'Yes Guv.' DS Jones gives Skelgill an old-fashioned look, but efficiently does as he requests.

After half a minute he glances anxiously behind them, but the road is dark and he says, 'That'll do – stick the lights on before we end up in a ditch.'

'Like you've not been in a ditch already, Guv?'

'Ha-ha, Jones.'

She stares across at him, too long for the good of safe driving, but the dishevelled state of his hair, features and attire demand such attention.

'Guv – you look like *Wurzel Gummidge*. What's happened? Are you okay?'

'You're not old enough to have heard of *Wurzel Gummidge*.'

'I'm old enough to have heard of *YouTube*, Guv. You'd be surprised what I know.'

'Maybe I would.'

DS Jones grins. 'Anyway, thanks for being on time.'

'That's no prob...' Skelgill stops himself and falls back into the seat. He allows himself a kind of laugh. 'Sorry – aye – thanks. You saved my bacon, there.'

'All part of the service. Though Alec... I mean, *DI Smart*... was none-too-chuffed when I told him I wouldn't be reviewing the day's findings over a nightcap.'

Skelgill stares straight ahead. He leans forward to massage his bruised knee. After a moment he turns to appraise his companion: she's still dressed for the nightclub in Carlisle she left an hour earlier – a short black skirt revealing most of her sheer silvery tights (or are they stockings?), matched by a tight-fitting sparkly bodice, and striking eye make-up that belies any possibility that she might work for the CID.

'You don't look like a copper.'

'I'll take that as a compliment.' She glances at Skelgill. 'Guv – it's a deadly boring gig.'

'Aha.' Skelgill's tone is flat.

'Are you sure you're okay?' She turns again to inspect his condition. 'You've got a hell of an egg on your forehead.'

'Which came first?'

'The chicken?'

'That was me – I had to do a runner.'

'What on earth were you up to, Guv?'

'Same as you, really – doing at bit of a recce.'

'Without permission?'

'Right to roam, and all that.'

'I though that was Scotland, Guv.'

'It's near enough.'

'Did you get spotted?'

'You know,' Skelgill rubs his scalp with both hands, dislodging small items of vegetation, 'I actually think I got away with it – by the skin of my teeth.'

'Find anything?'

'I'm not sure.'

'How can you be *not sure*, Guv?'

'Well – sometimes, nothing can be something.'

DS Jones gives him a cross-eyed look that says she's heard his double-speak before.

'Where are we going, by the way?'

'Peel Wyke. My car's down by the boat.'

'Oh. How did you get to the school?'

'I swam.'

'You're kidding?'

'Why would I joke?'

'Well – you *are* wet through, I can see that.' She sniffs. '*Smell*, actually.'

'Cheers, Jones.'

'Sorry, Guv.'

'No offence taken.'

'What would you have done if I'd not managed to pick you up?'

'A triathlon?'

She chuckles.

Skelgill adds, 'And then throttled Smart.'

DS Jones raises her eyebrows, but does not respond. Perhaps she takes the opportunity to change the subject, for she says, 'Guv – about Singapore.'

'Aye.' Skelgill sounds as if he is not listening.

'You wanted to know about the Head and his Deputy?'

'Oh... yeah. But you can't have heard already?'

'No, it's not that.' She brushes a couple of strands of hair from her eyes. 'While I was in the club... there was a wifi signal, so I was looking online. Google Oakthwaite plus Singapore and guess what?'

'Snyder?'

'Actually, Guv – no. The Head.'

'How come?'

'There's an educational convention in Singapore this week. He's the keynote speaker and Oakthwaite's got one of the main exhibition stands – you know, to recruit overseas pupils.'

Skelgill is silent, but evidently digesting this news. After a few moments he says, 'He was catching the London train this afternoon. That must be where he was heading. He never mentioned it to us.'

'Maybe nothing in that, though, Guv? You said he was pretty circumspect.'

Skelgill nods ruefully. 'Aye, maybe.'

'You can see why they don't want adverse publicity, Guv. When there are all the schools in the world to choose from. Bad news costs money.'

Again Skelgill has to concur. He says, 'Do you reckon they charge more to foreigners?'

She shrugs. 'I'm sure I can find out – but it can't be a huge difference... must be quite a competitive market.'

'Whatever it is, it's enough to merit a beano in Singapore. Alright for some, eh? When do we get a junket like that, Jones?'

14. SALE FELL

'Morning, Guv – where are you, squire?'

'Leyton...?'

'Guv – you alright?'

'Aye... I... er... something came up.'

Skelgill's thick voice and sluggish wits tell the listening DS Leyton all he needs to know: his superior has overslept. This is most unlike the DI Skelgill who, among his various nicknames of 'Mallory', 'Dan Dare' and 'Dirty Harry', is also referred to among his colleagues by the less flattering epithet 'Badger', for his general disregard of the protocols of the eight-hour sleep and the concept of retiring and rising at civilised hours.

'Guv – you should get down here.'

'Steady on, Leyton.'

'But, Guv – I'm at the school. It's urg...'

Skelgill interrupts. 'Start without me Leyton. Do the next interview.'

'But, Guv...'

Skelgill is becoming irate. 'Leyton,' (he coughs heavily) 'What's your problem?'

'Guv – it's Hodgson – you know, the groundsman?'

'What about him?'

'He's dead.'

'What?'

'Looks like *he's* topped himself, too.'

Skelgill breathes heavily, but does not respond.

'Guv – *sure* you're okay?'

'Leyton, I'm fine. Shut it.'

'Sorry, Guv.'

'Why didn't you call me earlier?'

'I've been ringing for the last forty-five minutes, Guv.'

Skelgill clears his throat again.

'How did he do it?'

'Shotgun, Guv – one of those little four-tens.'

'Where?'

'In the gatehouse – Querrell's cottage.'

Again there's silence.

'Who found him?'

'Local jobbing chippy, Guv. He comes in once a fortnight to do all the handyman stuff. Snyder had asked him to sort those shelves you pulled down.'

'What time?'

'About an hour ago. Eight-thirtyish.'

'Is Herdwick there?'

'On his way, Guv – he had to finish an autopsy first thing.'

'So we don't know when he died.'

'That's right, Guv – not yet. The light was on, though – suggests it was during the night.'

'Was it locked?'

'Apparently so. Snyder loaned the chippy the key.'

'Is the place sealed off?'

'Yes, Guv – I've got PC Dodd guarding it – keeping a low profile, like.'

'No signs of foul play?'

'Not at first sight, Guv. He sat in the armchair. Shot through the mouth. Looks like he might have used the poker from the hearth to press the trigger.'

After a few moments Skelgill says, 'Get a photo of the gun on your phone – find out if it's from the school.'

'I've done that, Guv – the picture, anyway. I've arranged for us to see Snyder at ten.'

'You might have to do that on your own.'

'But, Guv – ain't this the connection we've been looking for?'

'Maybe.'

'So, Guv...'

'And call SOCO in.'

'What are you going to do, Guv?'

'Me, Leyton? I'm going for a walk.'

*

Skelgill parks at his regular spot at Peel Wyke, tucking his car away from prying eyes among the trees that surround the hidden and largely unknown slipway. The day has dawned calm and clear, and his attention is easily won by the gentle rises that puncture Bassenthwaite Lake's taut margins. The air still holds its night-time chill, and a residue of foxy mustiness. Through this resonant ether a great tit and a chiffchaff – approximately homophonic – mark their respective territories. Skelgill is drawn to the water's edge, and now lingers beside the boat: there's always tackle in the back of his car.

Suddenly, from above his line of sight, hidden by the canopy, an osprey crashes into the glassy surface about fifty yards from the shore. There's a moment of life-or-death tumult, a frenzy of white water, whence the raptor emerges, its great dark wings bowed by the effort, a twenty-inch jack pike rigid and staring in the iron grip of its talons. The strike seems to dislodge Skelgill from his reverie; he nods admiringly at the uncompromising angler and turns on his heel, eschewing his car and heading back along the lane.

A minute later he's striding past the frontage of the old coaching inn, a long, crouching relic, its low undulating roof an irregular warp of mottled tiles seemingly woven into the fabric of the landscape. Some of its ancient mullioned windows are already flung open as the chambermaids set about banishing stale night fugs from the snug bedrooms. The clink of empty bottles being dropped one by one into a recycling bin rises from the back of the building, returning as an echo from the steeply banked ground beyond.

Skelgill skirts the old barn connected to the distempered hostelry and vaults over a protesting wire fence, panicking a cock pheasant into an explosive getaway. He picks a path into the dense hazel thicket immediately behind the inn. The north-facing ground here is damp, and his boots sink into black peaty bog until he gains the rockier upslope, hauling himself vigorously by means of whatever saplings come to hand. Gradually, the underfoot conditions ease and the shrub layer thins, though the gradient remains punishing. In places there is a thick carpet of slippery bluebell leaves, and mosquitoes and midges rise from the bracken as he brazens his way through, climbing, climbing. High overhead, a pair of circling buzzards catcall to one another, their extended feathered fingers feeling for the first thermal of the day.

While Skelgill's unmarked route intersects with several easier tracks, he is unwavering in his unorthodox trajectory, his stride a steady rhythmical pull, his wiry frame springing off his toes at each upward step, his breathing surprisingly light. After ten minutes or so he reaches a dry-stone wall, and with swift agility swarms over it, taking care not to dislodge loose rocks. He has reached the edge of the wood; before him the open ground rises to its peak at just under twelve hundred feet, a little-visited hill known locally as Sale Fell.

He sets a course for its modest summit, crossing the reedy turf at a punishing pace. Beneath his downturned gaze tormentil, bedstraw and harebell must be a floral blur. Only when he attains the little cairn does he afford himself a glance around, as if he's been saving the surprise of the view. He unhooks his small weathered knapsack and lowers himself down against the irregular stone backrest, looking out over the woods that descend to Bassenthwaite Lake beyond. He produces a dented flask and pours himself a cup of piping hot tea. Sipping pensively, he stares eastwards.

Even from this altitude, Oakthwaite School is still only partially visible, guarded by great oaks and Spanish chestnuts that patrol its green parkland. Its wooded perimeter is more distinct, and Skelgill can just make out the boathouse. There is the route he took last night, along the bank of the lake, then inland towards the lodge, hidden somewhere within the dense belt of trees. He turns his attention back to the jetty; there's something he hasn't spotted before. A curious landform that might escape notice at ground level, it appears as if the site of the landing stage was once connected to the school – some half-mile distant – by a broad dyke, or perhaps a raised bank or thoroughfare. All that remains now is a low ridge of ground. This would be imperceptible if it were not for the slanting rays of the morning sun that reveal its presence as a line of shadow. In sections it is planted with trees, and it fades away altogether as it nears the school building. At its western end, closest to the lake, it disappears into a thicket not far from the boathouse and does not emerge.

Skelgill, as if coming to some decision, suddenly casts away the last dregs of his tea. He jams the mug and flask into the knapsack and slings it onto one shoulder as he swings to his feet. He sets off, retracing his steps down the hillside, but now with a more languid gait. Casually, he reaches into his back pocket for his mobile phone.

15. THE M6 MOTORWAY

'Not still on your walk, Guv?'

Skelgill pauses to peer through the windscreen of DS Jones's car. 'Just approaching Keele Services.'

'Come again, Guv?'

'You heard, Leyton.'

'On the M6?'

'Last time I looked they were.'

'Heading south?'

'Leyton, what is this, Twenty Questions?'

'Flamin' Nora, Guv – I'm blowing out of me jacksie. It's bedlam here.'

'Leyton, you're on loudspeaker. There's a lady present.'

'It's only me,' pipes up DS Jones.

'Oops.' DS Leyton coughs apologetically. 'So, er... Guv – since you're in Staffordshire I take it you won't be coming to the school?'

'No need, Leyton – you can handle it.'

DS Leyton suppresses a sigh of resignation.

'What's Herdwick had to say?'

'Time of death somewhere between two and three a.m.'

Skelgill glances at DS Jones, conscious she's watching him. 'Eyes on the road.'

'Sorry, Guv?'

'Not you, Leyton.'

'Right, Guv.'

'What about cause of death?'

'He's pretty certain it was the four-ten. There was a three-quarters-finished bottle of whisky beside the chair.'

'How many glasses?'

'No glasses, Guv. But Herdwick reckons he'll have some blood test results later. I suppose it was Dutch courage.'

'When was he last seen alive?'

'Greig left him to tidy up after the cricket match around seven – said he was staying to roll the wicket.'

'Did he go home?'

'No one seems to know, Guv.'

'What about the shotgun?'

'Belongs to the school, Guv. Snyder recognised it straight away. I got him to take me to the gun room – it's like a horror movie, down there in the cellars – he showed me the empty space in the rack. Right old arsenal, they've got.'

'What's his explanation?'

'He says he's certain it was there last time he checked.'

'When was that?'

'A couple of weeks back. He says they don't shoot in summer term.'

'And he's sticking to his story about being the only key-holder?'

'Yup.'

'What about Hodgson, did he have keys on him?'

'That's the strange thing, Guv – car keys and what looks like a house key, but nothing else.'

'Yet he was locked inside the gatehouse.'

'Well – kind of, Guv. I spoke again to the old boy who found him. He now says he couldn't swear on the Bible that the door was actually locked. It's got one of those clunky mortises and he reckons it's possible it was already open. He had to fiddle with the key to get in, and thinks he could have locked it and then unlocked it again.'

'Brilliant.'

'Sorry, Guv.'

Skelgill doesn't trouble to absolve DS Leyton of any misplaced blame. 'And how was Snyder?'

'Laying it on a bit thick, if you ask me, Guv. Slagging off Hodgson for sneaking his key away. Claims he must have nicked it from his desk while he was in assembly one morning. I suggested he could have left the gun room unlocked, but he was having none of it.'

'What about any connection between Hodgson and Querrell?'

'He pooh-poohed it, Guv. Except to say they didn't get on. I don't think it's a lover's pact if that's what you're driving at.' A note of hilarity creeps into DS Leyton's voice.

'Leyton, behave.'

'Sorry, Guv – but you never know these days.'

'I think it's a theory we can rule out.'

'Suits me, Guv.'

'So why did he go to Querrell's cottage to do it, Leyton?'

'Suppose he knew it'd be empty. Maybe he got some bad news?'

'Did he have a mobile?'

'Not that's been found, Guv.'

'No other clues at the property?'

'Oh – there was one thing.'

'Aye?'

'The toilet window was unfastened. Somebody could have locked the place on the inside then climbed out.'

'Bit obvious, though, Leyton. Stage a suicide then leave your signature?'

'Perhaps if they were in a hurry, Guv?'

'Or stupid.'

Skelgill realises DS Jones is again looking at him quizzically. He indicates with an impatient nod that she should watch the road ahead.

A moment of silence passes, then DS Leyton asks, 'What next, Guv?'

'You'd better get over to Hodgson's place. Is he married?'

'Snyder doesn't think so. Then again, he says he knows next to nothing about him.'

'What's the address?'

'Cockermouth, in the main street. I looked it up and it seems it's a flat above the newsagent's.'

'Ask in there first.'

'Will do, Guv.'

'Better mind how you go, Leyton – in case he's dismembered his missus and left her in the freezer.'

'Cheers, Guv – one corpse is quite enough for a day. I don't have your cast-iron stomach.'

Skelgill indicates with his left hand to DS Jones that she should take the approaching service station slip road. 'On that note, Leyton, I feel a burger coming on. We'll love you and leave you. I'll call you later.'

16. FLYING ECONOMY

'Think England will ever win the World Cup again, Guv?'

Skelgill shakes his head ruefully. They have the pair of seats on the starboard side of the aircraft. Skelgill's is adjacent to the window, while Jones's beside it is separated by one of two aisles from the central bank of four. They're watching the great arch of Wembley Stadium, highlighted in the afternoon sunshine, gradually disappearing as the jumbo banks away to find its easterly course.

'Don't depress me, Jones. It's bad enough to think I've got twelve hours inside this aluminium tube breathing recycled microbes.' He sits back in the chair and gazes at a cheongsam-clad stewardess who totters past with a tray of small white face-towels. 'Though it has its compensations.'

DS Jones gives him a playful nudge of her elbow. 'So that's why you booked *Singapore*, Guv.'

'Don't blame me – the Chief's office made all the arrangements. I just worked out we could get there and back without needing a hotel.'

'Talk about a flying visit.'

Skelgill shrugs. 'We can use the Police Club as a base – you'll be able to change there. They'll have showers and wifi and whatever we need.'

DS Jones shakes her head. 'I still don't know how you pulled it off, Guv.'

'Natural charm.'

'Guv – no one charms the Chief.'

'Well, I guess I'm on a roll.'

'There has to be something, surely – for her to approve the budget for flights? And to get DI Smart to spare me.'

'She must think so.' Skelgill, impassive, nods slowly. 'Which is more than I do.'

DS Jones looks at him questioningly. 'Come on, Guv – you must at least have a hunch?'

'Jones, you know me – I have more hunches than Nostradamus – but that doesn't mean a thing.'

'Guv – do you mean Quasimodo?'

'Maybe.'

'Surely he only had one?'

'You're getting picky now.'

'But we're tailing Goodman – meanwhile there's been another death at the school.'

Skelgill shrugs. 'The suicides could be incidental. What if the second is a total coincidence, and the Chief used the first purely as an excuse for us to poke our noses in?'

DS Jones puts her hands together prayer-fashion and brings her index fingers up to her lips. She frowns and after a moment's contemplation says, 'So there's some bigger picture in which Goodman could figure?'

'Maybe.'

'Only *maybe*, Guv?'

'Aye – whatever. Look – this is a chance to strike while the iron's hot – at least as far as Goodman's concerned. If we're wrong, nothing's lost. Except a few quid on flights.'

'I'm worried we won't see anything incriminating, Guv – it seems a bit of a long-shot just to try to observe him.'

'Don't worry, Jones, I've got a plan for that.'

DS Jones shakes her head. While he has told her she has been conscripted because – unlike DS Leyton, or Skelgill himself – she won't be recognised by Mr Goodman, she knows sufficient of Skelgill to suspect strongly that something unorthodox is afoot.

'Does the Chief know about this plan, Guv?'

'She knows enough.'

'Guv...' DS Jones sounds insistent.

'Listen – she forked out for the trip, didn't she? She has faith in me. Don't worry about it. I'll tell you more when we arrive. Once we get the lie of the land.'

DS Jones stoically shakes her head. 'And DI Smart's going to be livid.'

Skelgill glowers. 'The Chief said she'd deal with Smart. She wants the details of this trip kept under wraps. Even Leyton's supposed to think we're in London.'

DS Jones nods pensively.

Skelgill reaches forward and lifts a menu card from a flap in the seat pocket. 'When do the drinks come?'

'Dunno, Guv – I've never been on a long-haul flight before.'

'Me neither – but, look at this – *Singapore Sling* – when in Rome, eh? Better give that a go.'

DS Jones grins. 'Okay – so I know what to order with my sparkling water.'

'Alcohol 'till touchdown, black coffee thereafter.'

'I only hope we can sleep, Guv – I'm playing catch-up as it is.'

Skelgill shrugs, as if it were no concern of his.

'That was a bit of a late night, Guv.' DS Jones's tone is somewhat tentative.

Skelgill is staring at the menu card. 'What did you tell Smart?'

Now her voice is rather flat. 'I said my Dad's on medication – which is true – and he can't be relied upon to take it.'

'Right.'

Skelgill pushes his recline button. 'If asked, forget you saw me.' He slips on his headset and begins to jab distractedly at his remote control.

DS Jones sinks back into her own seat. 'You got it.'

*

Seasoned travellers have their well-tried strategies for surviving night flights, and immediately some passengers bed down, blindfolded and ear-plugged, recognising that it's already midnight in Singapore, and six hours sleep in the back pocket is the best insurance against jet lag tomorrow. For Skelgill and DS Jones, however, the little novelties of cold towels, warm towels, drinks and dinner, added to the in-flight entertainment system, keep them going well into the Orient's early hours. And, of course, it's still evening in the UK.

Eventually Jones, perhaps lulled into slumber by the dimmed lights and progressive settling down going on around her, drops off during the extended opening credits of her second rom-com. Skelgill, however, shows no signs of succumbing to fatigue, and periodically clambers over her unconscious form to wander to one or other of the washrooms, soon learning that he is *persona non grata* among the otherwise charming crew when it comes to infiltrating the business class section. Moving through the darkened cabin is rather like tiptoeing through some great celestial dormitory, a fantastic Land of Nod where individual sleepers have been gathered together, unknowingly to act out their private dreamtime routines, their bodies curled foetus-like, their faces sagging masks.

For a light sleeper such as Skelgill, there are also the various unsynchronised challenges of crying babies, heavy snorers, those with chronic coughs, and the occasional crash of luggage in the overhead lockers as the aircraft slices into a pocket of clear-air turbulence.

Whenever DS Jones tosses and turns in search of comfort, tugging her blanket close around her shoulders, she opens half an eye to see Skelgill, upright and staring, seemingly watching their progress across Eurasia on the map on his screen. And he is awake, too, when the lights come up and the cabin fills with the thick aroma of cooked breakfast – though as yet there is no sign of it – and the aisles become clogged with bleary eyed folk in crumpled clothes, stretching and yawning as they queue silently for the toilets.

The sun, too, has reappeared. One after another, window blinds are raised, and the great orange orb they waved away over the Atlantic now greets them above the South China Sea, a little miracle of circumnavigation. As they make a rapid diving descent Skelgill, holding his nose and swallowing hard, squints into the brightness, but there is ocean below and little to see. Only when the pilot lines up over the Straits to take them into Changi, does Skelgill make an exclamation, wowed by the mind-boggling flotilla of cargo ships assembled like a great Elizabethan armada.

Thus, as is the way with all long journeys, they suddenly arrive. The jumbo slams onto the runway without apology or explanation, passengers strain forwards against their belts, and lost mobiles shoot from beneath seats. Then, as the engines are cut, before even the fasten-seatbelt signs are switched off, all hell breaks loose. Collective lethargy and indifference suddenly transforms into every-man-for-himself argy-bargy, and a competition develops to drag bags from overhead lockers, and push and shove for pole position in the aisles.

Skelgill and DS Jones look on phlegmatically. They can afford to be a little complacent at this juncture; journeying on minimal hand luggage, they sense they have an easy passage compared to some overburdened travellers. In due course they filter into the line of departing passengers, and fall in with the general flow of the crowd as it snakes along pontoons, corridors and airborne glass-sided walkways, affording views of what looks less like an airport and more of a theme park blended into a shopping mall.

Perhaps one of the reasons for their fellow passengers' urgency to exit the aircraft becomes clear when they eventually draw to a halt in the substantial queue for passport control: had they got off quickly they certainly would have saved themselves some time here. Now they stand awed in the cathedral-like atrium, forced to admire its free-standing palm trees and towering walls clad with lianas and running water. If visitors harbour any doubts that they've arrived in the tropics, this is all the confirmation they need.

In the process of gradually shuffling forwards, Skelgill suddenly drops to his knees as if he's ducking a flying missile.

'Guv – what is it?' DS Jones is taken aback.

'Shush.' Skelgill shakes his head. He digs frantically in his bag, and after a brief search retrieves his limp-brimmed bush hat and a pair of outmoded sunglasses, donning both before rather circumspectly rising to his full height.

DS Jones gapes in amazement – it's as if he's going to pull some gauche disguise stunt with the immigration officials.

Cautiously he turns so that he is alongside her. Out of the corner of his mouth he hisses, 'Over there, in the VIP queue.'

'What, Guv – I don't get it?'

'In the grey suit, with the black briefcase. Third from the front. Don't stare – it's Goodman.'

DS Jones steps round to face Skelgill, 'You mean the Head?'

'It's him. Definitely.'

'I'll keep my back to him.'

'Aye, best do. He'll be gone in a minute.'

'So he was on our flight, Guv?'

'Looks that way.'

'But, Guv – that means he could have been at the school on Monday night.'

Skelgill nods. 'Something else for you to find out, Jones – did he really go to London?'

17. SINGAPORE

'Guv – I don't know if I can carry this off – what if he spotted us at the airport?'

'Jones – he didn't. And you can't get cold feet now – we've just flown the best part of seven thousand miles.'

'What if he checks my story?'

'He won't – he'll be flattered by the attention.'

'But it's paper thin, Guv. Literally. You made it up on the way here.'

'No it's not.' Skelgill brandishes the in-flight business magazine he has removed from the aircraft. 'Look – British education – there's an article on it to coincide with the convention. He probably read it. Just waggle your notebook and tell him you're the ace reporter.'

'But, Guv – one phone call to the editor and my cover's blown.'

'Jones – listen – if that happens – which it won't – you say you're a freelancer appointed by the owner – say he's a multi-billionaire and wants the inside track.'

'And just what is the inside track, Guv?'

'That's for us to find out.'

DS Jones shakes her head and looks up helplessly at the ocean liner marooned in the sky that is the Marina Bay Sands.

'For *me* to find out, you mean.'

'I've got work to do, too, remember.'

'Swap you, Guv.' But the note of resignation in her voice confirms her knowledge that only she may approach Mr Goodman without immediately arousing suspicion.

'You can do it, lass.' Skelgill reaches out and grips her shoulder. 'Look, get moving – I'll meet you in that shopping centre,' (he gestures across the broad modern highway to the expansive buildings opposite) 'there's bound to be a coffee bar in there. Say, four o'clock.' He holds out the magazine.

She nods and her features take on a set determination. She seizes the periodical and without a further word turns and heads for the sliding doors of the imposing glass-fronted entrance.

Skelgill watches until she disappears from sight: in her smart two-piece suit, with its close-fitting skirt and tailored jacket, plus heels that are just on the risqué side of business dress, she looks every bit the ambitious and successful twenty-something executive.

After a moment's contemplation he joins the nearby queue for taxis, and within a minute is heading for his own assignation.

*

'I'm sorry to disappoint you, Inspector Skelgill – and I sincerely hope it hasn't been a wasted journey – but I'm afraid to say that in the past decade we have not had anybody here by the name of Dr Snyder.'

Skelgill is impassive. Of course, this is something he could have established by telephone from England, but – although it is not what he was expecting – calling personally at the school had added a further raison d'être to his role in the trip.

'You're quite certain, sir?'

'Absolutely – I have been Principal for the past six years. Prior to that I was Assistant Principal for three years and Head of English for two – so you can see I have been here the whole time.'

This is one possibility that Skelgill has foreseen. He takes out his phone and locates a screengrab of Dr Snyder lifted from the Oakthwaite website. He slides it across the desk.

'He could perhaps have gone by another name.'

The Principal removes his stylish spectacles to examine the portrait. He looks briefly at the image and shakes his head.

'I don't recognise him, Inspector. Although you Europeans look much alike to us.' He returns the handset with the faintest hint of a smile on his lips.

Skelgill looks suitably nonplussed. 'Why might someone claim they taught here, sir?'

Dr Yeung replaces his glasses and blinks modestly. 'SIS is generally regarded as the finest international school in Singapore. Of course, we are the oldest.' He indicates with raised hands the whitewashed colonial style office in which they sit, a large wooden fan with varnished blades rotating silently above them. 'And we attract the sons of leading industrialists from all corners of Asia.'

'So he did his research.'

'Quite, Inspector. Perhaps he was employed at a lesser institution, and saw an opportunity to benefit from our brand name.'

'He must have banked on his references not being checked.'

'That would seem a little perilous, Inspector.'

Skelgill nods. 'To you and me, sir.'

The Chinese now looks typically inscrutable. After a moment he says, 'We should appreciate the opportunity to correct this misapprehension – especially if there were the possibility of some damage to our reputation.'

Skelgill holds up his palms in a placatory gesture. 'I quite understand, sir.' He slips his mobile back inside his jacket. 'But if you could bear with us on that for the time being.'

Dr Yeung nods his understanding. It can't have escaped him that he has in fact provided a potentially significant piece of information.

'I shan't take up any more of your time, sir. Thank you – and also for the tea – I could get a taste for that.'

The Principal bows graciously and rises with Skelgill to accompany him to the door.

'I see there's an education convention in town this week, sir.'

'Yes – we have a strong presence ourselves. Although we meet stiff competition from your British public schools.'

'Really, sir – I'd have thought you had the advantage of home turf?'

Dr Yeung shakes his head ruefully. 'It is hard to match the traditional connections with top universities – but we are trying our best to catch up.'

Skelgill grins optimistically. 'If the look of your city's anything to go by, you left us behind long ago.'

The Principal chuckles and bows a farewell.

*

Singapore International School is housed within the same complex of colonial buildings that includes Raffles Hotel, and Skelgill – now with an hour or more to kill – swinging his jacket by its coat loop, finds himself wandering past the famous Renaissance façade. He pauses and sniffs the air like an inquisitive fox sensing some easy pickings. The humidity – although not something that especially seems to trouble him – is bringing out beads of sweat on his brow, and a damp patch between his shoulder blades. His small travel holdall is deceptively hefty, and the prospect of an air-conditioned seat and a refreshing beverage must have its appeal. He turns into the palm-fringed driveway and makes for the pantiled veranda of the main entrance. Immediately he attracts the attention of a stocky British-looking attendant wearing an elaborate commissionaire's outfit.

'Are you a hotel guest, sir?' He's perfectly polite, but careful to block Skelgill's path with his sturdy frame.

'Just popping in for a drink.'

'In that case, sir – the Long Bar is around the side.' He indicates a paved route that skirts the building on its left.

Skelgill, though no doubt curious to see inside the iconic institution, and perhaps a little irked at being assigned what appears to be second-class status, gives a surly nod but obediently follows the commissionaire's instructions. It takes a couple of minutes navigating courtyards, stairways and balconies before the signs deliver him to the promised bar. Inside it is rather dark and has the ambience of a wooden ex-colonial mansion; bartenders busy themselves behind a befittingly long counter; palm-shaped fans flick in unison overhead. About half the seats are taken, though he is guided to an empty table in a corner position. He orders the obligatory *Singapore Sling*; it swiftly arrives as a rather ostentatious pink affair, its sweetness evidently concocted for the tourist rather than the purist (for whom the traditional *Straits Sling* is an altogether more challenging beverage). The copious supply of complimentary groundnuts does find immediate favour, and he amuses himself by tossing away the husks, as is the local custom. Moreover, by the time he leaves around an hour later, he would also appear to be a convert to the signature cocktail, its alcoholic effects serving to soften the blow of the bill.

Finding his way back onto Beach Street, he crosses the wide thoroughfare and, using the map on his mobile to guide him, begins walking in the direction of Singapore Cricket Club, whose extensive open grounds he had noted with interest on his taxi ride earlier. Gaining the sidewalk he pauses for a moment, looking directly ahead, then suddenly breaks into a canter, just in time to reach a bright red city tour bus that has pulled into the kerb ahead. Upon parting company with DS Jones, he had noticed the very same brand of transport at a stop outside the mall, the agreed locus for their impending reunion. Leaping aboard just as the doors are closing he hands over a fistful of Singapore dollars to the bemused driver and, eschewing the hastily proffered headphones, swings himself up onto the staircase as the vehicle pulls away. A few drops of warm rain are beginning to fall from the smoky skies, so as an expedient he opts for a seat at the canopied rear of the upper deck. The only other passengers are two camera-toting middle-aged couples, who appear to be white Europeans until their greeting of *g'day* reveals their antipodean provenance.

Skelgill picks up a glossy map from the floor beneath his seat. The tour is advertised to last an hour, and he can see that he's about half way around the circuit from Marina Bay – perfect timing. He settles back comfortably into his seat, and almost immediately falls fast asleep.

*

When he wakes the biggest shock is the darkness. Having travelled from a near Arctic Circle summer latitude to barely more than a degree from the equator, even a seasoned outdoorsman such as Skelgill can omit to factor the short day-length into his expectations. He sits upright in momentary panic – he must be thinking he's missed his flight, never mind his rendezvous with DS Jones – then checks his watch, staring at it disbelievingly.

In fact, it's only six o'clock.

Perhaps, with hindsight, he would confess that the combined effects of a two-night sleep deficit, a seven-hour jet lag, and three Singapore Slings, had ganged up to finally get the better of him. Fortunately it isn't necessary to be back at Changi until around nine. Nevertheless, DS Jones must be wondering where he is. He pulls out his phone and sees she has texted him – they'd agreed not to call one another in case either was at a key moment with a party to the investigation. He opens the text:

'Guv – developments – meet you at airport at nine x.'

His stern features are highlighted in the glow from the bright little screen. He begins to tap out a rejoinder, but half way through cancels it and returns the handset to his pocket. He gazes ahead, unseeing as the bus enters the bright canyon of Suntec City, its concrete-and-glass walls steepling into the darkness overhead. DS Jones's text is timed at five twenty-six; the convention was scheduled to break up for the day at five. Perhaps there is some kind of drinks reception to enable parents of prospective students to mingle with representatives of the schools? Equally, she could have hooked up with someone who can provide useful information. There are few plausible explanations: that her cover has been blown and she has been abducted, or that she has been charmed by some yacht-owning billionaire, might strike Skelgill as possibilities, distant and yet disconcerting as they are by equal measure.

As such, he looks uncharacteristically uneasy for one usually so implacable. An anxious Englishman abroad, tired, hungry and dehydrated, he watches blankly as sights flash past, a kaleidoscope of the familiar and the foreign, the sublime and the ridiculous. No sooner than there's a quaint church, then there's an ornate mosque, or a temple or a pagoda. The smart green-and-white road signs, slightly pompous in their Britishness – Stamford Road, Raffles Boulevard, Connaught Drive – speak of an age of understatement, in contrast to glib-sounding business names like Lucky Joint Construction, Darkie Trading Co., and

Top-Hole Employment Agency (specialising in maids from Indonesia and the 'Phillipines').

When the surroundings tell him this is Chinatown, he alights at the first available stop and begins to stroll along Tanjong Pagar Road. Right now the restaurants seem quiet and, though hunger causes him to linger outside a number of small eateries, he seems deterred by the lack of patrons. Indeed, for an island state whose geo-demographics are the equivalent of the entire five million population of Scotland being shipped over to the Isle of Mull, the streets are hardly teeming. Could this be a phenomenon of the little eastern nation's high per capita GDP: the widespread availability of air conditioning keeps the populace indoors?

A small rat runs ahead of him on the sidewalk, before toppling into the gutter with a flick of its tail for balance, and then it slides from sight into a drain. Cicadas are hissing from somewhere in the darkness between buildings. The stuccoed houses are relatively old here; he sees a date – 1903. With their heavy porticos it could be a street in London. Then he comes upon what at first sight seems like an indoor market – with open ends and side entrances – then the powerful waft of stir-fry overwhelms him and he is drawn towards its source. In fact the establishment is an oblong food court, lined on two sides with little stalls. Down its centre, diners have randomly taken up fast-food-style tables. They appear to be exclusively locals.

Skelgill begins to scrutinise the fare on offer. He recognises snake-like duck heads, lolling in drunken heaps, skinned and stained a shiny orange – but that's where familiarity begins and ends. Many of the counters seem to be advertising dishes of unappetising limp vegetables and displaying large unrecognisable fruits. As he weaves among slurping patrons, the glossy, soupy contents of their dishes are as much a mystery to him as he must be to their momentarily upturned gaze. Heads down, they're packing the stuff in, a pair of chopsticks in one hand and a spoon in the other.

Incapable of ordering, he reaches the exit. Here there's a separate stall, a mobile one on wheels. A friendly elderly Chinese woman squatting on a low plastic footstool engages him. His natural reaction is to reject her exhortations, but in the nick of time her wares catch his eye and on this impulse he buys a tube of *Pringles* and a bottle of *Coke*.

Thus provisioned, he regains the sidewalk and hails a taxi.

18. CHANGI

'Sounds like you're in an airport, Guv.'

'Nah – Euston.'

'Funny that – I could have sworn that announcer just said Kuala Lumpur.'

'Clapham Junction, I think it was.'

A hint of suspicion lingers in DS Leyton's voice. 'Must be going deaf in my old age, Guv.'

Skelgill would ordinarily have a somewhat vulgar retort for this suggestion, but now he quickly moves the conversation on. 'So what's the story on Hodgson?'

'Guv – the final lab report's not ready yet. I called Herdwick about an hour ago. He says cause of death was definitely the shotgun wound – instantaneous – and as predicted a shedload of alcohol in the bloodstream – about four times the legal driving limit. The only prints on the gun were his – but it was his job to clean and oil them after use, so no surprise there, really.'

Now Skelgill hurriedly tries to muffle the microphone with his jacket as a flight to Hanoi is called.

'Sorry, Guv – didn't quite catch that. Your voice is a bit distant.'

'I was saying *what else?*'

'Well – I went round to his gaff, yesterday afternoon – right state it was. A crate of empties – mainly vodka. No sign of her indoors – word on the street is she slung her hook years back on account of his drinking.'

'Seems like there's a theme developing there.'

'Too right, Guv. He was banned from the local about six weeks ago for threatening the staff – girl refused him a drink when he'd had a few too many. Bit of a Billy no-mates by all accounts. Then the newsagent told me he'd run up a fat tab for the *Racing Post* – so I asked at the bookies and the old dear there said he was a chronic loser, but couldn't keep away.'

'Chasing his losses?'

'That's it, Guv. And I reckon it goes further – there was a stack of final demands in the flat – couple of CCJs, by the look of the envelopes – and hardly any electricals – no telly or fridge even.'

'Could the place have been turned over?'

'No signs of a forced entry. More likely he pawned the gear.'

'Anything connected to the school? Letters or documents?'

'Not as I could see, Guv. But it was hard to tell with all the mess and bottles and old newspapers.'

'So we've got an antisocial alcoholic with gambling debts.'

'On the face of it, Guv, no real surprise he's gone and topped himself.'

Skelgill is silent.

'Guv – you still there?'

Skelgill rises to his feet, staring into the distance, his mobile held by his side. Then he seems to remember the conversation. 'Leyton, I've got to go – I'll see you tomorrow – keep up the good work. Follow your nose.'

He ends the call before DS Leyton can reply or protest, or even make the Londoner's observation that surely a train departing for Clapham Junction would mean Skelgill was at Victoria? Skelgill then leaves his bag and jacket on his seat, and strides towards the control point of the departure gate within which he has been ensconced for some thirty minutes or so. Beyond the security belts and x-ray machines, about a hundred and fifty yards into the seething mall, the high-heeled DS Jones is making uncertain progress through the milling crowds, glancing anxiously at overhead departure screens as she comes.

*

'Have you been drinking, Miss Jones?'

'Just a couple, Guv – I had to go with the flow.'

Skelgill lifts his head in seemingly reluctant assent. Certainly she appears a little inebriated, her hair and clothing dishevelled by the impeccable standards of earlier in the day.

'I was beginning to think I'd be flying alone. I reckon they'll board us any minute.'

'Sorry, Guv – my phone ran out of charge not long after I sent you that text.' She drops her shoulder bag onto the seat beside his.

'So, what kept you?'

Skelgill's tone is probably more severe than he intends, and for a moment DS Jones looks a little crestfallen.

He corrects himself, saying, 'I mean – how did you get on? You said there were *developments*.'

DS Jones slips off her jacket. Underneath she wears a close-fitting white blouse, with perhaps one button too many undone. Then she removes her strappy shoes and swaps them for a pair of sleek ballet pumps from inside her shoulder bag, her tanned and sculpted calves exhibited by her lithe movements. Skelgill becomes conscious that she's attracting surreptitious glances from two male passengers sitting opposite them. He coughs rather ostentatiously, perhaps in an attempt to create a proprietorial bubble around himself and his more photogenic female colleague.

She sits back, clearly the happier for making herself comfortable. 'Top line, Guv – I think the school is looking for funding, over and above the regular fees – and they're eye-watering enough, as it is.'

Now she has Skelgill's full attention. He says, 'You mean *illicit* funding?'

She puffs out her cheeks. 'I don't know – but I think it could be a kind of inside track, as you put it.'

'How did you reach that conclusion?'

DS Jones pulls her feet up beneath her, so she's curled kitten-like, half facing him. 'It all happened after the event, really, Guv. When I got there, they were in a big hall, with tables round the outside, and you could go up and speak to representatives of each school – they had their own roller-banners and display boards and brochures. Thing is, there was a queue at most of them, so you were only allowed a couple of minutes, and there was no way I could ask any tricky questions with people breathing down my neck. But, in the end, that worked in my favour – I introduced myself to Goodman and asked a couple of obvious questions.'

'Such as?'

'What makes Oakthwaite so special.'

'What did he say?'

'Oh, just the pat answers, really – they're always high up in the exam league tables... the emphasis on sport and outdoor experiences... that it's all boys so there's no distractions...'

'Ha! That's an advantage?'

'Maybe, Guv.'

'Can't see it myself.'

'No, Guv.' She knows Skelgill can fall a tad to the right of political correctness on issues concerning masculinity, and her reply is one of accord. She continues, 'Anyway – it meant I was able to introduce myself without being grilled about who I was.'

'I told you that.'

DS Jones gives him a patient grin. 'Yes, Guv. After that we all went into an auditorium for about an hour and a half of presentations. Goodman's not on stage until tomorrow – and it was starting to look like a waste of time. I thought the event was closing at five, but they announced a private cocktail hour through in the lobby of the hotel – you ought to see it, Guv – it's got this space age feel.'

Skelgill nods. Now he's looking at her a little warily.

'As soon as I walked in to the roped-off section Goodman came up to me with two drinks. He was acting kind of suave, and said something about us fellow Brits needing to look after one another. Then I had this brainwave.'

'Oh.'

'Well you know your back-up idea that I was sent by the owner, not the editor?'

'Aha.'

'I told him that was why I was really there, except I embellished a bit – that the owner was thinking about sending his son to study in England, and had heard good reports of three schools, one of which being Oakthwaite.'

'So what?'

'He suggested we went up to the bar – you know, right up on the roof, the Sky Park – they've got this infinity pool looking down from over six hundred feet – it's like you're flying.'

'You weren't in it?' Skelgill sounds irate.

'No, Guv – don't be daft – but I had to pretend I knew all about it – I'm a reporter that works here, remember?'

'So how did you manage that?'

'Fortunately I'd Googled the place while the speeches were going on – that's probably why my battery gave up.'

'What then?'

'We went to the Sky Bar – with Goodman being a resident at the hotel it was no problem to get in. I guess we had a couple of cocktails...'

'You guess?'

'I thought it best to act interested, Guv – I wouldn't normally drink on duty, or during daytime.'

'I should think not.'

'So he was asking me about the guy I represented – nothing really difficult – I think he was getting a bit tipsy. I basically made out my employer was a media mogul – billionaire type – and that seemed to satisfy him. Then he was quick to explain how there was a lot of demand to join the school, and there's only so many places each year and a tough entrance exam. He said his job was to select the boys that would most benefit from the school, and vice versa.'

'*Vice versa* – that's what he said?'

'Verbatim, Guv. Of course, he could have meant what personal qualities and varied backgrounds they'd bring to the community – he'd touched on that earlier – but I don't think it's what he was getting at.'

'Was he explicit?'

At this question DS Jones momentarily flinches, but she quickly regains her composure and says, 'He said they had such a thing as a 'VIP Application' – for parents whose sons were considered more likely to qualify for one of their places at Oxbridge.'

'*Their* places?'

'Yeah, Guv – like it's a done deal – like travel agents have so many seats on a flight, so many rooms at a hotel. That's how he made it sound.'

'That can't be right, surely?'

'I don't know, Guv – who really knows about this kind of thing?'

Skelgill is thoughtful for a moment. He shakes his head ruefully. 'Well no one from my comp got in, that's for sure. I reckon the best we did was a couple into St Andrews, and I thought that was a football ground until recently.'

DS Jones grins and, as if taking the opportunity of this moment of brevity, she draws a breath and says, 'So he suggested we went to his room and he could help me fill out a preliminary application. He said it ought to get me a promotion, at least.'

Thus Skelgill's recovering ambivalence is short-lived. He frowns and stares at the carpeted floor of the departure lounge. Earlier, when his taxi had passed beneath the twinkling towers of the two-and-a-half-thousand room behemoth, he'd gazed upwards at the Sky Park, seemingly suspended like an illuminated version of the Starship Enterprise, wondering if she were somewhere inside the great edifice and – if so – what she was doing.

'I didn't go, Guv.' Her tone is one of stating the obvious.

'What? Why not?'

'Well... I thought there might not be an application form.'

'Oh.' Skelgill seems to be grinding his teeth.

'So I said I was going to powder my nose and never went back to the bar. I'd already mentioned I was flying to London tonight for an assignment, so I just told the girl on the reception to pass on a message that I'd been called away and would be back later if I could make it. I don't think he would have been short for company, anyway, Guv.'

Skelgill now appears like he's trying to look unconcerned. He says, 'Maybe you should have given it a try – you might have got something concrete that could be useful as evidence.'

DS Jones shrugs as though she thinks probably not. But she humours him with, 'I was thinking about you, Guv – I'd been looking forward to us having a Chinese or something – it would have been good to see a bit of the city. How did you get on?'

Now it's Skelgill's turn to lift his shoulders. He says, 'I went to the school your aunt put us onto. As I half expected, they'd never heard of him – didn't recognise the mugshot.'

'So he's a fraud? What does that mean, Guv?'

'Dunno. Not yet – no idea. Maybe he just thought it was a crafty little white lie to put on his CV. They're obviously keen on recruitment out here. Would have made him sound more valuable to the school if they thought he had the right contacts.'

'But, Guv – why wouldn't they send him instead of the Head?'

'Maybe the Head pulled rank on this occasion – wanted the trip and the trimmings for himself.'

DS Jones raises her eyebrows. Her recent experience might seem to corroborate this hypothesis. 'What did you do then, Guv?'

Skelgill makes an effort to sound casual. 'Just had a bit of a wander, really. Nothing much. Came back here and got a burger.'

'When in Rome, Guv!'

'You know me, Jones – catholic when it comes to my tastes.'

The public address system at their gate suddenly crackles into life. Families travelling with small children and important executives may come forward for boarding. There's a rise in the level of the general hubbub, as passengers adopt the customary panic mode that will get them to London no faster.

'Oh, Guv – London.'

'Aha?'

'Goodman says he's got a flat in Covent Garden. He's kept it on from when he worked down there. I didn't manage to ask him directly – but he told me he uses it when he's at conferences or in transit.'

'So that would be his answer to where he stayed Monday night?'

'I think so, Guv – and no easy way of corroborating it.'

'Pity we can't check the place out while we're passing.'

'We almost could have, Guv – he offered me the spare key – said I could stay there for my trip and give it him when he arrives back in London on Friday night.'

19. THE BOTHY

The time gain on the homeward leg means that Skelgill and DS Jones, having originally left London on Tuesday afternoon, arrive at a ghost-town-like Heathrow in the very early morning of Thursday and, avoiding the commuting hordes that will shortly stream onto the M25, are back in the Lakes well before noon. It's an absence barely noted among the great mass of their colleagues, who would no doubt be flabbergasted to learn they had just 'popped' over to Singapore. DS Jones, driving, drops Skelgill at Penrith Police HQ. For the time being, at least, they must go their separate ways. Skelgill collects his car and heads home to shower and change, and file a report to the Chief. However, fewer than twenty minutes after his return, his garage swings open and he roars out aboard a large blue-and-chrome *Triumph* motorcycle, riding one-handed as he raises the remote over his shoulder to lower the door behind him.

Scotch mist has descended to resume its occupancy of Cumbria, and Skelgill has dressed accordingly, clad as he is in a threadbare *Belstaff* jacket, what look suspiciously like cut-off fishing waders to shield his legs, and biker's boots that have long since seen better days. His fisherman's hands need no such protection from the elements, but a distinctive orange full-face helmet completes the somewhat original ensemble.

Turning off the A66 at Keswick, he weaves his way through the bustling market town and joins the B-road that skirts the wooded west bank of Derwentwater and winds past the Bowder Stone due south into the depths of Borrowdale. The weather has driven the majority of tourists to their cars, and his progress is slow. His powerful machine at 900cc affords ample opportunities to overtake, but for whatever reason he eschews these; he seems content to go with the flow – perhaps in the knowledge he can take control whenever he so desires.

Neither is his journey a long one. Leaving Derwentwater behind he passes the turn for Grange, his eyes flicking right to survey the water conditions of the River Derwent. He continues for a couple more miles until, approaching Seatoller, he makes a sharp left into the track that leads up to Seathwaite. Within a minute he draws to a halt and dismounts and, helmet tucked beneath his arm, strides on towards a cluster of low-built grey slate and stone farm buildings.

A rudely lettered sign on splintering plywood sits askew in the verge, *TEK CARE, SHEEP ONT ROAD*, and second one – *CAFE* – is affixed to a canted post, with an arrow indicating across a liberally manured yard towards the farmhouse.

He's not alone here: there must be a dozen cars lining the lane, abandoned by hardy explorers who use this popular access route to Great Gable and Scafell Pike; and several motorcycles like his own, the café itself being a favoured haunt of the local bikers' chapter. It is in the latter capacity that Skelgill arrives this afternoon, and perhaps fortunately so, since the fells might as well not be there, for all there is to see of them. Only an intangible looming presence infuses the impenetrable mist with an air of foreboding, a sense of encirclement, of steeply banked terraces, a great cauldron of wild country that presses in upon the diminutive farmstead. Black water drips from the eaves and gutters. Sheep stand still, shivering and sodden in their walled pastures. All is silent but for the plaintive mew of a buzzard from some gnarled perch – perhaps a protest at its inability to fly today.

'Hareet, marra?'

Skelgill has entered not the door marked *OPEN*, but has ducked instead into the low back entrance of an adjoining stable-like structure that might once have been a smithy. Now it is put to use as a workshop, and the colloquial greeting comes from a grizzled, heavy-featured man in his sixties, clad in a boiler suit and smeared with grease, who kneels, wrench poised, beside a semi-dismembered vintage AJS motorcycle.

'Nice one you've got there, Art.'

'Should be – when she's wukn. Thew up fer a fry, Skel?'

'You know me. Never say never.'

'Our Jud's ovver ont' fell – else he'd join yer fer a chinwag.'

'I'll see him again. It's *your* brains I wouldn't mind picking, Art.'

'Shunt tek yer long, then.' The older man grins, revealing a crooked row of yellowed teeth.

Skelgill returns the smile. 'Old boy from over Bassenthwaite way – rode a black BSA Gold Star, pre-63 plate – I'm trying to find where he went on it.'

'*Went*, lad?'

'Suspicious death.'

The farmer nods. 'I'll put out a tweet t'lads. Black beezer, eh?' He reaches into the breast pocket of his overalls and extracts a state-of-the-art smartphone.

Now Skelgill shakes his head. 'Struth, Art – who said you can't teach an old dog new tricks.'

'Thu's life int this dog yet. Got ter move wi't times. How's t'ol lass?'

'Still peddling.'

'Aye – I've sin her. T'other day it were hossing it doon an' she wo' garn like t'clappers.'

'I'll tell her you were asking.'

'Get yer scran, lad – Gladis'll be pleased yer up.'

'Not as pleased as I'll be.' Skelgill raises a hand of thanks and begins to back out of the smithy.

'Skel – 'ey up, lad.'

'Aha?'

'That beezer – is it ont' market?'

*

Skelgill stares disconsolately in the direction of the footpath that meanders from the far gate of the enclosed farmyard and swiftly disappears into the mist that still crowds the dale. Replete with Gladis's legendary 'Cumbrian Fry' – in his estimation the first proper meal he has consumed in the past three days – he exhibits an uncharacteristic sense of indecision, a degree of inertia perhaps ostensibly brought on by the skyscraping saturated fat levels contained in the infamous all-day breakfast.

The snug café, which he has just left, is really nothing more than a parlour of the farmhouse, with its perennially steamed-up windows and strident nineteen seventies wallpaper. A group of damp-looking hikers and half a dozen sedentary bikers, none of whom exude any impression that they are in a hurry to take on the elements, presently inhabit it. Skelgill hadn't recognised anybody, but his own biker-gear, idiosyncratic as it might be, had nevertheless earned him immediate access to their little clique, motorcycling being a universal fraternity to which all participants automatically belong and, by virtue of this involuntary membership, are bound to help a fellow biker in any way that circumstances may require. Thus they made both space for, and conversation with Skelgill, and any doubts about his apparel were soon dispelled as they discovered first that he rides a decent 'hog' and second that he is clearly a favourite of the café's owner, Gladis Hope.

These days, while Gladis is still content to run the café, her husband Arthur Hope has the luxury of dabbling with his lifelong passion of old motorcycles, whilst coordinating the activities of the local bikers' club. This is thanks to their son, Jud – with whom Skelgill was at school – assuming responsibility for the running of farm and flock. Indeed, it was around this very farmstead that a young Daniel Skelgill had cut his teeth in the hills, helping out in the holidays and during lambing, impressing the incumbents with his natural stamina and alacrity about the fells. As an adult, Skelgill had further endeared himself to the family in a semi-professional capacity, intercepting in no uncertain terms an attempt at sheep rustling, and to Arthur especially when he took possession of a *Triumph* motorcycle, albeit the 'new-fangled' Hinckley variety. Thus always welcome, and sure of double helpings, Skelgill's only awkward moments come over the battle to pay for his food.

On this occasion, just as he was pressing his money upon Gladis, and insisting the change went into the collection tin for the mountain rescue (a somewhat curious donation, in that he is a member of the local team of volunteers), Arthur had limped through and confided that his tweet had generated several positive sightings. It seems that Querrell was most often to be observed tootling along the leafy lanes of the extreme western fells (perhaps where Skelgill had subconsciously noted his passing – certainly he had recognised the classic motorbike when he found himself face-to-face with it on Monday night), and that the distinctive black-and-chrome 'beezer' was occasionally seen parked outside a small climbing hut or bothy at the far reaches of Wasdale Head, the most isolated driveable outpost of the entire Lake District.

And therein lies Skelgill's present dilemma. Wasdale Head, from the spot on which he now stands, is a little over three miles as the crow flies: about twenty-five minutes were Skelgill kitted out in his fell-running gear. He knows the route well, and has covered it in darkness often enough: from here south to cross Stockley Bridge, a sharp westerly ascent to pick up Styhead Gill, topping out at Styhead Tarn, and finally a sweeping westerly traverse across Great Gable. He stamps his feet and looks down in frustration at his attire, holding out his arms as if in mimed protest to his incompetent valet who so ignorantly equipped him for the task in hand.

But it's no good. To attempt the run (or even walk) wearing ill-fitting biker's boots and heavyweight clothing would be futile, unthinkably uncomfortable, and Skelgill plainly knows this. He must go by road. But, by one of those quirks of Lakeland topography, while Wasdale Head might be three miles as the crow flies, it is forty miles by road, in a great north-westerly anticlockwise loop; perhaps an hour and a half's driving at typical Lakeland speeds. With obvious reluctance, he dons his helmet and turns to remount his *Triumph*.

*

The spectacular view along Wastwater has been voted the best in Britain, and Skelgill as always is forced to slide to a halt and cut his engine as the breathtaking vista opens out before him. Though today is not one for picture postcards; only a seasoned purist feels a thrill at such desolation. While the drizzle has lifted with the mist, far ahead the immense angular slab that gives Great Gable its name spears into the lowering cloud base, flanked by the titanic curving 'hull' of Yewbarrow and the sharply ridged Lingmell. Closer, to his right, the precipitous Wastwater Screes tower like some advancing tsunami of bare rock, their shadow blackening the still waters, the deepest in England, watery grave of who knows how many missing persons.

Indeed, as Skelgill surveys the silent scene, it would not seem incongruous were a sword-bearing arm to burst forth from the mirrored surface, pointing him in the direction of his quest. But he needs no *Lady of the Lake* to show him the way. He starts the bike and moves circumspectly onwards, as if in an act of reverence towards his preternatural surroundings (although perhaps it is simply in recognition of the abundant sheep 'ont road'). The narrow lane, now unwalled, clings to the north-west bank of the lake, cutting through the open fell that pours down to the water's edge. He crosses Overbeck Bridge and, leaving Wastwater behind, passes through Down in the Dale and continues, finally to park at the inn at Wasdale Head.

He locates the hut without difficulty – in fact he has noticed it in passing on occasions down the years, without particularly evaluating its likely function or ownership – set a short distance beyond the inn on a patch of common ground. Perhaps once a winter fodder store for sheep, it is little more than a rectangular stone construction, windowless apart from a narrow slit above head height at each gable end. The olive green door is heavily planked, and secured by what appears to be a well-oiled padlock; indeed all aspects of the building give the impression of it being well maintained.

Skelgill, after satisfying himself there is no possible means by which to engineer a glimpse inside, steps away to survey the property: a small chimney stack protruding through its low black slate roof is one certain sign that this is potentially more than just a conveniently sited repository for outdoor equipment. A ruddy male stonechat momentarily alights upon the little ochre pot, catching Skelgill's attention with its onomatopoeic *tack-tack* before it flits away. Perhaps its fleeting appearance sharpens his perceptions, because now he notices something that draws him back to the building. Upon the rough lintel above the door is a distinctive mark. Closer inspection confirms this to be the work of human hands: a whorl that could be the number six, although laterally inverted – the ascender curves off to the left. Skelgill reaches up to touch the motif. It has actually been carved into the stone, and lichen has settled in its recessed lines, highlighting its aged presence. Most curious of all, though, is that Skelgill has seen this symbol elsewhere.

'Thew'd best keep away – crabbit ol' gadgey as looks after tha' place.'

At this unexpected warning Skelgill spins around. Propped on a chin-high crook is a small wizened old man dressed rather like a Victorian farm worker. Behind him slinks an opaque-eyed border collie, its matted fur hanging in damp wads. Belying his decrepit appearance – the farmer, or shepherd, or whatever he is – has managed to approach to within a few yards without attracting Skelgill's notice.

'The old fellow who comes on the motorbike?'

'Thou one of his cronies?'

'Nah – just passing.' Skelgill raises his crash helmet and gives it a little shake.

'Not many as pass this way.'

'Good reason to come, in my book.'

The old man makes a small upward jerk of his head, as if accepting of Skelgill's remark. 'Thou frae Wukiton?'

'Pereth.' Skelgill uses the colloquial name for Penrith in response to his questioner's Workington diminutive.

His efforts to endear himself appear to be bearing fruit, since the old man says, as if by way of apology, 'Thought thew be an offcomer.'

Skelgill shakes his head. 'You said *cronies?*'

'Bunch a' rich folks.'

'How do you know?'

'Deeked their cars. Range Rovers and that.'

'Hillwalkers?'

The old man frowns. 'Ont bevvy more like.'

Skelgill inclines his head towards the bothy. 'In there?'

'Aye. After t'inn's called last orders. I've heard 'em.'

'Do they board at the inn?'

'Reckon.'

Skelgill hitches up his overtrousers. 'I was just going in for a pint.'

'Ars gan yam.' The old man says this as if to decline an offer unmade by Skelgill. He points with his crook at a cluster of small cottages a quarter of a mile distant, and without further formalities begins slowly to hobble away, the skulking collie in tow. After a few seconds, and without looking back, he calls out, 'You wunt get nowt out't landlord – *he's* an offcomer.'

*

As Skelgill clumps through into the reception area, a tall pale man of around his own age suddenly rises to attention from behind the counter. He wears a tattersall shirt beneath a quilted gilet. He's holding a newly opened ream of copy paper, and is perhaps in the process of reloading a printer.

'Sorry, chum – no boots or biker gear in the residents' areas.' The accent is refined; as the shepherd intimated, the hotelier is not a local.

'How about this kind of boots?'

No doubt resisting the temptation to include the patronising epithet 'chum' in his reply, Skelgill, without breaking stride, reaches into an inside pocket and produces his warrant card. Holding it at eye level he forces his protagonist to take a step backwards in order to read the details.

'Oh – of course – I had no idea you were – police.'

'We don't usually walk about with a sign saying CID, sir. Tends to reduce our effectiveness in protecting the public.'

'Naturally, officer.' There's a distinct flushing of the skin around his neck.

Skelgill drops his crash helmet on the counter top and rubs his hands together. He scrutinises the landlord, then casts about beyond him, as though he's expecting to see an item of lost property that has been handed in. His silence forces the other to speak.

'So... er... how may I be of assistance to you?'

'You are the proprietor, I take it, sir?'

'That's correct.'

'There's a little stone climbing barn about a hundred-and-fifty yards along the lane. Does that come under your ownership?'

'No – that's nothing to do with us.' This response comes quickly, as though the man is keen to distance himself from the subject matter.

Skelgill nods slowly. 'We're trying to trace the connections of the key-holder.'

'I can't help you there, I'm afraid, officer.' Again, the answer is rushed, when a qualifying enquiry such as 'Why?' or 'Who?' might have been expected.

'According to our information the people who use it lodge here.'

'Oh, I don't think so, officer. Our hotel prices are designed to deter the climbing types – they tend to go for the budget places, the B&Bs.'

'Who said they were climbing types?' Skelgill sounds a little irked by the implied class distinction in the landlord's explanation.

'Well... er... since it's a climbing hut...'

Skelgill doesn't reply, and instead takes a leaflet advertising the inn's services from a dispenser close at hand. He raises an eyebrow at the slogan *'For the discerning foodie'*, and scans through the price list.

'May I?' He inserts the brochure into his jacket without waiting for a reply, and then picks up his helmet. Taking a step back he says, 'Is that your blue Defender parked down the side?'

The hotelier, sensing that Skelgill has finished with him, and for a moment beginning to relax, stiffens once more. 'Yes, it is, officer.'

Skelgill turns and begins to head for the exit. As he reaches and opens the door he looks back and says, 'I should keep an eye on your road tax – you can renew online these days, you know, chum.'

And with that he strides out, leaving the landlord staring disconcertedly at the spot where he had stood.

Skelgill heads directly for his motorcycle, hauling on his helmet and fastening his jacket as he goes. But when he reaches the machine, rather than climbing aboard, he goes down on one bended knee to examine the little disc-holder attached to the front-left fork. Tipping his head to one side as if in a gesture of confirmation he stands upright and pulls out his mobile phone. Quickly he taps out a text to himself, 'Bike tax expired.'

20. THE BURGER VAN

Throwing caution to the wind of his own warning that the Chief passes this way, Friday morning finds Skelgill parked in the layby that is home to the recently discovered burger van. Working through a bacon roll whilst waiting for DS Leyton to join him for breakfast, he is conducting a consequently disjointed telephone conversation with DS Jones.

'So what are you doing now?'

'I'm on my way to meet DI Smart, Guv.'

Skelgill tuts. 'Where?'

'Southwaite services – he wants to give me a de-brief.'

'I bet he does.' Skelgill mutters under his breath.

'Sorry, Guv?'

'I said keep mum – about Goodman.'

'Of course, Guv.'

Skelgill now has to finish a mouthful of food before he can speak again.

'You still there, Guv?'

'Yup. Look – I want you to contact him.'

'Goodman?'

'Correct.'

'Won't he be flying right now?'

'Just leave him a message. And if he rings when he lands, don't answer – see if he records a voicemail before you call back.'

'Can we use that, Guv?'

'I'm sure we'd find a way.'

'What should I say?'

'Sorry you had to rush off. Make it sound like you're in London. Tell him your boss is still keen on getting his son into the school, but wants something a bit more concrete on what the deal is. Cut to the chase, Headmaster.'

'Shall I use that expression?'

'Words to that effect – we need to hear it from him if he's bending the rules.'

'What if he wants to meet up?'

'Get the train?'

'But... Guv.'

'Jones – wait and see – play it by ear. At least make it *seem* like you could meet him for a drink later.'

Now it's DS Jones turn to remain silent.

'Tell him if he can give you a steer, you should be able to get a proposal back from your employer by tonight.'

'Okay.'

'You don't sound convinced.'

'Guv, Smart will go crackers if I go gallivanting off again on your case.'

'Look – *I* don't want you gallivanting, but...'

'It might get the Chief off your back?'

'Something like that.'

Skelgill holds up two fingers through the windscreen to the arriving DS Leyton who, rather than take offence, nods and walks away to place their order.

'What did she say about our trip, Guv?'

'Qualified success. Reading between the lines of her email.'

'Just between the lines?'

'You know the Chief. The only time she says 'Well done' is when she orders a steak.'

'I'd have thought she eats them rare, Guv.'

'You're thinking of her subordinates.'

'Ha-ha, Guv.'

'I'm not joking.'

'So we're to keep looking?'

'Continue fishing in the dark.'

'At least that's your forte, Guv.'

This apparent compliment could be metaphorical, literal or indeed an attempt at wry humour, but before Skelgill can fashion a response DS Leyton pulls open the passenger door.

'Look – here's Leyton – I need to go – keep me posted.'

*

'You already had one, Guv?' Leyton indicates the brown paper bag screwed up on the dashboard of Skelgill's car.

'Just a provisional, Leyton – didn't know how long you'd keep me waiting.'

DS Leyton protests. 'Like clockwork, me, Guv – I'm as keen on a bacon roll as you are.'

Skelgill looks across with an ironic expression as DS Leyton pats his ample stomach.

'I dunno where you put 'em, Guv.' DS Leyton sounds a little defensive. 'My missus reckons you must have a tapeworm.'

'It's called an appetite, Leyton – comes from the uneven terrain by which we're surrounded, in case you hadn't noticed.' Skelgill gestures with his roll in a circular motion. 'Not that there's a lot to be seen right now.'

'That suits me, Guv – stick to the level, that's my motto.'

Skelgill nods pensively whilst chewing. After a moment he says, 'Aye – I hadn't realised how flat London is until just the other day.'

'Home sweet home. The good old Smoke. How did you get on down there, anyway, Guv?'

Skelgill takes another bite of his roll, perhaps to buy a little time in composing his response. 'Let's just say it looks like Goodman might be up to something.'

'In what way, Guv?'

'Trading places at the school for more than the market rate.'

DS Leyton frowns in a perplexed manner. 'Is that illegal?'

Skelgill shrugs. 'Probably not. It's a private school.'

'Unless he's taking backhanders, Guv?'

Skelgill taps the plastic lid of his disposable tea cup. 'That could be tough to prove.'

DS Leyton nods, and for a while both detectives alternately munch and slurp their way through their takeaways.

After a while, DS Leyton pipes up, 'That cricket pavilion, Guv – that was paid for by a parent.'

Skelgill nods. 'Maybe he just liked cricket. Or was so impressed with the school.'

'Be nice to have that kind of bangers and mash to spare, eh Guv?'

'These people operate in a different world from us, Leyton. You should see the buildings in...'

Skelgill stops himself mid-sentence, presumably realising his next word would be Singapore.

DS Leyton looks a little bewildered, until he concludes his superior has finished speaking. Tentatively, he offers, 'Still, Guv – it could be the connection we're looking for – I mean, what if old Querrell was on to him? That Jacobson reckoned he was none-too-keen on Goodman's policies.'

'But Querrell committed suicide, Leyton.'

'Maybe Goodman had something on him in return – threatened to expose him if he came clean about he was up to? Enough to push him over the edge.'

Skelgill flicks a sideways glance at DS Leyton. Then he shakes his head and says, 'Where's the crime in that?'

DS Leyton looks a little exasperated. 'But, Guv – two suicides in a week – the second one in Querrell's cottage. There's something not right here – we both know that. It's beyond the normal.'

'The school isn't a normal place, Leyton.'

'I see that, Guv – but, look, take Hodgson. While you were down south I occupied myself with digging into his background – seeing as with Querrell we've hit a dead end. Turns out he was more than a nasty piece of work around the town.'

'In what way?'

'Remember I said he'd been sacked from his last job as a gamekeeper for intimidating some walkers with a loaded twelve-bore?'

'Aha.'

'Well, that wasn't the full picture.'

'So?'

'It was just the excuse his employer needed to get shot of him – no pun intended, Guv.'

'No, Leyton.'

'So I called round at the estate office, across in the Eden valley – talked to the factor. There'd been a catalogue of problems.'

'Such as?'

'Nothing they could pin on him for certain, but for instance they were losing a lot of game. A flock of ornamental Canadian geese were shot. They discovered some illegal pole traps set in the woods. Then there was a roe deer found dead in a snare. They suspected it was Hodgson, on a killing spree – flogging the meat on the black market.'

'Did they confront him with the evidence?'

'Yeah, Guv – but he just insisted it was poachers and went on the warpath. Apparently he came across a van parked in a gateway on the estate and slashed its tyres. Turns out it just belonged to a land agent who was doing some surveying.'

'You'd think they would have got rid of him at the time.'

'He denied it – though it wasn't all that long before the confrontation with the walkers, so by then the estate had had enough.'

'The school evidently didn't check his references too thoroughly, eh Leyton?' Skelgill squints thoughtfully out through the windscreen. A small queue has formed at the burger van and Skelgill seems to be scrutinising it for suspects.

'Maybe he spun 'em a different yarn, Guv. Appears he wasn't averse to the odd bit of fraud. The estate suspected him of embezzling from the petty cash – he had responsibility for buying the shooting supplies and the feedstuffs for rearing pheasants. And the factor said he'd heard talk that Hodgson short-changed the beaters – though with that being all cash-in-hand he came over a bit vague when I pushed him.'

Skelgill nods pensively. 'Sounds like Hodgson's financial crisis was nothing new.'

'What if he'd gone to Querrell's cottage to see if there was a secret stash, Guv – like as a last resort? I mean – the old boy – what did he spend his money on? Nothing that I could see – not even a telly, Guv.'

'His salary would have been paid into a bank account – we can get that checked out.'

'Maybe we should have looked under his mattress while we were there, Guv.'

Skelgill raises an eyebrow. 'I rather got the feeling we wouldn't have been the first, Leyton.'

'Snyder – you mean, Guv?'

Skelgill shrugs. 'Hodgson himself – when he was sent to look for Querrell. After that – who knows? It was the best part of a week between Querrell going missing and us turning up.'

'Still might be worth a proper search, don't you think, Guv?'

'Too late.' Skelgill's tone is decidedly fatalistic.

DS Leyton looks perplexed, as if how could Skelgill be so certain. But he shrugs resignedly and says, 'Well, I can't help thinking there's some connection, Guv.'

Skelgill cranes his neck and gazes wistfully up in the direction of where Skiddaw's summit ought to be. 'You ever tried to do a cryptic crossword, Leyton?'

'Blimey, Guv – I wouldn't know one if it came up and bit me.'

'Thing is – try too hard to look for a connection and you get stuck in a rut. If you misinterpret the clue in the first place, you can never reach the solution. You know the old Lakes joke where the shepherd tells the tourist you can't get there from here.'

'I had no idea you were a crossword guru, Guv'

Skelgill frowns philosophically. 'I'm not. Jones can do them. She was showing me, on the train coming up from London last week. She correctly came up with the name of a rare fish she'd never heard of.'

'You had me worried there for a minute, Guv. I thought crosswords were a bit anoraky for the likes of you.'

Skelgill's body language hints that he might disagree with this statement. 'There's a lesson, though, Leyton. About letting the clue unwind before you start pressing too hard.'

DS Leyton doesn't appear convinced. He says, with a note of irony, 'Have you tried this theory out on the Chief, Guv?'

'Ha-ha, Leyton. But I'll tell you something that'll make you smile. When Jones had explained the method to me – she had this *Daily Telegraph* or something – then she fell asleep. I noticed there was an old lady in our carriage doing the same crossword.

When she got off at her stop she left the newspaper, so I copied her answers and Jones thinks I finished the crossword.'

21. DR SNYDER

'Dr Snyder, thanks for making time to see us again. You'll appreciate we have to be meticulous about this investigation given there was a firearm involved.'

Dr Snyder nods somewhat reluctantly. 'Inspector, I believed I had provided all the required information to your Sergeant.'

Skelgill casts about the academic's study, as if there is plenty yet that he would like to know. There are few clues to be had, however, in the starkly furnished apartment. Apart from a precise geometric array of certificates testifying to Dr Snyder's qualifications, and – rather ominously – hung horizontally, an old-fashioned varnished cane curving above an oak mantelpiece, much of the remaining wall space is given over to ranks of unprepossessing grey filing cabinets marked with neatly typed labels too small to read at a distance.

Skelgill returns his gaze to the Deputy Headmaster. 'Since you spoke with DS Leyton, has any alternative idea occurred to you as to how Mr Hodgson got hold of the shotgun?'

'Unless he had a spare key, Inspector, I can only imagine he took advantage of my absence from my study and temporarily removed mine.'

'How would he have come by a spare key?'

'Well, of course, he was already employed here when I arrived – my predecessor supervised the important keys. I have no means of knowing how strict his regime was. For instance he may have put them in Hodgson's possession long enough for a copy to be made. It would take forty minutes to drive into Keswick and back. Given his gamekeeping background, ostensibly he was a person to be trusted with guns.'

'But you didn't see it that way, sir?'

'I wasn't prejudiced against the man, Inspector. But risk assessment is part of my responsibility – limiting access to certain keys seems a sensible precaution to take.'

Skelgill folds his arms and stares evenly at Dr Snyder. 'But not quite a sufficient precaution as it's turned out, sir.'

Dr Snyder appears piqued. 'I rather suspect, Inspector, that had the shotgun not been available, Hodgson would have found some other equally effective method to solve his problems.'

Skelgill now responds as if through gritted teeth. 'Well let's just say, sir – if I may use the word *lucky* in relation to this unfortunate event – we were all lucky that Mr Hodgson didn't decide first to take out his problems on the school population.'

He allows the import of this statement to reverberate about the room. Dr Snyder has no answer and, if it is possible, his cadaverous demeanour seems to take on a more haunted expression. He makes as if to speak but his mouth is dry and he reaches with his long hands to pour water from a decanter on his desk.

'You can see, sir, why our colleagues can be a bit jumpy when we know there are firearms around.'

Dr Snyder swallows rather uncomfortably. 'Yes, Inspector.'

'Was Mr Querrell involved with the shooting club?'

'No, he was a conscientious objector – wouldn't have anything to do with guns.'

'How did he get on with Mr Hodgson?'

'I believe they kept their distance from one another – although I imagine they crossed swords on occasion.' Dr Snyder seems to have regained his composure. 'Querrell would have required pitches prepared for his first form teams – and some of his outdoor activities took place in the school grounds. A case of obstinacy meets belligerence, Inspector.'

Skelgill sits back in his seat and rearranges his jacket. He says, 'Investigations suggest Mr Hodgson's private life was troubled – marriage, drink, finances. Does that strike any chords?'

Dr Snyder folds his fingers around the glass, as if to stabilise its contents. 'Nothing that reached my ears, Inspector. The boys probably were the butt end of any ill temper that spilled over into his work – you know how teenagers can be rather irritating. Our Director of Sport might be able to cast more light on this subject than I am able.'

'Mr Greig?'

'That's correct.'

124

'We had a brief chat earlier in the week. Sergeant Leyton and I got a little lost and found our way to your new cricket pavilion.'

Dr Snyder nods slowly, but doesn't offer a comment.

'He was telling us the building was paid for by a parent?'

Dr Snyder takes another gulp of water. 'Yes – we're fortunate from time to time to have pupils whose parents are in a position to create a significant legacy.'

Skelgill nods and leans forward inquiringly. 'How does that come about, sir? I mean, do you launch an appeal?'

Dr Snyder is already shaking his head, an expression of unconcealed distaste gathering about his haggard features. 'Oh, no Inspector – that wouldn't do. To hold out the begging bowl would send entirely the wrong message to parents.'

'In what way, sir?'

'Well, there are those who might be concerned if the school appeared unable to fund its investment programme. And on the other hand you have to bear in mind that many of our parents are stretched paying school fees as it is.'

Skelgill grimaces, as though he finds this hard to believe.

'So it's just a case of waiting to see who comes along with their chequebook?'

'That is my understanding of what has happened in the past, Inspector.

Skelgill appears to stifle a yawn. Then he points a finger towards the certificates on the wall behind Dr Snyder. 'What subject do you teach, sir?'

'My qualifications are in English Literature. I specialise in Shakespeare.'

Skelgill purses his lips. 'They make excellent spinning rods.'

Dr Snyder's blank expression suggests he fails to recognise this statement as a joke. DS Leyton, who has been assiduously taking notes, glances up from his scribbling with an amused twinkle in his eye.

Skelgill now reaches into his jacket. He produces the first edition *Wainwright* borrowed from Querrell's library and lays it on the desk between them. 'Not exactly literary fiction, sir – but as good as it gets in my book.'

'Ah – I shall replace it later.'

Dr Snyder begins to reach forward to draw it towards him, but Skelgill is quicker and places a palm flat on the book. 'It's okay, sir – we're going to take another look around Mr Querrell's cottage – if you can furnish us with the key, that is.'

Dr Snyder doesn't reply, but ponderously unlocks a drawer to one side of where he sits, perhaps over-emphasising his newly improved security measures. He locates the required item and slides it across the surface of the desk beneath the tips of his long pale fingers, their nails perhaps surprisingly bitten down. 'This was Mr Querrell's personal key. I am not aware that another exists.'

Skelgill scoops up the hand-made iron mortise key and weights it in his palm as he rises to his feet. DS Leyton snaps his notebook shut and follows suit.

As they move towards the door Skelgill turns and says, in a casual tone, 'Was English your subject in Singapore, sir?'

Dr Snyder hesitates for just a split second, as if he is carefully checking over the content of his intended reply. 'I have only ever taught English, Inspector.'

Skelgill nods. 'I'm surprised they didn't fly you out this week to the convention – given your experience over there.'

Dr Snyder's already-guarded body language hints at further retrenchment. 'As I believe I mentioned previously, Inspector, the Headmaster handles all of our external affairs.'

Skelgill shrugs sympathetically. 'Seems a shame – you could have popped into your old place – SIS wasn't it?'

Now the academic seems to recoil involuntarily, a tremor in his ungainly frame belying his stern countenance. In a rather strained tone of voice he declares, 'Maybe I shall have that opportunity in future, Inspector.'

'Let's hope so, sir.' Skelgill nods to DS Leyton to indicate he should exit, and then crosses the threshold himself. 'Well – thank you for your time – we'll return the key before close of play.'

He backs out, closing the heavy oak door behind him. He turns to find the inquisitive gaze of DS Leyton trained upon him.

'*SIS* ,Guv?'

'Singapore International School.'

Skelgill sets off briskly along the corridor, forcing DS Leyton to break into a jog in order to keep up.

'Since when did you become an expert on Singapore, Guv?'

'Leyton – you'd be amazed what I know.'

DS Leyton shakes his head and pulls a stoical face. 'Is that where you were, Guv?'

'Leyton – would the Chief pay for me and Jones to fly business class to the Far East and stay in a five-star hotel drinking *Singapore Slings*?'

'Well... no, obviously not, Guv.'

'There you are, then.'

Despite his forced retreat, DS Leyton does not appear convinced. He says, 'Well – you certainly touched a raw nerve, Guv – why might that be?'

'I suspect there are one or two white lies on his CV.'

'Significant, Guv?'

'That is something I wish I did know.' Skelgill vigorously rubs the top of his head with one hand. 'Then again, I wish I could get a cup of tea – those bacon rolls don't half give me a thirst.'

DS Leyton nods in agreement. 'Fat chance of being offered one by Snyder – he was itching for us to leave from the second we arrived.'

'Follow me.' Skelgill suddenly veers to the right, away from the main doors, which they are approaching, and enters the long corridor that leads into the opposite wing of the school. The walls are bare and heavily coated with generations of cream gloss paint. At intervals classroom doors provide limited illumination through their windowed upper panels.

'Where are we going, Guv? I thought the refectory was at the back?'

'Let's try Jacobson – he was good for a brew last time – and a gossip – who knows?'

DS Leyton shrugs in acceptance and shambles along in the wake of his superior. At this moment, a shrill bell marks the end of a period. Almost immediately classes break up and a seething tide of boys of different sizes, their dark uniforms in varying degrees of disarray, begins to flow around them. The detectives attract curious stares which, when returned, become expressions of respectful deference. To a man, the boys move politely aside to facilitate their elders' progress. Skelgill might reflect on this paradoxical arrangement, when many of these courteous young gentlemen are already multi-millionaires.

Skelgill accurately leads the pair to Dr Jacobson's quarters. As he raises his knuckles to announce their arrival, in an action replay of their last visit, before they can summon Dr Jacobson by the normal means, the diminutive Cholmondeley emerges from the doorway and darts off along the corridor.

'Leyton – there's that *Chumley* kid again. Go after him.'

'What for, Guv?'

'Off the record – see if there's any rumours going about. Querrell was his sports coach.'

'What shall I ask?'

'Leyton – you've got kids – use your loaf.'

'But, Guv – who shall I say we are?'

'Tell him we're inspectors.'

'But I'm a Sergeant, Guv.'

'Not police, thicko.' Skelgill raises his hands in a gesture of frustration. 'Then tell him *your colleague's* an inspector.'

'Blimey, Guv.'

'Here.' Skelgill digs the key that Dr Snyder has given him out of his pocket. 'I'll meet you at the gatehouse. On your bike!'

Cholmondeley, thanks to his distinctive ginger crown, is still just visible, bobbing in the sea of mainly dark heads, and DS Leyton launches his ample bulk in pursuit. Thankfully, the mass of pupils into which the boy has merged collectively senses the Sergeant's gathering momentum and parts in well-drilled fashion.

Skelgill momentarily looks as though he would like to give DS Leyton a parting boot in the backside, but he returns his attention to the door, which the boy had pulled to, and instead readies himself for the capricious Cleopatra.

22. DR JACOBSON

'No dog today, sir?'

'Alas, Inspector – Cleopatra is taking exercise with one of my pupils. She is a popular alternative to an everlasting – provided the weather is fair, of course.'

Skelgill raises his head in acknowledgement – it would be a no brainer for him, whatever the weather. Though not a dog owner, the extra impetus a canine provides in driving its owner out of doors has not escaped him as a reason to have one. In his case irregular working hours militate against such an arrangement, never mind the difficulty of finding a breed that would gladly run for hours over the fells, alternating with long sedentary spells spent sitting obediently in a boat – although the irrepressible Border Collie would probably fit the bill.

'What breed is she, sir?'

'She is in fact a cross – between a Staffordshire and a Boxer. She is actually very soft at heart – despite her rather intimidating appearance.'

'Yes, sir – it's something we often find – appearances can be deceptive.'

'I don't doubt it, Inspector.'

Skelgill nods and takes a sip of the tea with which, as he anticipated, Dr Jacobson has willingly furnished him. Indeed, his welcome is as effusive as that earlier in the week, although on this occasion the somewhat eccentric academic is more conventionally attired in pinstriped suit trousers and a plain white shirt; however the dickie-bow and carpet slippers are still in evidence.

Now Dr Jacobson coughs rather affectedly. 'They call them a Bullboxer, Inspector, but I can't say it's a name that trips off the tongue.'

Skelgill tilts his head in agreement. 'Lady I know keeps a Labradoodle.'

'Well at least that has a certain phonic ring to it.' He grins in a leering manner. 'But then there is the Cockapoo. Rather vulgar, don't you think?'

'Perhaps Cockadoodle might sound a bit better, Sir.'

'Quite, Inspector.'

'What will happen to the gun dogs that Mr Hodgson looked after, sir?'

'Oh, Inspector – I believe the janitor's brother-in-law is a gamekeeper over at Greystoke – he has apparently taken them under his wing for the time being.'

There's a *ping* sound from what must be the kitchen, and Dr Jacobson points a finger into the air and springs urgently from his armchair. 'That will be the scones, Inspector – always better warm, don't you agree? I shan't be a moment.'

'Certainly, sir.'

Dr Jacobson scuttles away, leaving Skelgill alone in the parlour. He takes a casual stroll about the room, as a tourist might when visiting a stately home. There are various artworks and ornaments, of a somewhat chintzy nature, but it is upon the collection of drinks displayed on the dresser that he homes in.

'Can I offer you a little sherry, Inspector?'

Dr Jacobson's silent carpet-slippered return seems to take Skelgill by surprise, and he needs two hands to replace the whisky bottle he's been examining.

'Oh, no thank you, sir.'

Skelgill edges between one of the armchairs and the settee in order to regain his seat; while Dr Jacobson lays out upon the coffee table the various items from the tray he bears.

'Or perhaps something stronger?'

'Naturally I can't drink on duty, sir. I have a friend who is a bit of a whisky buff.'

'Ah, I see. I'm afraid that is just a common-or-garden blend, Inspector.'

Skelgill resumes his position on the sofa and accepts a side-plate and scone from Dr Jacobson. 'I'm more of a real ale man, myself, sir.'

'And some very good local ones, I believe?'

'Not that I have much spare time for it, sir.'

'A policeman's lot is a busy one, to coin a phrase.'

'That's marginally better than the original, sir.'

'Well, Inspector – another day, another death – the excitement is getting too much.'

Skelgill begins to frown disapprovingly, but there's a mischievous glint in the eyes of his protagonist, and he's forced to grin in sympathy. He says, 'It is a bit of an odd one – I mean, we don't get a peep out of this place the last ten or fifteen years – and all of a sudden two suicides in a week.'

'Let's hope they are not like London buses, Inspector.'

Skelgill shakes his head ruefully to indicate he understands the allusion. 'I was wondering if you could tell me anything about Mr Hodgson, sir – we've done a bit of digging into his background and it doesn't look too clever.'

Dr Jacobson flicks at the tufts of hair above his ears and pulls a face of distaste. 'A thoroughly unpleasant character, Inspector – I'm not at all surprised to hear that.'

'Did you know him very well?'

Dr Jacobson suddenly looks alarmed. 'Heavens, no, Inspector – I'm simply passing on the word around the common room. I rather suspect he was one person who wouldn't have shied away from a drink whilst on duty.'

Skelgill nods. 'That corresponds to our findings. But it's still a bit of a leap from there to blowing your brains out with a shotgun – well, a four-ten, at least.'

'They're all the same to me, Inspector, I must confess.'

Skelgill lets this comment pass and continues with his theme. 'The thing is, sir, my Sergeant interviewed Mr Hodgson on Monday. Apparently he showed no sign of distress that would lead us to anticipate subsequent events.'

Dr Jacobson absently rotates his bow-tie in alternate directions, as though he is computing something. Then he says, 'But isn't that normally the way, Inspector? One reads the same thing in the papers. And look at old Querrell – he was right as rain on the day he drowned himself.'

Skelgill's ears prick up at this remark. 'What makes you say that, sir?'

Dr Jacobson ostentatiously throws his hands in the direction of Skelgill. 'He sat right where you are, Inspector. He called round to rope me into his infernal Skiddaw Challenge.'

'Sounds like something up my street, sir – a bit of fell running, I take it?'

'Quite right, Inspector. It's an end-of-term tradition – in fact it takes place tomorrow – in Querrell's memory for the first time, I suppose.'

'How does it work, sir?'

'It's a hill race for the first form – a test of their manhood, as Querrell would put it. To demonstrate to the rest of the school that he was handing them over into their second year battle-hardened and ready for anything.'

'And these are eleven-year-olds?'

'By now, generally past their twelfth birthdays – several their thirteenth – some boys drop back a year before they start at Oakthwaite – their parents believe it gives their offspring a developmental advantage over their peers.'

Skelgill nods. 'That's one way of looking at it, I suppose. And I take it, sir, this challenge involves scaling Skiddaw and getting back?'

'That's right, Inspector. There's a well-trodden circuit up from the school beneath Carl Side and home via Little Knott, if my memory serves me correctly.'

Skelgill tilts his head and looks up to the ceiling, as if he's assessing the viability of the route upon a map in his mind's eye. 'Presumably someone has to wait up at High Man to make sure there's no cheating?'

'Indeed, Inspector – and Querrell would post marshals at one or two other points to circumvent short cuts. Canny little devils, even at that age.'

'So he was trying to enlist you as a marshal?'

Dr Jacobson winces theatrically, as though the proposed assignment had been one of a much more distasteful nature. 'But there you are, Inspector – it bears out my point.'

'Sir?'

'That people who commit suicide often do it on the spur of the moment. Querrell was otherwise planning well ahead. I shouldn't be surprised if it turns out that both he and Hodgson departed on something of a whim. Have another scone, Inspector.'

Skelgill duly obliges, and helps himself to liberal dollops of cream and jam. 'Well, it's certainly looking that way, sir. Obviously with there having been a firearm involved in this last incident we're obliged to take a thorough look at things.'

'I quite understand, Inspector – in the meantime I don't suppose you have had any success in establishing whether in Querrell's case there are any surviving relatives?'

Something about the offhand tone of Dr Jacobson's question seems to put Skelgill on the defensive. He says, 'We may be getting closer, sir – these things can take a long time to check out – we're at the mercy of other authorities – they insist on all the formalities tied up with red tape.'

'Indeed, Inspector – and, of course, the modern fad for reports and appraisals and performance tables was another thing that old Querrell railed at. Drove him to distraction at times.'

Skelgill nods thoughtfully. 'Do you think he took things a little out of proportion?'

'Undoubtedly, Inspector. For instance, only a couple of weeks ago he was fuming over the idea to rename the school as a college. Although I have to agree with him on that one, it is a hare-brained idea.'

'Whose idea would it be, sir?'

'I rather suspect it is something the new bod they have recruited to do *marketing* has cooked up.' He emphasises the word marketing by crooking his index fingers into mid-air quotation marks, and rocking his head from side to side in oriental fashion. 'But these pronouncements officially emanate from the two-man policy committee comprising the Head and Snyder.'

'So it wasn't up for debate?'

The academic widens his eyes in an exaggerated manner. 'Certainly not, Inspector – the Head dismantled the old consensual regime the minute he arrived.'

'Had he worked with Dr Snyder before – I mean, since they joined at about the same time?'

Dr Jacobson purses his lips and looks rather vacantly at the ceiling. 'Not that I am aware of, Inspector – Snyder came in afterwards as part of an open recruitment process.'

Skelgill pauses for a moment before asking casually, 'Is that a job Mr Querrell would have applied for?'

'I shouldn't have thought he would have considered himself remotely in the running, Inspector.'

'No?'

'Apart from his age, he would have divined the Head's intentions to have his own man.'

'In what respect, sir?'

'Someone whose loyalties lie with him, rather than with the school and its traditions and its teaching fraternity. In Snyder he has an effective gatekeeper.'

'I see, sir.'

Dr Jacobson seems content to elaborate. 'In any event, Querrell would have been wholly unsuitable. His formative years at Oakthwaite occupied another era altogether – I believe we still had an empire and ration cards. One has to move with the times.'

'So do you generally support the new policies, sir?'

Dr Jacobson makes one of his erratic ducking movements, as though Skelgill's gentle medium-pace has suddenly come at him like a wayward full toss. 'Inspector, idioms such as one's bread being buttered spring to mind – in these straitened times one has to tread a line between the ideal and the commercial. But we should take care not to dilute our USP.'

Skelgill glances quizzically at the academic. '*USP*, sir?'

Dr Jacobson reaches to the heavens in affected horror. 'Good Lord, Inspector – they've got me doing it! I should wash out my mouth with soap. Confounded marketing jargon. Apparently it means unique selling proposition.'

'Ah, I see. And what exactly is it?'

Dr Jacobson picks up his cup and saucer and settles back in his armchair. 'Let me regale you with a short anecdote, Inspector. I was speaking with a parent during the drinks reception prior to the Michaelmas prize giving – a Chinese who owns a mall the size of a medium-sized English town in the city of Chengdu – he had travelled over by private jet to see his son accept an award, and fly him back for the vacation. He told me he had visited schools across Europe to find a suitable institution for the boy. And do you know why he settled on Oakthwaite?'

Skelgill opens his palms to indicate he has no idea. But Dr Jacobson remains silent and inclines his head towards him, imploring him to make an educated guess as he might do a reluctant pupil.

'Exam league tables... English language... Lakeland scenery?'

Dr Jacobson shakes his head gleefully at each of Skelgill's apparently incorrect guesses. He carefully balances his tea on the arm of the chair and leans forwards, elbows on his knees, hands together in a praying attitude. 'Manners.'

Skelgill reacts momentarily as if this is a rebuke, then he realises it must be the solution to the question. *'Manners?'*

'Indeed, Inspector. As he was shown around the school he was so impressed with the conduct of our boys that it made up his mind.'

'Really?'

'I don't doubt your other suggestions formed part of the edifice – but comportment was the keystone.'

Skelgill looks a little relieved that his answers have received some recognition. 'And that's the USP?'

Dr Jacobson holds up a finger, rather like an umpire giving the batsman out – in Skelgill's case as a bowler an act liable to prompt a Pavlovian celebration. 'And *that* is what is at stake, Inspector.'

'In what way, sir?'

'Breeding, Inspector. One can't teach it. Our indigenous boys are born with it. The little brats arrive here as if miraculously fully formed in this regard. The finished article requiring only the odd rough edge filed here and splintered bottom sanded there.'

Dr Jacobson makes a caressing motion with both hands, and Skelgill looks a little embarrassed by this simile. 'And the Chinese don't?'

'Nor the Russians nor the Mexicans nor the Germans nor the rest.'

Skelgill's expression is perhaps unintentionally disapproving, for now Dr Jacobson seems to backtrack a little. 'Don't get me wrong, Inspector – I harbour no xenophobic grudge – and most of these non-nationals hail from authoritarian backgrounds – all I'm saying is that the more we dilute our native population with little Johnny foreigner, the more we diminish the very reason that persuaded his parents to send him here.'

Skelgill nods. 'So you might say it's good business in the short term, but not necessarily the best thing in the long run.'

'Quite, Inspector.'

'And is this a policy that Mr Querrell particularly objected to?'

Dr Jacobson makes a so-so hand signal, his cup rattling in its saucer as the movement is transmitted through his sparse frame. 'We've always had a small overseas contingent – typically from the traditional colonies. But there is so much new money in the world. Are you au fait with Dickens' *Great Expectations*, Inspector?'

Skelgill looks like he's thinking about it, which is evidently sufficient for Dr Jacobson to assume the answer is no. He says, 'Inspector, down through the centuries successful merchants have yearned most for one thing: that their sons may be Gentlemen.'

Skelgill seems relieved that he is not about to be quizzed further upon a subject that was never one of his strengths. 'I certainly can't argue with your assessment, sir – based on what I've seen of the school myself. Though that little ginger-haired lad seems to be full of beans.'

Dr Jacobson's pale eyes narrow, as though he feels in singling out a specific pupil Skelgill has breached a convention. 'Ah yes, Inspector – Cholmondeley. A Blencathra boy. He can be a bit lively at times – but these first-formers settle down once they've had a couple of good thrashings.'

Skelgill, who is replacing his empty side-plate upon the coffee table, shoots a surprised glance at Dr Jacobson, only to find him grinning widely. 'Just joking, of course, Inspector.' He leans forwards and gives Skelgill's knee a vigorous squeeze, in confirmation of the jest.

Skelgill's unblinking expression belies the discomfort apparent in the stiffening of his posture. Only when the housemaster retracts his hand does he reply. 'Naturally, sir – though I couldn't help noticing that your Dr Snyder had a cane hanging in his office – it did make me think twice about what the position is in private schools.'

'If I recall correctly, it has been outlawed since nineteen ninety-eight – thankfully.'

Dr Jacobson says this in a rather wistful tone that might make Skelgill think he believes otherwise.

The contact upon his knee seems to have disconcerted Skelgill, for now he sits up in his seat and straightens his jacket. 'Well, sir – I'd better be getting along – my Sergeant will be waiting for me. Thanks once again for the tea and scones – much appreciated – you can't always rely on a regular meal in my line of work.'

'Glad to help keep the thin blue line intact, Inspector.'

They rise and Dr Jacobson precedes Skelgill into the corridor. As they pass the open door to his study Skelgill glances in, and a collection of trophies upon a bookcase catches his eye – there are one or two silver cups, and several pedestals adorned with what appear to be figurines of swimmers or divers.

'Ah, Inspector – you have spotted the *Querrell Quaich*.'

'Sir?'

Dr Jacobson steps into the small room and selects what is probably the least striking of the items – a small shallow silver bowl with a protrusion at either side. He turns and holds it out for Skelgill to see. 'Blencathra House currently holds the honour of getting a team back first from Skiddaw. Alas, I doubt we shall triumph tomorrow – I understand this year's crop is not for running.'

'You never know, Sir.'

Skelgill says this rather distractedly. He is looking beyond Dr Jacobson at what seem to be the obligatory academic certificates adorning the wall. They somehow lack the symmetry and precision of Dr Snyder's comparable qualifications.

Dr Jacobson now replaces the quaich, and shepherds Skelgill towards the exit, closing the study door behind him.

'Well, I mustn't keep you from your rendezvous, Inspector. Good luck with your investigation – and drop in any time you are in need of succour.'

*

'Wait 'til I see him. I'll swing for the Mancunian dork.'

'But, Guv – I thought he wasn't supposed to know I'm still working with you?' There is a mixture of guilt and panic in DS Jones's tone. 'It'll give the game away. I think he suspects, as it is.'

Skelgill seems to relent in the face of this logic. 'What the hell's Smart doing messing with your phone, anyway?'

'I didn't notice I'd left it on the table when I went to the ladies' – I was keeping it where I could see it in case Goodman called.'

'I thought you had a PIN code?'

'I do, Guv – he must have watched me. I've changed it now.'

'Sly bastard – he should keep his nose out of your business.'

'Sorry, Guv.'

Skelgill, who is making rapid strides along the slick tarmacadam that winds through the woods towards the gatehouse, stoops to pick up an itinerant pebble. Irritably he flings it left-handed at one of the round '10 mph' signs that line the driveway. His aim is unerring and there's a resounding clang. A little flock of chaffinches scatters from the verge beyond, flashing white in their wings and tails. As he nears the point of impact he pulls an apologetic face – the paint has chipped off and there's a distinct dent in the centre of the figure zero.

After a moment's reflection he speaks, saying, 'But he didn't listen to the message?'

'I think he just looked to see who'd called. Or he saw me coming back. But that meant the reminder was cleared from the screen – so I didn't realise until I checked my voicemails that there was one waiting from Goodman.'

'Do you have his name in your phone memory?'

'No, Guv – so DI Smart wouldn't recognise the number – he was probably checking it wasn't you.'

'Pillock. Just how long are you going to be stuck with him?'

'I don't know, Guv – he's saying this drugs case could take days or months.'

Skelgill tuts. 'I'd have a word with the Chief – if there were ever such a thing as a good moment.'

'More hassle, Guv?'

'Only the standard Friday email. Pull your socks up else you're demoted. The usual motivational stuff.'

'She's obviously been on a carrot and stick course, Guv.'

'I could live with that if there were some carrot.'

Skelgill remonstrates with nobody in particular, waving his arms about and casting his eyes up to the clearing skies. It would be questionable whether either carrot or stick have much impact upon his behaviour, but neither does he demonstrate that it's for love of the job that he works; it seems only a strong sense of justice drives him day and night.

He returns his attention to the call and says, 'Just run past me again what Goodman said.'

'Only that he got my message – and he was on a tight connection and that he'd be on the train from Euston in an hour unless he heard from me. Obviously I missed that opportunity.'

'Sounds like he might have stayed down south if you'd got hold of him.'

DS Jones hesitates before replying. 'He could have tried harder, Guv – maybe he's come home from Singapore with everything he wants?'

'I doubt it, Jones.'

There's a hint of innuendo in Skelgill's tone, but DS Jones does not react. 'I could still call him, Guv?'

Skelgill cuts down his pace. He is approaching the lodge and DS Leyton has spotted him. The Sergeant hauls himself backwards out of his car, blinking in the dappled sunlight like a bleary-eyed bear that has emerged from a spot of hibernation. Skelgill holds up a hand in acknowledgement.

'Jones – I've reached Leyton – I'd better find out how he's got on. Sit on the call for the time being. But let me know if Goodman decides to ring again.'

'Sure, Guv...'

'Aha?'

'I was just wondering...'

'Aye?'

The line suddenly goes dead. Ten seconds later a text appears on Skelgill's screen: 'Smart back – will call later.'

When he glances up from his handset a shirt-sleeved DS Leyton is recumbent on a bench just a couple of yards to one side of the front door of the building. The mid-June sun hangs directly overhead, and the sheltered glade in which the cottage stands is a little bowl of humidity. A blackbird takes advantage of the resonant air to proclaim its territory with a rich stream of liquid warbling notes. Above a hawthorn a shimmering column of St Mark's flies attracts Skelgill's eye: a sure sign that rapacious brown trout will be eminently foolable by means of a shrewdly cast *Bibio*. He saunters across and apes his Sergeant, slipping out of his jacket and swinging it onto his shoulder.

'You look pleased with yourself, Leyton.' He settles down gingerly upon the weathered seat; it appears fragile, and while it has borne the greater weight of his colleague, he doesn't want to be the straw that breaks the camel's back.

DS Leyton, an affable sort, evidently bears no grudge against his superior for berating him an hour before. 'How'd it go, Guv – any joy with Jacobson?'

Skelgill shrugs. 'He was good for tea and scones, but I couldn't draw him on whether the Head or Snyder or both are up to something – assuming he would know about it, that is.'

DS Leyton nods, but holds back, as if he's waiting for an invitation to speak.

After a moment Skelgill obliges, saying, 'What about you?'

DS Leyton's tone is self-effacing, perhaps so as not to sound competitive. 'I got free beans on toast, Guv.'

'What, in there?' Skelgill tilts his head back to indicate the gatehouse.

'No, Guv – with the kid, *Chumley* – it's spelt Chol-mon-del-ey, by the way.'

DS Leyton flips open his notebook at the page held fast by an elastic band – he holds it out so Skelgill can see the heading with the boy's name.

'What is it, Guv?'

Skelgill is frowning and staring intently at DS Leyton's notes. He looks away and gazes up into the trees. A family of newly fledged blue tits is feeding upon the abundant aphids in a mature sycamore. 'It strikes a chord. I can't think why, though.'

'Bit of a posh name, eh, Guv? Can't say we had a Cholmondeley in our school – I doubt even the borough.'

Skelgill shakes his head like a dog pestered by a bluebottle, as if he recognises the futility of racking his brains. 'It'll come to me when I'm not trying. Don't reckon it's one of our local villains though, you're right on that score.'

'He's okay, the kid – smart little nipper. Suggested we went into the communal kitchen to avoid eavesdroppers. They've got their own separate boarding block, the first formers. There's a woman – a Housemother – looks after them. They call her Mrs Tickle. Well sorted, they are.'

Skelgill nods and asks, still a little absently, 'How did you get on?'

DS Leyton leans over his notebook. 'I told him like you suggested – you were an inspector and I'm your assistant – he didn't seem too fazed about that. So I just said we were interested in how things are going at the school right now.'

'What did he say?'

'They know about the suicides, obviously, Guv – but I reckon it's all a bit of an adventure – for these young 'uns, anyway. Apparently legend has it that the school chapel is haunted by Mary Queen of Scots, and her ghost returns every so often to wreak vengeance on the Church of England.'

Skelgill takes DS Leyton's notebook and looks hard at the open page, as if to check whether his Sergeant has actually got this written down. 'So Mary Queen of Scots drove an atheist and an alcoholic to suicide?'

'I think they'd happily believe it, Guv.'

'I must put this in my email to the Chief this afternoon.' He hands back the notebook.

DS Leyton chuckles. 'Thing is, Guv – I don't reckon at this age they grasp the finality of death. And it doesn't sound like either Hodgson or Querrell will be missed.'

Skelgill purses his lips. 'Hodgson I can understand – probably all they got from him was *"Get off the effing square"*, but I thought Querrell was supposed to be *Akela?'*

DS Leyton shrugs. 'Not so sure about that, Guv. According to Cholmondeley he was a bit of a slave driver. Like when he refereed the rugby – if a kid got injured he'd just leave him lying there and play on.'

Skelgill lifts his head in acknowledgement. 'What about the official line?'

'They've been told they both had personal problems unconnected to the school.'

Skelgill puffs out his cheeks. 'That's stretching it a bit as far as Querrell was concerned.'

DS Leyton shrugs. 'Like I say, Guv – I think they're just taking it in their stride. BAU.'

'What?'

'Business as usual, Guv.'

'Did the kid say that?'

'Er... yeah, I reckon he did. Why, Guv?'

Skelgill shakes his head slowly. 'You keep giving me a *déjà vu*, Leyton.'

DS Leyton beams. 'I get that myself all the time with the missus, Guv.'

Skelgill reciprocates with a forced grin. 'So no indication that anything was amiss with Querrell?'

DS Leyton looks hopefully at his notebook, as if willing something hitherto unwritten to materialise. Then he jolts and says, 'Oh, Guv – Cholmondeley did say he'd heard raised voices while he was waiting to see Jacobson, and Querrell had come out with a face like thunder.'

'When was this?'

'He couldn't remember exactly – last week. Seems he has to go to Jacobson every day to collect a diary sheet for the first-form noticeboard. He's the house rep.'

'I take it he doesn't know what they were arguing about?'

DS Leyton shakes his head. 'He just said it wasn't unusual for Querrell to be bad tempered.'

Skelgill purses his lips. 'Did he mention this hill-race they've got tomorrow?'

'No, Guv – what's that about?'

'Something Querrell normally organised – Jacobson told me about it. That could be what the fuss was over. The first years have to run to the top of Skiddaw and back.'

DS Leyton shifts uncomfortably in his seat. 'Blimey, Guv – the more I hear about this place the more I reckon I got off lightly in my day. No wonder he was unpopular if that was the sort of stunt he put them up to.'

Skelgill nods. 'What did the boy say about Jacobson?'

DS Leyton shrugs. 'Nothing we don't know, Guv. Said he's a queer old bird – but that he's a soft touch for tuck and forgetful when it comes to punishment exercises.'

'Think he was holding anything back?'

'Nah, Guv – I don't. He's very open and quick to answer. A bit too talkative for his teachers' liking, I shouldn't wonder.'

'Well he was right about the scones. Jacobson eats more than me. You'd think he'd carry a bit more padding.'

DS Leyton leans back and proudly pats his ample stomach. 'We're not all designed to survive a shipwreck, Guv.'

Skelgill glares disapprovingly at his Sergeant. 'Except you'd still be stuck on the desert island long after I'd built a raft and sailed to safety.'

'Then you'd come to rescue me, Guv – just as the coconuts run out!'

Skelgill chuckles and gets to his feet. 'Come on – thankfully it's Friday.'

He strolls across to the doorway; while DS Leyton, following, pats his pockets for the key that Skelgill had given him earlier.

'Here we are, Guv – I thought I may as well wait for you before going in.'

But Skelgill's attention is fixed upon the stone lintel above the entrance. He reaches up and brushes his fingertips across the uneven surface.

'What is it, Guv?'

Skelgill steps back and points with an index finger. 'What do you reckon that is?'

DS Leyton squints hopefully at the chiselled marking that Skelgill indicates.

'Dunno, Guv. A backwards number six?'

'Wouldn't make sense, though, would it – number six on a gatehouse in the middle of nowhere?'

'Could just be a design, Guv – looks a bit like those prehistoric markings on the rocks at Copt Howe.'

Skelgill shoots a surprised glance at DS Leyton. 'How do you know about them?'

'Ah, you see, Guv – one of our kids is doing the Stone Age as a project at school. We drove down and had a look last weekend. They made axe heads there, too – traded them all over Europe.'

'Well, you're certainly turning into a fount of information, Leyton. You'll be teaching me about fishing next.'

'No fear, Guv – you know me and hydrophobia.'

'You should give it a try sometime. I shall be on Bass Lake on Monday morning bright and early if you want to come.'

'I'm all out of leave, Guv – 'till my next holiday year starts.'

'Pity we can't trade – I'm going to forfeit two weeks at my present rate.'

'You just off Monday, Guv?'

Skelgill nods. 'I was going to cancel it, but we seem to be grinding to a halt on this case. Maybe I'll have some inspiration while I'm fishing.'

'Guv, I reckon I ought to follow up those livestock thefts over at Appleby – the file's been burning a hole in my in-tray. Unless you want me to come and talk to someone else here?'

Skelgill's shoulders have slumped and he has a defeated look about him. He shakes his head. 'Nah – you'd better keep the landowners happy. I'll try to do the same with her majesty.'

DS Leyton pulls in his head in tortoise fashion. 'Rather you than me, Guv.'

Skelgill sighs. 'Hopefully she'll be in her Friday heads-of-departments meeting for the rest of the day. I'll leave it as late as I can to send her a report.'

DS Leyton nods, and reaches with some difficulty over his shoulder to pull his shirt away from his skin. 'I'm sweating like a pig, Guv. Think the heatwave's coming back?'

Skelgill gazes up to the skies and watches the movement of the clouds. 'Doubt it – not with these westerlies. The outlook for the weekend's not too clever. I've got a run on Saturday and a mountain rescue exercise on Sunday.'

'Maybe they'll get it wrong, Guv. I'm supposed to be cutting our grass before the pigmies move in. Reckon I might already be too late.'

Skelgill forces a smile. 'Come on, Leyton – let's get this door open. I can't see us finding anything here, but I'd better return this *Wainwright*.'

23. BASSENTHWAITE LAKE

Rather in the way of Manchester, whose reputation is such that the climate is sometimes styled as *'raining, or about to rain'*, the Lake District experiences precipitation approximately every other day, with little respite in summer. This phenomenon provides the forecaster with a fifty per cent chance of being correct, before any meteorological skill or local knowledge is applied. Not surprisingly, therefore, the forecast to which Skelgill had referred has been borne out as accurate. Friday's mid-afternoon sunshine proved to be a false dawn, so to speak, and the weekend something of a washout for those who had outdoor activities in mind: a state of affairs that probably suited DS Leyton. Though the worst of the downpour restricted itself to Saturday and Sunday, a slow-moving occlusion has bequeathed a stubborn blanket of cloud and low-hanging mist that drapes the fells; complemented by a light but persistent drizzle, the conditions are such to merit the colloquial epithet *mizzlin*.

On the damp bankside shingle Skelgill, something of a doppelganger for Tove Jansson's *Snufkin*, crouches beneath a makeshift shelter fashioned from a length of painter and a rather maggoty tarpaulin. The rope is strung between two springy alder saplings, and the gabled canopy held fast at its four corners by a quartet of heavy mudstone boulders – it is a far cry from the luxury bivouacs enjoyed by today's cosseted carp anglers, but it does the job as far as Skelgill is concerned. Like a Neolithic hunter at the mouth of his cave, he sits contentedly amidst the grey smoke that billows from his soot-blackened *Kelly Kettle*, poking with a twig a pan of fresh brown trout fillets that spit and pop and threaten to leap from his battered *Trangia* stove. The still air is thick with the aroma of their burnt skins, mingled with wood smoke and methylated spirits. As the tall aluminium storm-kettle reaches its boil he expertly sweeps it off its flaming base and decants a stream of steaming lake-water into a tin mug charged with the requisite two tea bags and powdered milk. Then he takes up a chipped enamel plate and, using his fingers as tongs, seemingly unaffected by the heat, lifts the fillets into a pair of hand-torn white buttered rolls. The finishing touch is a squirt of *HP* sauce from a plastic bottle that he fishes from the forces surplus knapsack at his side. Preparations complete, he stretches out his legs, his boot-heels gouging furrows into the shingle, and readies himself for his fisherman's breakfast.

It's ten a.m. as, nursing the surely scalding mug, he contemplates the scene before him. A gentle ripple laps lightly against the hull of his boat, grounded in the shallows. From its stern a single coarse rod with a *DayGlo* reed-tipped waggler float bobbing gently offshore pays lip service to his continued angling. But it has been a successful morning. Out on the lake since five-thirty, Skelgill has landed four pike for almost a hundred pounds, including one venerable specimen that eventually came aboard with two silver treble-hooks and a multi-coloured plug (not one of his) and their corresponding wire traces hanging like gipsy jewellery from its jaws. He cleaned it up and proprietorially set it back in the water, to fight another day bigger. The brace of brown trout he caught out of necessity when he realised he had left his much-loved Cumberland sausages in the fridge.

Chewing, he stares thoughtfully at the tiny orange blur of the float, although whether he sees it or looks right through it is hard to discern. Perhaps a bite will tell. There's a distant swishing rumble of wet tyres as the Monday morning delivery traffic gets going on the A66 beyond the tree-lined far bank. The small songbirds that might ordinarily be expected to bear territorial ambitions seem subdued by the dank conditions. Such avian silence is punctuated only by the occasional *plunk* of a trout sinking an ovipositioning daddy longlegs, and the hysterical cackle of a Mallard that finally gets last night's joke.

Also unclear is whether Skelgill's angling success has been matched by the inspiration he desired would come to him, as outlined to DS Leyton on Friday. Certainly his taciturn features provide little indication of such. Yet his thoughts must be drifting to the intractable Oakthwaite case. As Dr Jacobson rather cruelly remarked by allusion to London transport, for suicides to be coming along in plural, and for the Chief to have some unspoken reason for him to investigate... there is surely something afoot? What would be her motivation, however, is difficult to divine – other than logic suggests the link is either through her son, a pupil, or Mr Goodman, with whom she is evidently acquainted at the level of local dignitary. Each of these connections could explain her reluctance to state some overt rationale.

Skelgill, with his superior's patronage, has determined that the Head may be lining his own pockets, and that Dr Snyder is not all that he seems. Other masters have their idiosyncrasies – the effusive Dr Jacobson, and the tough little South African Mike Greig – although such singularity seems to be par for the course for Oakthwaite. Edmund Querrell's suicide lacks an explanation and circumstantially is suspicious, while Royston Hodgson's death is curious for its locus and Skelgill's illicitly acquired inside knowledge. Information may have been deleted from Querrell's computer (yet it is perhaps as likely that this was Querrell's own habit). And at various twists and turns Skelgill's antennae have been set twitching by subtle clues and red herrings – with seemingly no way of knowing one from the other.

Rather as in the travel of the waggler float out in the surface film, perhaps a hidden hand is at play. Wherever Skelgill might carefully cast, believing there to be a sunken shelf or submerged patch of weed that might harbour his prey, factors unseen determine that it shall drift and bobble its way back always to the same undesired point. Whether driven by some undertow or unfelt breeze, some tension in the line or vibration conducted through the rod, the pattern defies perception. And what seem to be tentative bites – even to his highly trained eye – may only be the bump of the slowly shifting bait against innocuous subaquatic obstructions, or invisible zephyrs that tease at the surface tension.

If indeed his ruminations mirror the same inexorable yet unfathomable path, then his dissatisfaction can be no surprise: nothing tangible is forthcoming, and he must leave his colleagues disappointed and himself frustrated. It is one thing to sail to a tempting conclusion, but without a clearly charted course it is a port with no name.

And now Skelgill is shaken from his reverie by the shrill ringtone of his mobile.

The phone is inside a polythene bag in a buckled side-pocket of his rucksack, and he knows he can't get to it before the call diverts. Unhurriedly he places his plate on top of the *Trangia*, and drills the half-full enamel mug of tea down into the shingle at his feet. Then he extracts the now-silent handset and sets it upon a stone, as if to wait for the voicemail notification – but when the screen springs once more into life it's the same caller trying again: DS Leyton.

'Yep.' Skelgill does not sound best pleased.

'Guv, Guv...' His Sergeant's voice has a breathless wheeze. 'You're needed.'

'What?'

'Bit of an emergency, Guv – it's the Chief's boy – the one at Oakthwaite.'

'What about him?'

'He's gone missing, Guv.'

Skelgill rises abruptly, catching his head on the apex of the bivvy and almost toppling onto his cooking paraphernalia. He manages to leap over the still-hot items and regain his balance with a controlled stumble and little trot into the water's edge, accompanied by a selection of expletives mainly of the A to C variety.

'Guv? You okay, Guv?'

'Leyton, I'm fine – just a bit pissed off, as you can imagine – what do you mean he's gone missing?'

'Sorry, Guv. What it is, in a nutshell – the school thought he'd gone home for the weekend – after that fell-running jaunt – and at home they thought he'd stayed at school.'

Skelgill stamps about in the shallows.

'Has he got a mobile?'

'They're not allowed 'em, Guv.'

'When was he last seen, then?'

'I don't know, Guv – I'm on my way now. The Chief's going apoplectic. We're just to get there and find him fast. Sounds like she's ready to call in the army.'

'When did they notice he'd gone AWOL?'

'In the past half-hour, Guv. He didn't turn up for registration, so they phoned home to see if he was sick or whatever. The housekeeper said he'd never been back.'

'He's probably skiving off around the school somewhere.'

Skelgill's tone is a blend of the sceptical and the unsympathetic. DS Leyton, conversely, can't conceal a growing note of desperation in his voice.

'Guv – I know – I'm sure it's a false alarm. But what with these suicides... it's a three-line whip. I'm to phone her back to confirm you're on your way.'

Skelgill takes a kick at a rock, but his contact is rather better than he perhaps intends and it flies across and knocks over his *Kelly Kettle*, spilling some of its contents hissing into the embers in its fire base. He surveys his equipment and shelter and the boat. It will take him a good hour to decamp, row back to Peel Wyke, chain up the boat, drive home, shower and change and make it over to the school. But his temporary camp is pitched on an isolated and overgrown promontory of the lake's largely untrodden east bank: inaccessible from all directions but the water, inconspicuous and probably safe from looters. There's little to prevent him from heading directly to the landing stage at Oakthwaite. He holds out his arms and inspects his attire.

'Leyton – tell her I'll be there in fifteen minutes – but I shan't be looking like I've arrived via Savile Row.'

DS Leyton lets out an audible sigh of relief. 'Thanks, Guv – I don't think she'll be too bothered if you turn up in your boxers.'

'Leyton – it might come to that.'

'Actually, Guv – now you mention it, I've got me other whistle hanging in the back – the missus's been nagging me to put it into the cleaners in Penrith.'

There's a pause while Skelgill contemplates this offer.

'Wait for me in the school car park.'

24. OAKTHWAITE SCHOOL

The intensifying howl of the approaching two-stroke engine must reach some critical threshold, for it diverts a frowning DS Leyton from his private misgivings as he examines the grey pinstripe suit hanging in the opened rear doorway of his car. He cranes around to be greeted by the oncoming sight of Skelgill, standing Steve McQueen-like in the saddle, riding a quad bike at full throttle across the manicured lawn that forms an apron around much of the main school building. Without decelerating Skelgill swerves onto the ornamental gravel border, the machine's back end snaking alarmingly, jinks between neat box hedges that mark the entrance to the parking area, and slides to a grinding halt beside DS Leyton.

'Blimey, Guv – where'd you learn to do that?' DS Leyton has to shout to be heard above the popping of the twin exhausts.

Skelgill dismounts and kills the ignition. He shrugs and wipes damp grass-cuttings from his forehead. His reply is a touch oblique. 'Most of the shepherds round here have them.'

'Who does it belong to, Guv?'

'Dunno, Leyton. Formerly Hodgson's maybe. It was at the back of an equipment shed on the far side of the cricket pitch, just up from the boathouse.'

DS Leyton shakes his head, his expression one of wonderment. 'I've only just got here myself, Guv – I thought you were stringing me along, saying fifteen minutes.'

Skelgill manages a wry grin. 'Leyton, I thought pretty much the same about you and your Cockney gobbledygook.'

'Whistle and flute, Guv.' DS Leyton gestures towards the said item. 'Suits you, sir.'

*

Whether it's the spectacle of Skelgill attired in an outfit substantially too wide and yet equally too short, or the latter's mud-encrusted boots off which drying flakes now cast, or the glint of fish scales that spangle the Inspector's unkempt hair – or none of the above – Mr Goodman is either unable or unwilling to disguise the expression of distaste that creases his prim features as he silently watches the two detectives cross the expensive-looking carpet that floors his capacious study.

It is probably Mr Goodman's practise to leave the majority of visitors to his room standing. In the absence of an invitation to make themselves comfortable, Skelgill leads the way in taking one of the seats on their side of the Head's ample desk. For a second or two he wrestles with the folds of DS Leyton's jacket; it clearly does not want to settle around his unfamiliar frame. Beneath it he wears a short-sleeved shirt and his bare suntanned forearms protrude well beyond the cuffs, giving him the look of a schoolboy whose wardrobe has not yet caught up with his latest growth spurt. But if he is embarrassed he doesn't let it distract from his purposeful demeanour. Mr Goodman, however, is first to speak.

'This is becoming an unfortunate Monday morning habit, Inspector.'

Skelgill appears momentarily taken aback, as though the last thing he should expect is an implied complaint of inconvenience from the person he is ostensibly assisting, especially when delivered in a tone redolent of the berating of an errant pupil reoffending.

'Though rather a more urgent issue this time, wouldn't you say, sir?'

'I am sure we shall resolve this between ourselves and the family, Inspector. I have just concluded a telephone conversation with the boy's father. Mobilising the CID seems a little heavy handed, don't you think?'

Now Skelgill shoots an accusing glance at DS Leyton, as if he is wondering whether his colleague has summoned him under somewhat false pretences. But DS Leyton appears not to notice, and doodles in his pocket book.

Skelgill turns back to the Head. 'It's not for me to question the powers that be, sir. Given the circumstances of the past week or so it seems reasonable that we should be called in.'

The Head is impassive. 'Inspector, I don't see what bearing an incident of truant has upon the now-closed matters to which you refer.'

Skelgill's features take on a look of puzzlement. He places his elbows on the surface of the desk and leans his chin upon his interlocked fingers. 'Are you not concerned about the missing boy, sir?'

The tendons in Mr Goodman's neck become more defined. Perhaps it is Skelgill's brazen intrusion onto his territory that vexes him. His eyes narrow as he shakes his head. 'Inspector, what I'm concerned about is the reputation of this great institution. I have no doubt the unauthorised absentee will surface. Meanwhile the last thing I need is some great hullaballoo with policemen combing the school when we have exams in progress. Imagine the reaction of parents if they discover their sons' futures have been jeopardised by the foolish antics of one boy.'

Skelgill is silent for a moment. Then he nods and sits back, and shakes a finger to himself, as though the penny has dropped. 'Yes, you wouldn't want the media getting hold of this, sir. You know how they seize upon the slightest morsel of news where a fee-paying school is concerned. Next thing they've syndicated the story and it's halfway round the world before you can say Jack Robinson.' He pauses, perhaps for effect. 'We've had the local press sniffing about only this morning.'

As he hears out this short monologue, Mr Goodman's stern visage seems to whiten. Whether the cause is annoyance or discomfort it is impossible to judge, but though he seems about to speak, he only succeeds in grinding his teeth.

After twenty seconds or so DS Leyton breaks the silence. He asks, 'Are you certain that he's not still somewhere in the school, sir?

The Head looks as if he is affronted that someone of a lowly rank should question him. Perhaps in confirmation of this impression, he directs his reply at Skelgill. 'As I just informed his father, Inspector – it is perfectly possible. We have labyrinthine accommodation – and extensive grounds, of course.'

Skelgill doesn't respond, but instead turns to DS Leyton, who obliges with a follow-up question.

'And has anyone looked for him, sir?'

'If you must persist, gentlemen, I suggest you speak with Dr Snyder. He deals with all these matters and no doubt has been in touch with the various housemasters and staff who would know.'

DS Leyton carefully writes this down in his notebook. The Head glances impatiently at his wristwatch. Then he drops his hand out of sight when he notices Skelgill is staring at it.

'I am expecting an important international call any at moment, Inspector.'

Skelgill, seemingly heedful of the hint, rises to his feet. 'We shan't detain you any longer, sir. We should be out and about detecting.'

The Head takes this cue to employ what is no doubt an effective method of dismissing visitors. With a swift movement he reaches for the intercom on his desk and in response to the female voice that inquires how she may help he replies, 'Please see the officers out.'

Then with a forced smile that barely troubles the corners of his mouth he says, 'Good morning gentlemen.'

As the door opens Skelgill pauses midway across the room and turns back to look at the Head.

'We understand, sir, that the boy went missing after the Skiddaw Challenge?'

Mr Goodman shrugs indifferently. 'I believe Mr Greig coordinated the event. I wasn't here on Saturday morning.'

'Ah – Mr Goodman. I meant to inquire how you got on at Marina Bay. But that will keep. Goodbye for now, sir.'

*

'The guy barely gives a monkey's, Guv. The Chief'd go crackers if she knew.'

Skelgill, leaning against the polished wall of the corridor that leads from the Head's study, puffs out his cheeks in affirmation.

'Look, Leyton – you take Snyder. I'll go and have a chat with Greig – I think the fell race is more up my street.'

'Righto, Guv.'

'Make sure they've checked all the obvious places. See what they know about his movements. Ask if there's a best pal he might have confided in.'

'Think we should call in help, Guv?'

Skelgill purses his lips, then shakes his head slowly. 'Assuming he's not suddenly going to pop up out of a desk like a jack-in-the-box, we need to establish where and when he was last seen. That shouldn't take long. Until then we can't just randomly commit resources. The Chief would know that.'

'The Chief's on tenterhooks, Guv.'

Skelgill inhales through gritted teeth and seems to steel himself. 'See if you can get a photo of the boy from Snyder – or the school office. They must have something on their system. Probably better coming from here than the family.'

DS Leyton nods willingly, understanding the subtext that underlies a request for a picture of a missing person.

Skelgill stares, almost vacantly. 'And find out if he can swim.'

'Blimey, Guv – you don't think...?'

'Worst case scenario, Leyton.'

DS Leyton blows out his cheeks and drops his hands by his sides, as though the potential ramifications are just sinking in: the extra weight of a case in which their commanding officer has the strongest imaginable vested interest, and the unthinkable repercussions if the outcome is negative.

Rather hopefully, he says, 'Surely it's right, though, Guv – about him being somewhere around? Easy enough to hide, size of the place.'

'For the best part of forty-eight hours?'

'But, Guv – he might only have vanished this morning. Maybe he's bunked off because he doesn't fancy the exams?'

Skelgill shrugs. His immediate suggestion to this effect had been informed by the prospect of his fishing trip being wrecked. 'Let's hope so, Leyton. On which note, speak to the Housemother – see what she knows, and if it's possible to tell from his belongings what he's wearing, what he's taken with him.'

'Sure, Guv.'

'And put in a call to HQ – get one of your DCs to check out family and friends – anywhere he might have gone.'

Skelgill studies his wristwatch. 'Failing other developments I'll meet you at the burger van at one.'

*

Mike Greig's office sits at the rear of the upper deck of the cricket pavilion. It boasts an impressive outlook directly onto the rain-soaked lower slopes of Skiddaw. Though Skelgill has telegraphed word and purpose of his impending arrival via the school reception desk, the diminutive Director of Sport is nonetheless momentarily startled as the detective enters his airy modern quarters. Standing behind his desk, and engaged in listening on the telephone, a flicker of recognition disturbs his relaxed features. Still clasping the handset to his ear, he leans forward as far as the tangled cable allows, and reaches out to shake Skelgill's hand, and then gestures for him to take a chair. He holds up an index finger, as if to indicate only one minute, and picks up a pen to jot down a series of brief notes upon the desk pad before him. He ends the call with a 'Thanks, Jim,' replaces the handset and resumes his seat opposite Skelgill.

'Inspector, welcome – again. When reception phoned through, I didn't realise we'd already met.'

'As your Headmaster put it, sir – if it's Monday it must be the CID.' There's the hint of a twinkle in Skelgill's eye.

Greig grins knowingly, as though he's amused by the fact that last week Skelgill had gone along with his erroneous conclusion that the detectives were parents supporting the opposing school. 'Please, Inspector – call me Mike.'

'Sure.' Skelgill nods, but doesn't remind the South African that he'd previously introduced himself by his own Christian name.

Greig seems keen and able to get to the point. He gestures to his telephone. 'The missing boy – that was one of my colleagues. I was just trying to find out what we know about Saturday.'

'He made it back?'

'We're not certain.' Greig punches a fist into the opposing palm in a gesture of frustration. 'The official finishing line was just in front of the main school – but the conditions were so bad, as soon as the trophy was won they packed up and went inside. There were *Mars Bars* and hot chocolate laid out in the junior common room.'

'When you say the trophy was won, Mike, how does that work?'

Greig drums the desk with his pen. 'The winning house is the first to get four boys back, ja? Helvellyn are really strong this year – they had four finishers in the first ten.'

'So the rest of them weren't recorded?'

'Let me tell you this, Inspector.' Greig employs the ostensibly aggressive form of delivery characteristic of his countrymen. 'In the circumstances – understandable. In light of the outcome – an oversight.'

Skelgill sits impassively, and the short silence succeeds in drawing an explanation from Greig.

'You see, Inspector, this was Querrell's bag. They say he'd organised the challenge single-handed since the nineteen seventies. It wasn't until Friday night after chapel that it dawned on me that it was on our plate. I was left with a skeleton sports staff on Saturday because most of the masters were away with their cricket teams at Ampleforth and Durham. If I'm honest with you, we were flying by the seat of our pants.'

'What about the boys reaching the summit?' Skelgill squints past Greig through the long landscape window where the green bracken of the fellside is darkened by the lowering sky. 'Presumably you had to count everyone through the trig point?'

'Correct, Inspector. I did it myself. Brutal it was – made the Highveld seem like the Bahamas. My waterproofs didn't live up to their billing.'

Skelgill nods sympathetically. He was out running himself, and had surely spared a thought for the small skinny schoolboys for whom the wilds of Cumbria were far from a natural habitat.

'They all made it to the top, Inspector – all sixty-two of them. I admired their guts, if not their fitness in every case. Querrell had certainly done a fair job whipping them into line.'

'What were the timings?'

'A good three-quarters of an hour between the first and last.'

'No wonder you got soaked.'

'I'll tell you this, Inspector – I tried an umbrella, but it took off and I reckon it must have landed on the Isle of Man.'

Skelgill grins. He refrains from correcting the South African's geography (given the prevailing wind direction), and instead replies, 'The hillwalker's brolly has yet to be invented.'

Greig shrugs sheepishly and continues, 'I made sure they all went the right way, then after the last runner came through I followed the course down to the school – in case there were any stragglers needing a kick up the rear.'

'And were there?'

Greig shakes his head. 'No – they couldn't get home quick enough.'

Skelgill nods. 'There was some mention of a marshal?'

'Ja – we had another master stationed where the downhill path crosses the lane that leads back to school – to make sure they carried on into the grounds.'

'And what was his report?'

'Same as the other, I'm afraid – once he'd seen four blue Helvellyn shirts come through, he called it a day. He phoned me for approval – I'd had to draft him in from weekend leave as it was, so I felt a bit guilty about keeping him out there to no purpose. I figured if a few of the boys cut the corner at that stage it didn't matter – it wasn't going to affect the result. Much as it goes against my principles, I think being soaked to the skin put me in a conciliatory frame of mind.'

Skelgill nods. 'So the last record you have is the boy made it to the summit of Skiddaw – what time would that be?'

'They went off at ten a.m. – I'd say about eleven forty-five, ja.'

'Was he alone?'

'To the best of my memory, ja. The gaps between them got bigger.'

'And after that he may have completed the proper course or could have used the short cut along the lane?'

'Correct.'

'What about when you walked back – did anything strike you as unusual?'

Greig considers this question for a moment, but shakes his head. 'Nothing I could put my finger on. I can't say I was at my most observant – near the path I would have noticed anyone in trouble, but I had my head down like everyone else, ja?'

'How familiar are the boys with the route?'

'Pretty well – Querrell had them running it every month – so they've been up there, what – eight or nine times? The first time they walked it as a group to identify the landmarks.'

'Do you have a map?'

'Nothing formal – but I can show you.' Greig gestures to the wall behind Skelgill, who turns to see it is papered floor to ceiling with the complete set of two-and-a-half-inch Ordnance Survey maps of the Lake District.

Skelgill admires the neatly dovetailed compilation. 'I'm getting office envy, Mike.'

'Ja – it's an impressive sight when you see it spread out like that. I tell my folks back home: it might be small in the scale of Africa, but it's not to be taken lightly on foot. Never mind the weather.'

Skelgill nods proprietorially, and automatically gravitates to the north-western quarter that holds Skiddaw and Bassenthwaite Lake.

'You got it, Inspector.' Greig points with a finger at a red circle. 'There's Oakthwaite. The route basically uses two public footpaths... this one to go up... and this one to come down.'

The circuit is roughly triangular, and its main landmarks correspond to those outlined to Skelgill by Dr Jacobson.

'Here's the lane where we had the marshal. Across that and they're in the grounds of Oakthwaite. They run down to the lake and pick up the jogging track that follows the shoreline to the gatehouse, then it's left along the main drive to the school.'

Skelgill is nodding thoughtfully. He says, 'So apart from the lane, there's no advantage in trying to take a short cut across the fell at any point.' It's a statement rather than a question.

'I reckon you're right, Inspector. I believe old Querrell devised the route with cheating in mind – wander off track and you just make it more difficult for yourself.'

Skelgill takes a hard look at the map and then closes his eyes, as if he is committing its contents to memory. Then he turns to face Grieg. 'What did you do when you got back?'

'I came directly here to shower and change – all my dry gear was in the locker room downstairs. Then I spent a couple of hours doing admin and ringing round the other schools to check the weather status, agreeing how long to wait before calling off the matches. Turned out it stayed dry over at Durham – hard to believe when you consider what it was like here.'

'They have to have some advantages, over in the east.'

Grieg smiles, enjoying the competitive remark. 'After that I locked up around mid-afternoon and that was me finished for the weekend.'

'Do you live in at the school?'

'No – my girlfriend and I rent a cottage at Grasmere – she's working as a water sports instructor for a firm in Windermere, so it's a good halfway house, ja?'

'So you didn't see the boys after the event?'

'To be honest, Inspector, I don't have a lot to do with the first-formers – by tradition Querrell broke them in. The PE Department gets involved from second year onwards – when they move up into the main school. One of those Oakthwaite quirks, I guess.'

'What did you make of Mr Querrell?'

Grieg produces a short ironic laugh. 'Oh – he soon put me in my place. I figured since I was only here on a short-term exchange there was no point rattling his cage. He was a tough old cookie – didn't stand any nonsense as far as I could see. Decent enough underneath, though, I reckon.'

Skelgill watches thoughtfully, but Greig seems quite relaxed in formulating his responses. Assuming a confiding tone he says, 'Mike – this latest incident aside – we've obviously had the sudden deaths of Mr Querrell and Mr Hodgson. As someone who is a bit more detached from the school than most, can you cast any light on these events?'

Greig digs his hands into the pockets of his tracksuit bottoms and turns out his lower lip. He swivels about and steps across towards the window, head down as though he's trying to wrestle up some intractable notion from the unyielding depths of his perception. After a few moments he turns again to face Skelgill and says, 'Inspector – don't get me wrong, this is a bit of a strange place compared to what I'm used to, ja? There's more than a touch of the cult about being a member of the Oakthwaite community. But I reckon you've just got a string of coincidences on your hands. I'm sure the boy will surface – don't be surprised if it turns out to be a dare among him and his mates.'

Skelgill's shoulders perhaps slump a fraction in response to what is a popular but unhelpful theory. He takes a couple of strides about the room and picks up a cricket bat that leans in a corner. He weighs it for size but replaces it; perhaps before the temptation to attempt a practise shot becomes too great. Then he asks, 'What about the groundsman – with the cricket season in full swing aren't you going to miss him?'

'I might have to do a bit of mowing and rolling myself – but I certainly shan't miss him, Inspector.'

'No?'

'He was not what you would call Oakthwaite material – even for ancillary staff. Not keen on taking orders, especially when he'd been out to the pub at lunchtime. I'm amazed they let him loose with the shotguns.'

'Were you surprised to hear what happened to him?'

Greig shrugs nonchalantly. 'Ach – you never know what's going on in people's minds. Where I come from an unexpected death rarely hits the headlines.'

Skelgill makes a face to show he comprehends the statistical divide that in this regard separates Johannesburg and the Lakes like a great rift valley.

'Look, Mike – I ought to get going – I think you've told me all you can about the boys – I better see how my Sergeant's getting on in tracking him down.'

'Sure – if I can be of further help just give me a shout.'

Skelgill reaches into his top pocket for a card, but to no avail since of course the jacket is not his. Indicating the desk pad and the pen lying upon it, he says, 'Can I write my number here?'

'Be my guest.'

Skelgill obliges, and then says, 'By the way, I borrowed what I assume was Mr Hodgson's quad earlier – I put it back when I came over just now.'

'I was watching as you went past – another of your hidden talents, ja?'

Skelgill pulls the ignition key from the pocket of his baggy jacket. 'Probably best if you keep this away from the machine – in case one of the boys gets the same idea.'

Greig wrings a wry grin from his thin lips. 'Let me tell you this, Inspector, we don't want any more accidents.'

25. THE BURGER VAN

'Blimey, Guv – it don't half pen. That's rotten fish, that is.'

'You're getting it cleaned, aren't you, Leyton?'

'Just as well, Guv – the missus wouldn't let me bring this back into the house.'

'I can only smell bacon – I think it's your imagination.'

DS Leyton's complaint might be more vigorous if he knew the full circumstances. Skelgill, in furiously rowing his boat back to Peel Wyke, had rather carelessly arranged the borrowed jacket on the bow thwart, only for it to slip off onto his sodden slime-and-scale encrusted landing net and spend a good quarter of an hour mingling with its questionable delights. Of course, he has not related this detail to DS Leyton, who therefore seems only mildly regretful about his generosity. Now he holds the suit still scrunched inside the plastic carrier bag passed to him by Skelgill, who has clambered into his car clad in waterproofs, gaiters and walking boots.

But at this moment the mobile phone mounted upon the dashboard lights up to indicate an incoming email. DS Leyton stoically tosses the suit into the back seat and takes up the handset.

'From the school, Guv – it'll be the photo and the boy's personnel file.'

Skelgill, however, is already distracted by the task of finding his way into the brown paper bag that holds his order of bacon rolls.

'Holy smoke.'

'What?' Skelgill sounds only vaguely interested.

Guv – you won't believe it – it's Cholmondeley!'

'What's he done?'

'No, Guv – the missing kid – the Chief's son – it's Cholmondeley!'

Skelgill squints at the grinning flame-haired boy whose image fills the screen.

'Bloody hell – of course.'

'Guv?'

'The name – I knew it rang a bell.' He snaps the fingers of his free hand. 'The Chief goes by her maiden name, doesn't she? That's right – her old man's a Cholmondeley. I've seen him once or twice with her in photos – you know, in the local rag, the court and social pages.'

'And the ginger hair, Guv. Stone me.'

Skelgill nods. 'Aye, the ginger hair.'

'Guv – it explains why the Housemother gave me a queer look when I referred to him by the Chief's surname.'

Skelgill nods. 'They'll know both names – she probably assumed we use the mother's.'

DS Leyton shrugs. 'Yeah.' He scratches his head rather distractedly. 'Guv...?'

'Aha?' Skelgill takes a substantial bite of his roll.

'You don't think we spooked him, do you?'

Skelgill swallows with difficulty and pauses to take a swig of tea before replying. 'You mean *you* spooked him?'

'Aw, Guv – give me a break – I was really diplomatic – I've got kids, remember? He was happy as Larry when I last saw him.'

Skelgill shrugs, conveniently glossing over the fact that it was at his behest that DS Leyton was despatched to hunt down Cholmondeley.

'If it's any consolation, Leyton – no, I don't.'

DS Leyton looks thankful. After a minute, while Skelgill continues to work his way through his meal, DS Leyton says, 'Strange to think I know him, Guv – he's a pleasant little nipper.'

'Must take after his father.'

'Guv, that's harsh.'

'But accurate.'

DS Leyton feigns a flinch, as if they are being overheard. Then a worried look clouds his features. 'Think it'll land us in it, Guv – talking to him, I mean?'

Skelgill is pulling a recalcitrant face. He shakes his head.

'But we'd better report it?'

'In good time.'

'But, Guv...'

Skelgill holds up a hand like a traffic cop. 'Leyton – we're the investigating officers. We know. If it's useful information, we'll turn it to our advantage. If you were the last person to see him – different matter – but you weren't.'

DS Leyton again appears relieved. 'Do you reckon there's any connection, though, Guv? It's a bit of a coincidence – four hundred kids and our one goes missing.'

'Maybe the Chief's pulled a flanker.' Skelgill tips the second roll from the crumpled bag, showering himself with crumbs. DS Leyton seems not to notice, and perhaps has long given up despairing of the daily mess his superior deposits in the footwell of his car.

'How do you mean, Guv?'

'What if she's spirited him away to give us an excuse to turn the place upside down?'

DS Leyton acts a little shocked at this suggestion. 'Surely not, Guv? I spoke to her myself – she was on the verge of tears.'

'I'd say that was impossible, Leyton – but I'll take your word for it.'

'But you can't be serious?'

Skelgill casually shakes his head. 'It's not a theory I'll be suggesting to her, Leyton. But perhaps now we know why she sent us into Oakthwaite in the first place. Remember Jacobson told us Cholmondeley was sixth generation.'

'So the kid's father would have been a pupil there.'

'And the rest of them.'

'They would have known Querrell, Guv.'

Skelgill nods thoughtfully. 'They would, Leyton.'

DS Leyton leans back in his seat and exhales heavily. But before he can expound his thoughts Skelgill says, 'Anyway, park that for now – we've still got to find the kid. Give me the lowdown on your interviews.'

Two handed, Skelgill determinedly tucks into his bacon roll. DS Leyton pulls his notebook from his inside jacket pocket. He flips through several heavily annotated pages and settles upon one headed 'Saturday'.

'What happened was, Guv – because of the weather they abandoned having the finishing line outside the front of the school...'

Skelgill cuts in, 'Aye – I got that from Greig – they only recorded the first ten. Cholmondeley was near the back of the field.'

'That's right, Guv. So the rest of the runners went straight to the changing room in the first-form block. They were trailing in for the best part of an hour according to Mrs Tickle.' He breaks off to glance at Skelgill. 'It really is her name, Guv.'

Skelgill forms a silent expression of surprised acceptance.

DS Leyton continues, 'The boys have free association on Saturday afternoons, so they could go to the junior common room, or to their dorms, or off to do activities or whatever. There was a film being shown in one of the other houses that they could watch.'

'And what mention of Cholmondeley?'

DS Leyton shakes his head. 'Nothing, Guv.'

'Nothing at all?' Skelgill sounds disbelieving.

DS Leyton winces as if he's being accused of laxness. 'Straight up, Guv. They've questioned the boys – but because they arrived in dribs and drabs – they weren't looking out for anyone in particular. Then they assumed he'd been picked up.'

'Picked up by one of his parents, you mean?'

'That's it, Guv. It was optional weekend leave for any boarders whose families live near enough to get them home. Apparently there's up to a dozen that do this – couple of times a term – Cholmondeley being one of them. They can go at one p.m. on a Saturday and have to be back in for Headmaster's assembly on the Monday morning, followed by registration – that's when he was missed.'

'What made the school believe he went home?'

'Natural conclusion, I suppose, Guv.'

'You'd think they'd have a notification system.'

DS Leyton taps his notepad on the steering wheel. 'They've got a signing-out book at the entrance to the first-form house. It's self-administered by the boys. Part of the idea is to teach them to be responsible. I got Mrs Tickle to show me – there were eight other kids who definitely *did* go home – and three of them forgot to sign themselves out.'

Skelgill raises his eyebrows, as if to acknowledge he would have been one such boy, had he benefited from a similar scholastic opportunity as Oakthwaite. 'They'll have to tighten that up in future.'

'They know, Guv. I just think what with Querrell and then Hodgson and it being exams and this fell-running event and whatnot – things have got a bit on top of them right now. Even Snyder admitted that.'

Skelgill pouts, as if disinclined to believe this declaration. 'So what did he have to say?'

DS Leyton turns a couple of pages of his notebook. 'Between you and me, Guv – I know he's a miserable sod – but he's been pretty efficient. He'd already gathered all the details of Saturday, so I got the same version of events from him as Mrs Tickle. And he's had the place searched.'

Now Skelgill's expression is one of reluctant approval. 'To what extent?'

'He knows they can't look in the likes of attics and cellars – and that the grounds are too big – but he organised for the staff and prefects to simultaneously search their own areas – cupboards and under beds – the obvious places a kid could hide.'

'And nothing?'

DS Leyton nods. 'No trace, Guv.'

'What about his gear?'

'Doesn't appear to be anything missing, Guv. Clothes-wise Mrs Tickle thinks all his uniforms are there. But they don't have an inventory of casuals to check against.

'How about sports kit?'

DS Leyton shakes his head, his loose jowls giving him a despondent hangdog look. 'Sounds a bit chaotic, Guv. Everything goes into a communal laundry, and they rely on it all being labelled at the start of term. Trouble is, kids lose stuff, labels fall off, and she says by the end of the year they're all wearing one another's kit, cobbling together whatever they can.'

Skelgill looks displeased. 'Are his trainers gone?'

'Same thing, Guv – I don't reckon it's going to be possible to establish if he's wearing casual clothes or his PE kit – unless we find a witness.'

'Bloody brilliant.'

'Sorry, Guv.' DS Leyton apologises, as though in establishing this ambiguity the cause of it is his fault, which is the suggestion carried in Skelgill's impatient undertone.

'Did you ask Snyder – is this a common occurrence?'

'For a boy to go AWOL, Guv?'

Skelgill nods.

'Not common, but not unknown – first time this academic year. He said the most usual thing is for a new boy to get cold feet or be homesick in first term. Then they might do a bunk. Unless they're Chinese, I suppose.'

'Can't be easy to keep tabs on everyone.' Skelgill sounds a little more conciliatory.

'They have a strict rule – up until sixth form they're not allowed to leave the school boundaries. Except on official trips and accompanied walking and running events like this Skiddaw Challenge. But he did say kids sometimes go off the radar in the grounds, especially at weekends when they've got free time. Or they might be doing project work and forget to come back to assembly or chapel service and whatnot.'

Skelgill peers up at the fells to their left. The drizzle has thinned to the faintest of opaque hues and there's a semblance of brightness in the cloud. He blinks slowly a few times as if he's trying to accustom his eyes to the improving light. 'Sounds a bit like an open prison, don't you think, Leyton?'

DS Leyton ponders, tilting his head from side to side. 'I reckon prison's a softer option, Guv – no fell-running and no exams.'

'Maybe there's a lesson there, Leyton.'

'I reckon a fair few of the kids at my school learned it pretty quick, Guv.'

Skelgill swallows the last of his tea and crushes the polystyrene cup, which he absently hands to DS Leyton rather like a child would to its parent.

'So what's Snyder's view?'

'He reckons the boy's not on the site, Guv.'

'Which matches Goodman's opinion.'

'Suppose they've discussed it, Guv.'

'Goodman was more concerned with PR as usual.'

DS Leyton nods. 'He looked a bit shocked when you mentioned that Marina place, Guv – where did you pull that one from?'

Skelgill winks. 'Did you notice his *Rolex*?'

'I did, Guv.'

'I don't recall him wearing it last week.'

'Think it's a fake he picked up in Singapore?'

'I think it's from Singapore.'

DS Leyton purses his lips and nods thoughtfully.

'How was Snyder – did he seem concerned?'

'I wouldn't say concerned, Guv – but he's obviously taking it seriously. I'd say he considers the ball's now in our court.'

Skelgill drums a *rat-a-tat-tat* with his fingernails on the dashboard. 'That would be fine if we knew Cholmondeley left the school like the other boys. At the moment it seems like the last sighting we've got is by Greig at Skiddaw High Man just before noon. You'd better speak to the teacher who was marshalling the lane – get his details from Greig.'

'Sure, Guv.'

'And make arrangements for a proper search – maybe later this afternoon if nothing comes in on the family and friends front. You'll need plans of the school – loft access, roof ladders, outbuildings, old wells – they'll have them for contractors and maintenance.'

'Probably Snyder, Guv.'

'And we'll need to get top-line statements from all the staff – and any of the boys that might have seen him on the route – especially on the way down.'

'Right, Guv – I'll draft in a couple of DCs from the farm thefts case.'

Skelgill slaps his waterproof-clad thighs and unlatches the car door.

'What are you going to do, Guv?'

'Climb Skiddaw.'

DS Leyton shakes his head. 'The Chief's going to be frantic, Guv – thinking he's been out on the hills for two days. Could he survive?'

Skelgill compresses his lips. 'Depends. But no reason why not. It's been mild. Cold wouldn't be too much of a problem if you kept out of the wind. Drinking water might be an issue.'

'Could he just be lost, Guv?'

Skelgill shakes his head. 'You can't really get lost in the Lakes – not in summer. Sooner or later in you come across a farm or a walker with a mobile. Someone missing is more likely to be injured and trapped out of sight.'

Skelgill boots open the door with his chunky *Vibram* soles and slides out of the seat. He turns and bends back into the car.

'Better put the underwater search unit on alert.'

DS Leyton is silent for a moment. Then he puffs out his cheeks and says, 'I meant to say, Guv – they don't think he can swim.'

26. SKIDDAW

Skiddaw and its non-identical twin sentinel Blencathra squat ominously like a pair of great muscle-bound bouncers, guarding the northern gateway proper of the Lake District. The former is one of only four mountains in England that rise above three thousand feet, on a clear day it is visible from the Devil's Beef Tub north of Moffat, a good seventy miles as the crow flies. However, from an aesthetic perspective Skiddaw would be low on most hill-baggers' lists of favourite peaks. Though impressive for its sheer bulk, critical examination reveals it to be somewhat nondescript, an undistinguished massif marked in ascending bands of grass, bracken, heather and mudstone scree. Its redeeming feature is the view it commands of almost every other summit in Lakeland, and a good part of Scotland, to boot.

Had young Cholmondeley gone missing on neighbouring Blencathra, Skelgill might have harboured altogether different fears about his fate. Blencathra may not be in the 'three thousand club' (standing one hundred and fifty-three feet short), but from an adventurer's viewpoint it is blessed with shattered escarpments and razor-like arêtes, such as the infamous Sharp Edge, site of many a scrambling mishap down the years, and deaths in double figures. While Blencathra is not a mountain to be taken lightly, to fall off Skiddaw takes a particular talent.

Skiddaw's approachability extends to a car park at the end of Gale Road, just beneath the more modest Latrigg, where the ill-equipped tourist may alight at an altitude of one thousand feet. This means the summit can be gained in little more than a gentle amble along a wide and well-worn path over mildly ascending and undemanding terrain, which, as Wainwright noted, has been 'derided as a route for grandmothers and babies'.

Despite Mike Greig's account of Cholmondeley having made it through the checkpoint at the summit, Skelgill eschews the easy ascent, and instead opts to follow the course of the entire Skiddaw Challenge. He parks at the school and, leaving the grounds by a rather unconventional route of his own making, joins the footpath that forms the upward leg, striding out at a pace that would leave most schoolboy runners trailing in his wake.

From a seasoned walker's angle the weather is steadily improving. The occlusion is giving way to the remnants of its cold front: the cloud is breaking and a stiff south-westerly breeze is picking up. The air might have a bite to it, but between abrupt showers of sleet the visibility is sharpening, bringing the wider surroundings into focus. By the time Skelgill reaches the triangulation pillar at Skiddaw High Man, the cloud base has lifted from the tops.

A raven knifes into the headwind, barking *brok-brok* to an unseen companion, while a plucky meadow pipit attempts an aerial display with limited success. A couple of distant bent walkers are poling slowly from the direction of Skiddaw Little Man, perhaps having heeded Wainwright's advice about its viewpoint. In the immediate vicinity there is no human trace, no remnant of Saturday's checkpoint – not that Skelgill would have expected anything. Nonetheless he carefully inspects the ground for any clue, before widening his search with a thorough 360-degree scan of the broad grey pebble-beach-like summit area.

After a minute he returns to the pillar and places both hands on the brass plate, closing his eyes as if he's trying to divine some otherwise intangible vibe, to tap into the mountain's memory of footsteps felt and voices heard two days earlier. His own contemporaneous hill experience, albeit at a kinder altitude, was of light but persistently driving rain, corroborating Mike Greig's estimation that it was a time for putting one's head down into the wind. The restricted visibility at three thousand feet – perhaps as little as ten yards – might have been irrelevant when the runners were simply following the path beneath their dripping noses.

This tactic would have served the boys fine provided they held to their course – and clearly most of them did just that. Greig had sent them off on the correct bearing – directly into the westerly – along a heavily worn pathway that quickly descends into a smooth-sided gully, before emerging on the obvious track that runs down to Little Knott. It is a route, as Skelgill already knows without re-tracing it, which is simple to follow, regardless of the visibility. In any event, well before Little Knott the mist would have thinned sufficiently to afford a wider view and enable the runners to keep their bearings. Moreover, as Skelgill noted and Greig confirmed, Mr Querrell had cleverly designed the challenge to make redundant the notion of taking short cuts. Quite simply, the best way home was to stick to the official course.

Naturally, had a boy gone off in the wrong direction on the summit plateau, there would be considerable scope to get lost. To the north and east of Skiddaw lies a great moorland wilderness, largely disregarded by hillwalkers, a good fifty square miles of undulating territory strewn with lesser-known peaks whose names seem to invite the hapless orienteer: Meal Fell, Longlands Fell and Great Cockup. As Skelgill is wont to put it after a few pints, only 'sniffing dogs or seeker helicopters' could effectively locate a missing person in these heathery wastes.

Having apparently satisfied himself that there is no more to be learned at the summit, Skelgill begins to pick his way down the return stretch, albeit at a more measured pace than he came up. He has extended his walking poles to their maximum limit, and – thus not needing any longer to watch his step – continuously scans the landscape on the downhill side of his course (presumably on the principle that people rarely stray against the influence of gravity). If he were descending Grey Knotts over at Honister there would be plumbago adits to worry about – horizontal shafts from which graphite was mined as far back as the sixteenth century. Nearby Blencathra bears similar scars, chiselled out by zealous Victorians in search of lead and other precious ores. Such mines might tempt the curious schoolboy, unmindful of their perilous part-collapsed tunnels and pitch-dark passageways that open into unguarded vertical pits. Elsewhere, many of the region's popular prominences are marred by man's longstanding demand for its world-renowned slate.

But this is Skiddaw, one of the oldest mountains in the Lakes, a great pile of Ordovician mudstone that flakes and crumbles when exposed, and which is consequently of no commercial value. While much of Skelgill's training – and indeed live action – in his voluntary capacity as a member of the local mountain rescue team has seen him hauling dummies from dank pits and dangling in water-filled shafts throughout the district, Skiddaw has not featured in such endeavours. Thus unblemished as regards intrusive human excavations, and in combination with its relatively benign topography, Skiddaw must be one of the safest mountains on which to get lost.

As such, Skelgill spends precious little time off the beaten track. And, while the mountain rescue team remains a resource upon which he could swiftly call – their familiarity with the terrain giving them an advantage over a police unit mobilised for the same purpose – for the present he has evidently decided to conduct the preliminary assessment solo. Perhaps he is not convinced that the boy is missing on the hill, and is merely retracing his steps to satisfy himself that this hunch is correct: a frustrating but necessary use of time, though minimised through this strategy.

Indeed, on only three occasions does he divert to inspect a passing feature – a small bluff, a rocky beck, a boulder patch – where perhaps a person might lie concealed. In general the terrain offers little to suggest someone might have strayed from their true course: no trace of stones dislodged, no path thrashed into the springy green bracken.

And so, uneventfully, Skelgill reaches a stile beyond which is the lane. The thump of his boots upon the tarmac disturbs a foraging woodpigeon; it departs with a battering of wings flashing white. He stands facing in the direction of the school, which lies out of sight about a mile distant. Then he surveys the immediate environs: dry-stone walls border the narrow roadway, backed by gnarled hawthorns and the odd spindly ash. There is no place for a car to park, nor even a suitable sheltered spot for a marshal to station himself – perhaps small wonder the teacher in question was keen to call it a day at the earliest opportunity.

On the opposite side of the lane a new-looking gate with a galvanised hunting latch marks the entrance into what must be the grounds of Oakthwaite. A discreet private property sign with the school's acorn logo confirms this supposition. Skelgill wanders across and gives the gate a shove: it is well balanced and recently oiled, and swings back easily into the closed position. Now he stares again down the lane, as if trying to decide which route he should take – or, perhaps, which option Cholmondeley would have chosen: the easy short cut to a warm shower and hot chocolate, or the looping jogging track that is twice the distance? He has not spoken to the boy himself, and has only DS Leyton's account to go on – though he knows the Chief's nature well enough. If the boy has inherited any of her grit (a quality Skelgill grudgingly admires), then – combined with the ethos no doubt drummed into him by the likes of Mr Querrell – he will surely have taken the 'honourable' route, despite his low ranking in the field. He will have completed the challenge in full.

After a few moments it seems Skelgill may have come to this conclusion. He takes a last look at the lane and then vaults the gate into the grounds of Oakthwaite.

27. OAKTHWAITE SCHOOL

'Ah – there you are, Guv. I thought I might find you coming back about now.'

Skelgill, standing one-legged and leaning on his car for support, momentarily glances up from inspecting the boot that he appears to be sniffing, an expression of distaste creasing his windswept features.

'Everything alright, Guv?'

Skelgill makes a scoffing sound and flings the heavy item of footwear onto the gravel of the school car park. 'Careless dog owners, Leyton. Got a carrier bag on you?'

DS Leyton digs into his pocket for his keys, and pops open the trunk of his own vehicle. From a bulging plastic bag he extracts one of many others screwed up inside it. He pulls it into shape and expertly gloves the offending boot, inverting the bag and handing it to Skelgill.

'I'm doing this all the time with the kids' shoes, Guv – used to be nappies, now it's shoes.'

'Where are the dog wardens when you need them.' Skelgill says this as a statement rather than a question, and his tone sounds flat and despondent.

DS Leyton inhales rather apprehensively, before saying, 'Nothing on the kid, Guv – not beyond Greig seeing him during the race.'

Skelgill hops around to the back of his car and fishes out his shoes from beneath the opened tailgate, then lowers himself onto the protruding flatbed to complete the change of footwear.

'He's not on the hill, Leyton.'

DS Leyton frowns. 'But, Guv – surely you can't know that? I've got a search team lined up to start – once you give them the nod.'

Skelgill remains seated. He licks his lips and casts about over his shoulder as though he is looking for something to drink. 'So tell me about nothing.'

DS Leyton looks a little crestfallen. 'In a way, Guv – it's as good as a positive sighting. I reckon there's only a slim chance that he came back to the school buildings.'

'Nobody saw him arrive, change, leave?'

DS Leyton shakes his head, but now he becomes more animated. He paces to and fro before his superior. 'It would have meant the boy completing the last stretch with a gap of at least three or four minutes between him and the runners either side of him.' He chops out the time intervals in mid-air with his chunky hands. 'Otherwise someone would have seen him get changed. It's not impossible, but seems unlikely. They also think if he were planning to leave, he'd have gone through the internal changing room door and along to his dorm to collect some gear – even just a jacket or his wallet or watch. He'd have to pass the housemother's day-room, and she says she was sitting there with the door open while the boys were coming back.'

'What about the teacher who was marshalling the lane?'

'As we thought, Guv. He walked back down to the school and drove straight home in his car. Lives over at Pooley Bridge. Reckons he was there before twelve. Then he went up to Carlisle for the rest of the weekend to stay with the in-laws, with the missus in tow.'

Skelgill nods. 'Make a note to cross-check those timings with his wife.'

DS Leyton pulls his notebook from his jacket. As he begins to write, he says, 'We've already spoken to several of the boys who were towards the back of the race, Guv – they confirm there was no marshal in the lane when they came through.'

Skelgill inclines his head in acknowledgement that his Sergeant has appreciated the potential significance of this point. 'And none of the other boys who were picked up by their relatives saw anything of him?'

DS Leyton shakes his head. 'We're contacting all the parents. But I reckon we'd have heard about that straight away, Guv.'

'I know, Leyton.'

'It's got to be somewhere round the course, Guv. Either he's become lost or got injured along the way.'

'Did you speak to Greig again?'

'I asked if he could be mistaken, but he said definitely not – Cholmondeley being the only ginger-nut in first form. Swears blind he turned him round at the summit.'

'He would say that, though, wouldn't he?'

DS Leyton looks startled. 'What do you mean, Guv?'

'Wouldn't look too clever for him if sixty-two boys set out and only sixty-one made it through his checkpoint – then he goes home as though nothing's amiss. That would be a bit of a blot on his copybook.'

DS Leyton puffs out his cheeks. 'Blimey – I hadn't considered that, Guv. Now you mention it, I had a quiet word with Jacobson – I reckoned with him being Cholmondeley's housemaster he might have known something about the boy's state of mind – but he was all for having a dig at Greig.'

'Such as?'

'Well, you know, Guv – I thought he was just being an old gossip, stirring it – but he did say something about watching your back where Greig's concerned. Apparently there was friction between him and Querrell.'

Skelgill shrugs. 'Greig more or less admitted that to me.'

'Jacobson reckons they weren't on speaking terms. Evidently when Greig reported for duty at the school he kicked up a fuss about the office they'd given him – being Director of Sport and all that – and so they had to boot Querrell out of the room he'd been using in the new pavilion.'

Skelgill raises his eyebrows. 'That probably explains the maps. I didn't get the impression that a love of the fells was Greig's bag.'

'Jacobson says the Skiddaw Challenge was a shambles, Guv – badly organised, like. He reckons Greig just wants two years at Oakthwaite on his CV and doesn't give a toss about the school. I think he's hoping we'll give Greig a hard time if he turns out to be the last person who saw Cholmondeley. He says no way would anyone have been allowed to go missing if Querrell had still been around. Claims Querrell never lost a boy in the hills in over forty years – overnight camping, trekking and whatnot. He blames Greig for a failure of supervision.'

Skelgill sighs. 'At the end of the day, Greig got himself to the top of Skiddaw and stood there for an hour or more in foul weather. I should remind Jacobson he'd declined to be a marshal.'

DS Leyton screws up his face to indicate he is accustomed to operating on only partial information as far as working with Skelgill is concerned. 'That might have shut him up, Guv.'

Skelgill does not react. He says, 'And does he have any theory about Cholmondeley?'

DS Leyton shakes his head. 'Nothing we haven't considered, Guv. He said the usual procedure if you wanted to find out who'd been picked up from school was to ring Querrell, because he watched all the parents' cars from his window at the gatehouse.'

'We shan't be doing that.'

'No, Guv. Be handy to know who came in and out on Saturday, though. I was thinking it's a pity they've not got CCTV.'

'Evidently the Singapore dollars haven't stretched that far yet. On which note, when did Goodman get back from his junket?'

'He says just after three p.m. on Saturday afternoon, Guv. Apparently he's got a flat in London – from when he used to work down there. Says he came up on an open return and got a taxi from the railway station.'

Skelgill chews his lower lip for a moment. 'See if you can get confirmation of that.'

'Should be easy enough to check out, Guv.'

'If he paid cash it's a fair bet the taxi ride wasn't metered. You know what goes on, Leyton.'

DS Leyton shrugs. 'Put it like that, Guv – if he wanted to fake a journey he could nip down to Kendal and catch the train there.'

'True enough. What else did he have to say?'

'He just kept banging on about bad publicity – threatening to call the Chief. He's like a record that's stuck. He insists the boy's done a bunk and it's not the school's responsibility.'

'And Snyder?'

'He's well narked, Guv. Looked like thunder when I told him we'd be combing the place. He said the Head would explode if he heard his house was going to be searched.'

Skelgill pulls a face to show he's not bothered.

'Snyder seems to think the police ought to take his word for it – that the boy isn't somewhere in the school. Says it's not any old state comprehensive that we can come swanning into.'

Now Skelgill scowls to signal his disapproval. 'What did you say?'

'I asked him to account for his movements over the weekend. I think he got the message, Guv.'

'And what were they?

'He reckons he never left the building. Spent the time between his office and his quarters. Had a meeting with the Head on Saturday evening. There was a chapel service on Sunday morning. Says he did his usual inspection rounds on both nights at nine-thirty. But they leave it up to the housemasters and prefects to make sure everyone's accounted for and that they get to bed on time.'

'What about the other staff – anything there?'

'Not really, Guv. The masters in charge of cricket teams left early on Saturday morning. Those off duty who don't live in went home on Friday evening. A couple of the resident teachers drove into Keswick on Saturday morning – before Cholmondeley was last seen. It seems like pretty much everyone at the school stayed indoors because of the rain. Jacobson was complaining that even the naughty lads took detentions instead of walking his dog.'

Skelgill grimaces. He stands up and strides a few yards from his car. Hands in pockets, he gazes out across the gently falling school grounds, a manicured parkland of cricket pitches and spreading sweet chestnuts. Flashing black and white, a magpie drops down from the boughs of one such *Castanea*, to relieve a foraging blackbird of its hard-won worm. The index and middle fingers on Skelgill's left hand momentarily twitch as the mugging takes place and the masked robber returns to a cackling accomplice hidden amongst the foliage.

DS Leyton looks on anxiously. Perhaps trying to guess Skelgill's thoughts, he asks, 'What about the search team, Guv? They need your guidance for where to start. We hadn't better leave it too long. The Chief's been onto me three times since lunchtime – she said your mobile was off.'

Skelgill shakes his head a little forlornly. 'I didn't need the distraction, Leyton. I know what we're looking for.'

'She's arranged a media conference for eight p.m. – she wants you to front it, Guv.'

Skelgill spins around, grinding gravel beneath his feet. 'Well that's a great use of my time.'

DS Leyton winces, as though this is his fault. 'She doesn't want it coming out that it's her son, Guv. Think of the press – they'll have a field day – misuse of limited resources and all that. It could distract from saving the kid.'

Skelgill walks across to DS Leyton and pats him on the shoulder. He perhaps appreciates that his Sergeant, as the father of a boy of similar age to Cholmondeley, is likely to experience an occasional unprovoked assault from his sensibilities. 'Let's think about this, Leyton. Statistically, you're right, he's most likely to have got lost or had an accident. I doubt it – but if he has, we'll find him – it's safe up there. If he's done a bunk – he'll turn up – but he was probably wearing wet sports kit. I don't think he's done a bunk.'

DS Leyton is listening carefully. 'But that only leaves abduction, Guv. Or worse.'

Skelgill shrugs, resignedly. He turns away, perhaps to conceal his grim expression from his colleague.

'Thing is, Guv... it would take a vehicle. And it's not like he's a nipper – a twelve-year-old takes some shifting.' DS Leyton seems to be striving to strike an optimistic note.

Skelgill remains phlegmatic. 'Leyton, there's nowhere to park where the route crosses the road. If you waited there you'd block the traffic. And, as you've confirmed from the boys that were interviewed, there was nobody about.'

'What if Cholmondeley were walking back down the lane and accepted a lift from someone he knew, Guv?'

'It's possible. Obviously that could explain a lot.'

But now the sombre note returns to DS Leyton's voice. 'Guv, there must be locals that use the lane – and plenty of tourists out in their cars, given the rain. He might have just been picked off by a random nutcase.'

'The odds of that are so low, Leyton. Think of the location. Predators hunt where they know they'll find prey. The only living thing you're likely to meet on one of these lanes has four legs and goes *baa.*'

DS Leyton ponders for a moment, then says, 'Guv – what if it were a hit and run? Shouldn't we be checking the undergrowth, and the road surface for signs of an accident?'

Skelgill doesn't appear convinced. 'It's too narrow and winding to drive fast. And if you'd knocked someone down you'd have to heave them over a six-foot wall.'

'We'd better look, though, Guv?'

Skelgill doesn't answer. Instead he returns to his vehicle, and begins to scrabble about in one of several plastic storage crates that hold an unruly jumble of fishing tackle and camping equipment. He lifts out his soot-encrusted Kelly Kettle and shakes it to check how much water it contains. 'I'm parched, Leyton – I need to make a brew. Got a newspaper in your car?'

DS Leyton looks a little dismayed, though whether this is because his unread daily is about to go up in flames, or the impression his superior gives of not having his heart in the investigation, it is impossible to discern. Perhaps Skelgill's mind is on the media conference, something he is well known to detest.

Within two minutes, and using only the outside half of DS Leyton's red top, Skelgill has boiling water spitting from the spout of his cherished contraption. Lifting it by its bucket-strap handle, and tipping it by means of a chain attached near its base (the other end of which is fixed to the large cork that seals in the water when the kettle is not in use), he expertly fills the pair of tin mugs he has already loaded with tea bags and dried milk.

'Blimey, Guv – that's impressive.'

'These newspapers have their uses, Leyton – and not just in the toilet department.'

DS Leyton grins sheepishly, but none the less retrieves the crumpled remnants of the said journal and stuffs it inside his jacket. Meanwhile Skelgill is stirring the tea. He hands a mug, still containing its tea bag, to DS Leyton and takes the other for himself, slurping thirstily over the hot liquid.

DS Leyton follows suit, but is immediately forced to spit out his mouthful. 'Crikey – it's boiling, Guv! I just about took the roof of my mouth off.'

Skelgill grins. 'You get used to it, Leyton. When you're out fishing it's better too hot than too cold. Take a seat.'

He settles back down on the sill of the estate car, and indicates for DS Leyton to join him. The latter obliges, the leaf springs creaking alarmingly as they take his weight. They sit and sip in silence for thirty seconds or so.

'It's a strange one, this, Leyton.'

'Guv?'

Perhaps the calming tea-ritual and the salving of his dehydration has relaxed Skelgill. He picks up a steel rod-rest that lies at his side and scrapes an unrecognisable pattern into the gravel between his feet. 'I feel like I know what's going on. It's like there's a mountain in the clouds, right in front of us – we can't see it, but we know it's there.' He reaches out to grasp a clutch of thin air. 'If only the mist would clear.'

DS Leyton nods, frowning philosophically.

'But the Chief wants answers – and we need to find the boy, no matter that he's her son.'

'Yes, Guv.'

'Look, Leyton – they can search the hill – a downhill sweep below the path from Skiddaw High Man – concentrate on the upper section. There's plenty of daylight – it won't be dark until ten tonight. And – yes - while you're at it, find out which local farmers use the lane.'

'Should we put in a checkpoint, Guv – same time of day?'

'Probably wise, Leyton.'

'Then what about the railway station – and the services on the motorway, Guv?'

'Do the usual – get photographs round to the staff, shop assistants, toilet cleaners – you know the routine.'

'The press conference will help, Guv – it could jog the memories of people who were travelling on Saturday afternoon. The Chief wants to get coverage on the late news.'

Without overtly admitting it to his partner, Skelgill appears to have capitulated in the face of DS Leyton's persistence. However, now he falls silent for a few moments, as though he is drawing upon his own intuitions.

'We could really use a detection dog, Leyton. Not just for the grounds, and the school – but all these staff cars.' Skelgill waves loosely at the vehicles parked in their vicinity.

'I'll see what's available, Guv.'

'We've got a PC on the gate, right?'

'It's young Dodd, Guv. He's based in the cottage. We're keeping the gates closed and he's checking everyone in and out. More for reassurance than anything.'

Skelgill nods. 'See if we can organise a plain-clothes tail to wait out of sight. If Goodman or Snyder or Grieg leave I want to know where they go.'

DS Leyton bites one cheek, as if he suspects this might be a tall order – then again, he will realise they do have their commanding officer onside in this matter. 'I'll ask the question, Guv.'

'And I'd like another uniform, visibly patrolling the perimeter of the school buildings. Twenty-four seven. Using a flashlight in the dark. Team of two or three on shifts, whatever it takes – remind her Smart's got plenty of resources we can commandeer.'

DS Leyton raises his eyebrows, but doesn't ask for further explanation. He's accustomed to his senior officer keeping his cards close to his chest, even if sometimes they prove to be a busted flush.

'And get the underwater unit moving, too.'

DS Leyton inhales like a rehabilitated smoker. 'That would be a shocker, Guv.'

'We have to do it – even if it's only going through the motions.'

'How do you mean, Guv – going through the motions?'

'Remember the lady of the lake?'

'Come again, Guv?'

Skelgill snorts. 'You've obviously never been trapped next to George at a police dinner. It's his specialist subject in case he ever gets invited onto *Mastermind*.'

DS Leyton shrugs, as if he still has no idea to what Skelgill refers.

'Murdered woman's body dumped in Wastwater lay undiscovered for eight years. Another one in Coniston Water took over twenty years to find.'

DS Leyton affects a shudder. 'I never knew that, Guv.'

'Mind you, Leyton – Wastwater's the deepest lake in England. And Coniston's not far behind.' Skelgill casts a hand in the direction of Bassenthwaite Lake; they can't see it, but the wide valley marks its presence. 'Bass Lake's a mere puddle in that respect – twice the area of Wastwater but average depth only five metres.' He scratches his head Stan Laurel fashion. 'Which is probably why it's excellent for fishing, now I think about it. All the shallows – good light for plant growth.'

'So a body would be easy to find, Guv?'

Skelgill folds his arms, as if he's now backtracking. 'Not necessarily. See, Leyton – you have to think of Bass Lake as just a widening of the Derwent – and it's one of the fastest rivers in Europe. Rises just below Scafell Pike and drops two-and-a-half thousand feet in twenty-five miles. There's a heck of a flow when it's in spate. Hidden currents. I've had whole trees overtake my boat like they've got outboards attached. Unbelievable.'

'And the rain, Guv.'

Skelgill seems lost in reverie for a moment. 'What?'

'The rain, Guv – with all this rain – the river will have been in flood?'

Skelgill nods ruefully. 'Aye, you're right. Bass Lake is on the move.'

DS Leyton sinks into silence.

After a minute, Skelgill says, 'You know it's the only lake in the Lake District?'

'You did mention that once before, I think, Guv.'

28. THE PRESS GANG

'Daniel?'

Skelgill hurriedly swallows the mouthful on which he has been contentedly chewing and, after an uncomfortable-sounding moment, manages to reply, 'Jim?'

'It is, Daniel. Where are you just now?'

Skelgill stares at the line of truckers and tourists waiting in orderly file for their burgers, their implacable queuing faces no doubt belying the hunger pangs that are inevitably triggered by the mouth-watering aroma of frying fat. He presses the button to raise his electric window: though the weather has cleared a straggling shower has left the road surface slick, and the metronomic swish of passing traffic interferes with his hearing.

'I'm, er... just below Skiddaw – on the A66.'

'Are you by any chance free to meet for a few moments?'

Skelgill checks his watch; it's after six and he has been summoned by the Chief for a briefing at seven. 'I've got to do a media conference – I'm just on my way to prepare.'

'Ah, I see.' There's a note of disappointment in Professor Hartley's voice.

'Was there something...?' Skelgill seems unsure as to how he should phrase the question.

'I'd rather not elaborate over the telephone, Daniel. It concerns the matter you were asking me about last week.'

'Right.'

'I extended a few feelers – but by what seems a remarkable coincidence someone else has got in touch – literally minutes ago. But they are somewhat reticent about anything being spoken over... how could one put it – the police airwaves? It does, however, appear to be a matter of urgency.'

Skelgill jams the remains of his roll into a space designed as a cup-holder, and reaches for the ignition. 'Jim, I don't think they're bugging me – but I hear what you're saying. Where are you?'

The professor gives a little cough. 'Ah – this is mildly embarrassing, Daniel.'

'Oh?'

'Well – you know the magnificent spot you mentioned on the Derwent – where you bagged all those brownies?'

'Aha?'

'I thought I'd give it a try – water's a bit high today, of course – but here I am. I didn't think you'd mind.'

Skelgill chuckles. 'Ever a fisherman, eh Jim? I don't blame you – if I had your free time I'd have a rod permanently strapped to my left hand.'

Now the professor has a smile in his voice. 'Right hand in my case – you always were a devil to teach.'

'Ah, you did a good job, Jim. Look – I can be there in ten minutes, tops – I'll just have to risk the wrath of my boss.'

'Perchance she will appreciate your efforts in due course, Daniel.'

'That'll be the day, Jim. Look – I'm on my way. I'd better ring off in case some keen young patrolman spots me on the phone.'

'I quite understand, Daniel. But – before I forget – I was doing a little research of my own. Would you believe that the name River Derwent translates as River of the Oaks? It has its origin in Celtic – they would say *derwen* for oaks. To this day the word in Welsh for oak is *derw*.'

Skelgill shows limited interest in this linguistic gem, though perhaps it is the process of performing a U-turn into a gap in the speeding traffic that restricts his attention. All he manages by way of response is, 'Great, Jim – I'll be with you shortly.'

*

'Jones, can you talk?'

'Sure, Guv – I'm just getting ready to go out.'

'To work?'

'The usual, Guv.'

'I need some back up – tonight.'

'What time?'

'Pick me up outside the Moot Hall in Keswick at eleven-thirty.'

DS Jones pauses for a moment. 'Guv – I'm supposed to be on with Al – DI Smart – until one.'

'Make an excuse, get sick – it's essential.'

'Guv – how about DS Leyton?'

'Have you seen him run?'

'Run? What's it about, Guv?'

'Jones – I'm joking. But he's a family man – I can't drag him out at midnight.'

'Whereas...'

'We work well as a team after dark.'

DS Jones is silent, although she is moving about, presumably in her bedroom, and there's the rumble of what might be a drawer being opened in the background.

'Jones?'

'Guv – I'll think of something. But please don't send me any texts, okay?'

'Sure.'

'The Moot Hall, Guv?'

'Correct. I'll park in the public car park and walk through one of the ginnels.'

'Isn't Market Square pedestrianised now?'

'Don't worry – the bollards will be unlocked when you arrive.'

'Right, Guv. And what should I wear?'

'What you had on the same time last week was pretty impressive.'

'Guv – I meant like trainers.'

'They always come in handy.'

*

'Inspector Skelgill, why can't you give us the boy's name?'

'Or tell us who the family are?'

'Is he a local, Inspector – or a tourist?'

'What was he last seen wearing?'

'How about lines of inquiry – you must have a theory?'

'Are you going to be charging the parents with neglect?'

'Inspector – why won't you tell us more?'

Skelgill, though not quite at the rabbit-in-the-headlights stage, certainly might be compared to a stag at bay. Rendered virtually dumbstruck by the concerted baying of the media pack, there's a hunted look about his taut demeanour. In contrast to his glib colleague DI Alec Smart, for whom weasel words and the slick put-down of the heckler come easily in these situations, Skelgill is cornered outwith his natural habitat. Frustrated too, since no doubt he wishes to lay flesh upon the bones of the sparse skeletal statement his commanding officer has forced upon him (backed, he surely suspects, by additional pressure from Oakthwaite's Headmaster). While he would feed the press hounds, it is not within his power so to do.

He might be alone on stage in the small purpose-built auditorium, but he knows the Chief is listening-in over the conference call unit on the desk before him. There is an 'agreed' party line, from which he may deviate at his peril. And yet, while the Chief is probably right in fearing that the media would sensationalise the potentially lurid aspects of the story – the commitment of public resources in search of the son of a senior police officer who attends one of England's most prestigious private schools – Skelgill must rue the handicap this places upon their ability to be of greatest assistance. Hyperbole usually translates into greater publicity and attention. Thus Skelgill appears a weary figure, perhaps half-willing the Chief to carry out her symbolic threat to revert the case to DI Smart.

'Gentlemen... and ladies – lady...'

Skelgill glances apologetically towards the sole female member of the media corps. A striking dark-skinned brunette, she reclines nonchalantly at one end of the curving front row of seats. She wears a black silk jacket and a short matching black dress decorated with cerise half-moons and festooned with an elaborate toothed necklace. From Skelgill's panoramic perspective he can see that her sculpted lower limbs draw the surreptitious glances of the pack-dogs among her male colleagues. A locally based freelance reporter, she shows no sign of being intimidated by the unruly masculine mob. Such self-confidence, in fact, is in keeping with her reputation for ruthless global syndication, and the rumours that she is a regular ghost contributor to the likes of *Private Eye* and *The Huffington Post*. Instead, she inclines her head gracefully towards Skelgill in acknowledgement.

Now he squints into the arc-lights erected for the benefit of the regional television unit that is covering the media conference. Addressing no single face in the crowd of twenty or so journalists, he clears his throat and then declares, 'All I can ask is that you assist us in communicating the boy's photograph to the public, and to request information from anyone who may have seen him after midday on Saturday, either in the vicinity of Keswick north of the A66, or alternatively at a railway station on the West Coast Line, or motorway services, most likely on the M6 in England and the M74 in Scotland.'

Perhaps out of growing desperation, driven by the need to provide their voracious editors with a high-value kill, the hacks now begin to speculate by revealing some of their own embryonic and ill-informed theories.

'Does he have Scottish connections, Inspector?'

'Is this a runaway or an abduction?'

'Has he been kidnapped, Inspector?'

'What about a ransom – have you received a ransom demand?'

'Inspector Skelgill, is he the relative of a celebrity?'

'Felicity Kendal?'

This quip causes a small splutter of amusement.

'How about a rock star?'

'Joe Cocker.'

A collective titter ripples back and forth as these local puns are understood.

'Nah – Greg Lake, more like.'

Now the titter becomes a guffaw.

'The Home Secretary's got a holiday cottage in Ambleside – *she's* a redhead.'

'No chance, mate – that's dyed.' This retort is yelled from one pressman to another.

'How come you're so well informed?'

'I read it in *Hello*.'

There's another approving peal of laughter, and it seems that the journalists have invented their own version of a Mexican wave: a response to the poor fare on offer centre stage. This sideshow provides Skelgill with a moment's respite in which to gather his wits. As the hubbub dies down he says loudly, in a firm tone of voice, 'Colleagues of the media – Cumbria Constabulary believes it is in the best interests of the missing boy that his identity is not disclosed at this time.'

There's a further growl of discontent, albeit accompanied by a murmured acceptance that this is all they are going to get for the moment. There's the slap of notepads being shut and the snap of briefcases. One disillusioned-sounding voice pipes up, 'How do you expect us to run a story when we don't know what it is?'

There is a renewed chorus of agreement with this sentiment, and Skelgill is beginning to look as if his will to withstand the onslaught is waning. He leans forward onto the desk over folded arms, and must be wondering why he had planned no means of retreat. As he affects a cough and takes a drink from the glass of water beside him, a text evidently comes though on his mobile, which lies on top of his case file. As he glances at the phone a perplexed frown creases his brow, and then – as it suddenly rings – he picks it up, answers the call and holds it to his ear, apparently listening intently. He says something in the affirmative into the microphone, ends the call and stands, hurriedly gathering his papers.

'Gentlemen,' (this time he appears to circumvent decorum and omit mention of both sexes) 'there's something urgent – I must leave you. Thank you in advance for your co-operation.'

Purposefully he sweeps towards the side exit of the auditorium, en route passing close above the still-seated female reporter. She seems preoccupied with her own mobile, and is in the process of completing an operation. She bends over to drop the handset into the designer handbag at her heels, momentarily revealing a glimpse of cleavage. As she sits upright she catches his eye; Skelgill averts his gaze and departs the room.

There are one or two hopeful shouted exhortations, last-gasp attempts to get Skelgill to reveal an off-guard or off-the-record detail, but he manages to make his getaway without falling victim to one of his own devices.

*

'Dutch courage, Danny?'

'Isn't that supposed to come beforehand?'

'That depends what's going to happen next.'

Skelgill inhales and quickly takes a gulp of his pint, before standing to admit the woman into the space beside him on the upholstered bench seat. She's both slender and shapely, and her lithe movements attract his scrutiny. He slides across in front of her a Collins glass; it contains a clear iced drink garnished with a slice of lime.

'How sweet, you remembered my favourite.'

Skelgill allows himself a wry grin. 'I seem to remember it was in your text about twenty minutes ago.' He takes another pull at his beer. 'Thanks for the rescue.'

'You're welcome — as an old friend I couldn't bear to see you limping about hamstrung in front of that pack of sour old hyenas.'

'Did it look that bad?'

'Danny — I know a stitch-up when I see one.' She raises her glass. 'Cheers.'

'Cheers.'

After another mouthful, Skelgill seems to relax, and sinks back into his seat. The woman apes his movement, stretching out her legs so that her hemline slips another inch or so up her suntanned (or fake-tanned) thighs.

'When you say stitch-up?'

The woman twists to face him, perhaps so she can see the reaction in his eyes. 'I'd venture that, to say you were operating under a three-line whip, would be an understatement.'

Skelgill doesn't look at her. He shrugs, and says, 'You know the score – there are times when we all have to be diplomatic.'

The woman laughs, a deep throaty chuckle that belies the soft tones of her voice. Two middle-aged men seated at the bar turn inquisitive faces towards the couple. Skelgill stares them down and they return to their game of cribbage.

'It's bollocks, Danny, and you can't deny it. When the boy's identity gets out – which it surely shall – I'll be intrigued to discover which authority is going to be embarrassed'

Skelgill's eyebrows register an upward shift, perhaps a clue that she is getting warm. 'What makes you say that?'

'Come off it, Danny – it's plain as day. The police wouldn't withhold an identity at the whim of parents, no matter how high profile they are – certainly not when they're distributing a photograph.' She takes a slow sip of her cocktail. 'Sure – let's have radio silence when a kidnap is in progress – but this isn't it. It takes a greater power to do this – and what power might that be, I wonder?'

Skelgill tilts his head momentarily towards her, as if to acknowledge her deduction. 'You always were top of the class.'

The woman's reaction to this compliment is a feline movement that seems to flow out from her core to her neatly painted fingertips. She leans forward to take another drink and then settles closer to Skelgill, playfully resting her head against his shoulder. 'Is it the police, Danny?'

Skelgill visibly stiffens, and the woman recoils with a mock defensive gesture of her mauve talons.

'Ouch.' She smiles coyly over her glass and says, 'Come on, Inspector, I pulled you out of the fire.'

'Aye – but straight into the frying pan wasn't what I had in mind.'

'What *did* you have in mind?'

Skelgill slumps back and once more reaches for the cover of his drink. After a moment's reflection he says, 'Oh, you know me – I'm not a great one for forward planning.'

The woman nods and smiles. 'See where the path takes you.'

'That's about it.'

'Surely there's something you can tell me?' She presses a hand onto his thigh. 'It can't all be top secret, Mr Bond.'

Skelgill looks anxiously about the pub. It's a little-known bolt-hole, thus a popular haunt of his, tucked away down a narrow one-way street on the edge of Penrith's old town centre. Frequented only by locals, now late on a Monday evening its clientele comprises half-a-dozen patrons quietly going about their drinking, soon to be turning in on this, a work-night. The lights are low and the atmosphere warm and humid. A drink or two ought to lower the inhibitions and loosen the tongue. Perhaps Skelgill is feeling this sense of freedom, in the little alcoholic haven.

Yet still he shakes his head. 'Look – right now, it really could be dangerous for the boy if I were to tell you any more.'

'So you *do* know something?'

Skelgill pouts, ruefully. 'That's the trouble – I *feel* something, alright. But I can't risk putting a foot wrong.'

'Maybe another drink would help – it's my shout, Danny.'

The woman reaches for her handbag, but she is at the mercy of Skelgill in order to extricate herself from her place at the end of the bench. With spread palms he repels her efforts to rise. 'I'll get them.'

He returns within a couple of minutes and carefully places the refills on the uneven pitted surface of the heavy oak-and-cast-iron table. In the meantime the woman has slipped out of her jacket and augmented her make-up; her cheeks show a fresh blush, her lips glisten like a sticky crimson flytrap. Casually she shakes her glossy chestnut locks, partially veiling her dark irises with their dilated pupils.

'Thank you, Danny.'

'I owe you – better to clear the slate. Before you try to suck me dry.'

For a second the woman looks pretend-shocked at this remark. Then she turns towards him over her bare shoulder. 'You could always owe me again, Danny.'

*

195

'Guv – is that blood on your neck?'

Skelgill appears surprised by this observation, though nonetheless he accurately locates and rubs vigorously at the spot when DS Jones's inquisitorial gaze rests.

'Must have nicked myself, shaving.'

DS Jones turns to stare ahead through the windscreen. She sits in silence while Skelgill settles himself. He claps his hands together.

'Okay, so drive east as if we're going to Penrith. Do you know Chestnut Hill?'

DS Jones is slow to reply; the interior light fades out and she squints into the streetlamp neon of the night.

'The Windermere road?'

'That's the one.'

She slides the car into gear and they move off. Market Square is devoid of its daytime tourist throng; only a scattering of late-night revellers totters towards curtained B&Bs. DS Jones has to brake while an elderly man in a greatcoat erratically crosses their path. He doffs his cap and then, when he gains the kerb, with surprising sprightliness he shadow boxes his reflection in a gift shop widow.

'Bollards.'

'Guv?'

'I need to lock the bollards.'

They stop for a moment for Skelgill to secure the pedestrian zone posts with a key that he has somehow acquired. When he hops back into DS Jones's car, his manner is as if she's just picked him up for the first time.

'How did you escape from lover-boy Smart?'

DS Jones scoffs at this question, as though she detects his diversionary tactic but is just sufficiently amused by its naivety. 'I told him you were taking me clubbing.'

Skelgill laughs nervously. 'You know me, Jones – if at first you don't succeed.'

Perhaps this hint of humility softens her displeasure, and her mood seems to lighten.

'So what are we doing, Guv?'

'I'm meeting someone – in connection with the Oakthwaite case.'

'Who is it?'

'That I don't know.'

'A man or a woman?'

'No idea. I'm assuming a man, though.'

'Well – where then, Guv?'

'Castlerigg stone circle.'

DS Jones is silent for a moment. 'In the dark?'

Skelgill shrugs. 'Midnight. Not my choice of rendezvous.'

Again DS Jones ponders for a while. 'Isn't the way to the stone circle along Eleventrees? That's the turn after Chestnut Hill.'

Skelgill glances across the shadowy interior at DS Jones. As she concentrates upon the road, her prominent cheekbones and smoothly curving brows catch the headlights of an oncoming vehicle. Her implacable features endow her profile with a classical chiselled appearance. He observes her for a moment before answering.

'I have a cunning plan.'

A smile creases the corners of her mouth. 'Not like you, Guv.'

Skelgill thumps his thighs three times in rapid succession, as if he is readying his quads for action. 'Aye, well – just in case it's a trap. I don't want to be another unexplained statistic.'

'So what do you need me to do, Guv?'

'First and foremost, to know where I am.'

'Do I come with you?'

Skelgill shakes his head. 'I want you to wait in the car – getaway driver. But I'll show you when we're nearer. Here's Chestnut Hill.'

They follow the road as it winds up out of Keswick over Castlerigg Brow. After half a mile he directs her to turn off, a left-hand switchback so sharp that she has to shunt to enter. The lane is walled, and barely more than a car's width across.

'Wow, Guv – this takes some doing.'

'The bad news is, now I need you to switch off your headlamps.'

'You're joking?'

'Just slow down – your eyes will adjust.'

For a while they crawl at something less than walking pace, until Skelgill's prediction proves correct and DS Jones is able to speed up a little. It helps that the lane is straight and bordered by treeless enclosures.

'You wouldn't want to meet anyone coming the other way, Guv.'

'That's the idea, Jones.'

After a couple of minutes he tells her to stop. He hops out of the car and hauls open a five-barred gate. Then he directs her to perform a three-point turn using the field entrance, before closing the gate again. He returns to the passenger door but remains standing.

'What now, Guv?'

'You wait here. Cut the engine.'

'But I'm blocking the road.'

'Correct.'

'What if someone comes along?'

'Send them back – you're a policewoman, remember?'

'They'd have to reverse, Guv. It must be a half a mile.'

'It's in the driving test, isn't it?'

'Right, Guv.'

'Seriously, Jones – this route is barely used by day, never mind this time of night.

DS Jones nods reluctantly. 'Is this part of the cunning plan?'

Skelgill looks like he's eager to set off, but he glances around and slides into the passenger seat, keeping the door open. 'I had to agree to come alone, with no police stakeout. This is the back-way – the stone circle's about a quarter of a mile further on. My guess is that whoever's meeting me will park up at the normal entrance. If I need to do a runner, we control this road.'

'What if you become trapped, Guv?'

Skelgill reaches inside his jacket and pulls out a cylindrical object. 'Know what this is?'

'A distress flare?'

'Correct. If you think you've seen a comet, dial 999.'

'Are you allowed to have one of those – I mean, on duty?'

Skelgill purses his lips. 'Are we on duty?'

'I think you're always on duty, Guv.'

With rather alarming force Skelgill raps on the windscreen with the flare. As DS Jones flinches, he says resolutely, 'We could be investigating a triple murder here. I'll take my chance.' He checks his watch. 'It's a quarter to twelve – time to creep along and see if anyone's about.'

As Skelgill makes to heave himself out of the passenger seat, DS Jones leans across and kisses him on the cheek.

'Be careful, Guv.'

Skelgill spins out of the car and, resting on his haunches, peers back inside. He touches his face. 'First blood, now lipstick.'

'Yes, Guv – you match DI Smart.'

'Ha-ha, Jones.'

29. THE DERWEN

As Skelgill drops catlike into the sheepfold that holds the Castlerigg megaliths, a screech owl floats noiselessly from an adjacent slate upright – a single plough-scarred outlier reputedly erected by a farmer in modern times. The presence of the secretive nocturnal raptor is perhaps an indication that the detective is first upon the scene.

He squats in the shadow of the dry-stone wall, watching and listening. There is just the barest hint of breeze and the sky is cloudless and star-spangled. The moon, though now a waning gibbous, casts sufficient light to reveal the ring of stones: from his angle a line of dark silhouettes and silvery highlights like the waiting ghosts of an ancient tribe. No vehicle is in evidence in the lane beyond; no soul stirs.

After a minute he rises and strides swiftly across the close-cropped pasture. A rabbit sentinel thumps the earth as it detects his approaching tread, and with its family scampers to safety. Skelgill enters the circle; he walks more slowly, but does not come to a halt until he reaches the worn patch of bare soil at its centre, as if drawn there by some special localised gravity.

The monument is set upon a raised plateau within a magnificent natural amphitheatre. Even by day few traces of civilisation are visible from its heart. Under cloak of darkness it provides a panoramic vista unchanged for five millennia – no sheep, no walls, no farms – just the inner teeth of the grey stones, and the great gaping jaws of the primeval fells ringing the skyline beneath a twinkling firmament. Skelgill slowly rotates on his heel, perhaps trying to pick out familiar peaks on the faint line of demarcation where black rock becomes dark sky.

In the south the moon sails high above Helvellyn. To the west is the distinctively pointed Grisedale Pike, Keswick's mini-Matterhorn. Straddling the northern quarter, where the sky is at its palest, is the great looming bulk of Skiddaw merging into Blencathra. And in the east, as Skelgill's clockwise rotation is completed, stands not a mountain – but a man.

Tall, cloaked and hooded, the wizard-like figure seems magically to have materialised. Indeed, all he lacks to complete this fantastical impression is a long wooden staff. Perhaps he was pressed close to one of the loftier uprights, and has now detached himself to announce his presence. Stock still, he seems to be waiting for Skelgill to make the next move.

Arms akimbo, Skelgill has the look of a gunfighter poised to draw. He must be disconcerted that he did not detect his opponent. Instinctively his hand reaches into his jacket.

'Inspector.'

The accent is at once refined, and the voice clear and confident. Most striking of all, its tone is warm and engaging.

'Not many sightseers about, this time of night.'

Skelgill's answer, though a little oblique, seems to satisfy his antagonist. The latter bows once and walks steadily into the little inner cove of stones that mark out a kind of chamber within the main circle. Belying his outward garb, which is suggestive of an elderly monk, he moves robustly, with military bearing, and like a man of no more than early middle age.

'Perhaps we should be seated, Inspector.'

He indicates a suitable shin-high stone to Skelgill, and then backs away a few paces to take one opposite. Skelgill approaches cautiously, glancing up at the moon, perhaps noting his adversary has taken advantage of its capacity both to spotlight, and to enhance the featureless shadow beneath the folds of the great hood. All around them, pale lichens adorn the surfaces, giving the impression that individual moonbeams dapple the pitted rocks, while glistening dew like a silvery film coats the grass and tells of a rapid fall in temperature.

'I see you employed local knowledge in your line of attack, Inspector.'

Skelgill lifts his palms in a gesture of mild apology. 'I've never been one for the beaten track, sir.'

'So I am led to understand.'

Skelgill raises an inquiring eyebrow. 'Who are you, sir?'

The man shifts a little uncomfortably. 'I do not believe it will assist either of our causes for you to know my identity,

Inspector. My apologies for this ceremonial costume – although we are not acquainted you would recognise me and I should prefer that not to be the case.'

Now Skelgill shrugs. Ordinarily he might be tempted to quip, 'Don't bank on it, buster,' but diplomacy prevails and he simply nods in acceptance.

'And you have no recording device?'

Skelgill chuckles. 'This is Cumbria Police, sir, not MI5. But in any event you have my word.'

'That, I also believe, stands for something.'

'You obviously haven't met my boss.'

The man does not reply directly, and instead, with a melodramatic sweep of the arm through the great hanging sleeve of his robe, he indicates their surroundings. 'One wonders what Arthurian parleys and tribal rites have taken place on this spot through the epochs, Inspector.'

His voice has taken on a wistful note, and for a moment or two it seems he is lost in the role of Neolithic chieftain or soothsayer.

The prolonged silence causes Skelgill to speak. 'You said *both* our causes, sir?'

This interjection brings the man's attention back to the moment. Now there's a hint of a regret in his voice. 'Indeed, I represent those who need your assistance.'

'And who are they?'

Again the man pauses, and for a second or two his breathing is audible as he formulates his response. 'Are you familiar with the ownership and control of Oakthwaite, Inspector?'

Skelgill shakes his head. 'Not really, sir. I'm guessing it's not the local authority.'

The man leans forward and gathers in his cloak. 'As is widely recorded, the school was established in the early Victorian era by a sole benefactor.' He breaks off and nods slowly several times, as if convincing himself that he should tell Skelgill what comes next. 'What is less well known – indeed undocumented – is that the institution was saved from bankruptcy shortly after the first Boer War, when its founder's heir speculated and lost heavily. At that time a score of Oakthwaite's supporting families came to its rescue. To ensure its survival, the ownership was transferred to a trust. Thereafter, control passed into the hands of a Board of Trustees.'

'And you represent the Trustees?'

'In part, Inspector. One might say, the hereditary faction.'

Skelgill nods obligingly.

'These families – let us call them the new founding families, for that is what they essentially were – deemed that they had earned a right of advantage. They determined they should reap the lifetime benefits that may stem from their not-insubstantial investments.'

'The old school tie?'

The man must read some disapproval in the tone of Skelgill's response, for he harrumphs before formulating a rejoinder. 'Inspector, where ancestral hegemonies are replaced by so-called democracies they invariably descend into an even more abhorrent form of corruption. One only has to glance around the world today.'

Skelgill shifts uneasily upon his ancient pew. Though his features are set like stone in the moonlight, his body language suggests he rocks on the horns of a dilemma.

'You'll understand sir, that my priority right now is the missing child.'

'Indeed, Inspector – and that is where our paths may well intertwine.' He points a long index finger to the heavens. 'If you will humour me for a little longer, it may prove helpful in your quest.'

Skelgill's jaw is jutting well beyond its normal resting position. But he opens his palms in a gesture of accord. 'Please – go ahead.'

'In order for the school to continue to serve our purpose it must thrive – and to thrive it must be a vibrant combatant in the vanguard of modern education. But the battle grows stiffer by the day. Survival is a function of funding – and therein lies the temptation. While some of the old families struggle to maintain their estates, and charitable status comes under attack, new money threatens to invade from around the globe. And such affected generosity arrives with conditions attached. Investors expect a return – not financial, you understand, but a share in the spoils – a share of what that control delivers.'

'Such as Oxbridge places?'

It is difficult to tell if the man is embarrassed by this suggestion. He raises both hands in what could be a gesture of submission, but his tone is very much that of the king to a commoner. 'Inspector, I do not expect you to condone the perpetuation of privilege, but it is the way of the world. Our intentions are lawful – if not always perceived as fair. Until the politicians deem otherwise the status quo is likely to prevail.'

'I believe they're part of it, sir.'

'You may be right, Inspector. But there are other forces that conspire against us. The old families, you see – not all have reproduced, or at least not always patrilineally. And there has been emigration, ruination... annihilation.'

'Annihilation?'

'We have lost one of our number in almost every conflict since the Great War, Inspector. There is a strong military tradition at Oakthwaite. Fallen oaks decay in many a foreign field. And so our influence has waned. Twenty has become a dozen. This has not been a critical issue, however, while we have continued to hold sway among the Trustees.'

'A voting majority?'

'In effect, yes, Inspector.'

'Who appoints new Trustees when positions become vacant?'

'The Board itself, of course.'

Skelgill nods.

'The Headmaster, naturally, has a seat on the Board. Our last Head – he was one of us, so to speak. And so was his Deputy, whom we anticipated would succeed him.'

'But they left together.'

'An unfortunate coincidence – their respective infirmities were entirely unconnected.'

'And Mr Goodman...?'

'At the time it was a wholly necessary practical expedient. Given the benefit of hindsight, I confess it was a regrettable decision. But without its two most senior staff Oakthwaite could not have functioned. An appointment had to be made. Perhaps the selection committee could have been more rigorous. Impeccable credentials on paper – including an OBE, no less – do not always tell the full story.'

'And Dr Snyder?'

'Dr Snyder was Mr Goodman's choice. He insisted he needed a strong lieutenant, a disciplinarian, an organiser, to allow him to operate freely in his strategic role.'

'And Mr Goodman is the problem?'

The man flaps his large pale hands as if to suggest this is not entirely the position. 'It would be accurate to say that Mr Goodman's policies have not found universal favour.'

'But he has some support?'

'You see, Inspector, not all Trustees are from the old families. And even those that are – the younger generation – they can on occasion fail to consider the traditional perspective, or to appreciate the importance of the bloodline. For some, money is the new god.'

'Also worshipped by Mr Goodman?'

The man coughs and takes a few seconds to compose a reply.

'Though a proportion of Mr Goodman's day-to-day initiatives have given cause for concern, strategically there was not a problem – while Querrell was alive.'

'Querrell?'

'You sound surprised, Inspector.'

Skelgill does not answer immediately – perhaps he senses the risk of closing off a vital line of detail. Cautiously, he says, 'I had the impression Mr Querrell was in the process of being pensioned off.'

The stranger seems reluctant to respond, and wrings his hands as though he is wrestling with a difficult decision. Beneath the hood there's a faceless void, and he could be uttering a silent prayer, for all Skelgill can discern. Then he sits to attention, and pulls back his shoulders.

'Querrell was Grand Master.' The phrase rings out into the night like an announcement at a formal dinner.

'Grand Master? Of what, sir?'

'Of the *Derwen*, Inspector – the Ancient Oaks. The brotherhood of the founding families. Each has one hereditary position.'

'So – this is a kind of... secret society?'

'It is certainly not advertised, Inspector.'

'Who would have known of Querrell's role?'

'Only the *Derwen*.'

'Can you be certain of that?'

The man waves his hands dismissively. 'Naturally, Inspector, one cannot sustain a brotherhood such as this for more than a century and a quarter without rumours and speculation. But all *Derwen* are bound to silence.'

'I take it the remaining Trustees are unaware of the organisation?'

'Correct.'

'Was Mr Querrell also a Trustee?'

'No, Inspector – that could have revealed our hand.'

'Yet his death is significant?'

'The loss of Querrell is profound, Inspector. He was our eyes and ears within the school. Little escaped his attention. This meant we were able quickly to marshal resources when there was a danger of being outflanked. But his real importance lay in his influence upon – how should I put it? – potential dissenters among those *Derwen* serving as Trustees. Querrell taught most of them, you see, their fathers in some cases, and his father taught theirs before him. The Querrells have always been held in high regard at Oakthwaite – and thus, when Edmund Querrell spoke, doubters followed.'

'So he kept the modernisers in check?'

'That is one way of phrasing it, Inspector.'

'But not any longer.'

He shakes his head and there is a note of despair in his voice. 'His demise has shaken our order to its core.'

'Was there anything about his behaviour or circumstances that might explain what happened to him?'

'Inspector – knowing Querrell so well, suicide seems entirely improbable. And there is the timing – in two weeks we hold our termly Trustees' meeting – at which there is tabled a controversial motion concerning admissions policy. Now there is a high risk that the vote will go against the old families.'

Skelgill nods. 'If I may cut to the chase, sir – do you or your colleagues suspect someone in particular of having a hand in his death?'

The man sinks back, his shoulders slump and he sighs audibly. Slowly he shakes his head. 'I wish I were able to help you in that regard, Inspector. I am unable to point an accusing finger at any of my 'colleagues', as you put it. And, as regards those members of staff for whom Querrell's departure may not be unwelcome: without him, we have no source of information.'

'Except the boy.'

'I beg your pardon, Inspector?'

The man's response is plainly evasive, as if he has anticipated this fact, but would prefer not to acknowledge it.

'I take it he comes from one of the old families? I understand the Cholmondeleys are sixth generation.'

'Well, Inspector – there are indeed several pupils at the school who fall into this category. But it is strict convention to shield them until they come of age. They are innocents as regards the existence of the *Derwen*.'

'But not everyone would know that.'

The man sighs, and nods pensively. 'It is possible, Inspector – I grant your deduction – a boy identified with such heredity may be perceived as a distant threat. But such a fact should not be known outwith the *Derwen*.'

'Surely it wouldn't be difficult to guess, sir? Aren't the old family names among those displayed on the honours board?'

The man shrugs, and sighs again, as if he is fatigued by futile speculation. 'You presuppose both knowledge of the *Derwen*, and that the boy's disappearance is connected to our order, Inspector. It seems highly improbable.'

'You'd be surprised what daft theories sometimes solve crimes, sir.'

The man holds up his hands and tilts back his palms as if in an appeal to the celestial gods. 'Inspector, it is the greatest wish of the *Derwen* that he is safely found. Indeed, it is the primary reason that I am here facing you tonight, revealing information that has never been disclosed in over a century.'

Skelgill nods, though whether this statement convinces him is not clear, for his countenance remains taut and anxious.

'And that's why I'm here, sir – in my own time, at one o'clock in the morning, miles from anywhere, meeting with – if you don't mind me saying so – someone whose job could be to put me off the scent.'

'Touché, Inspector – although I trust you are not truly serious about my mission.'

'I'll keep an open mind, sir.'

'That is good. There is one thing, however, that may provide further assistance.'

The man rises carefully to his feet and reaches inside the folds of his long gown. He produces a manila foolscap envelope and holds it out to Skelgill.

'Querrell was not a schoolmaster who set great store by computers, Inspector. His motto was 'one copy, one lock, one key'. But in this instance we have a duplicate.'

Skelgill takes the envelope. 'What is it, sir?'

'The complete alumni for the past century. Querrell maintained a rolling one-hundred-year record. There are no addresses, I'm afraid, just name and year of leaving. Nevertheless, I hope it is of use.'

'Thank you, sir. It may well be.'

The man twists and reaches out a hand to Skelgill. As he does so, a motif embroidered in gold thread upon his sleeve glints in the moonlight. It is the same curious symbol that Skelgill has noticed on the stone lintel of the bothy at Wastwater, and above the door of Querrell's humble gatehouse residence.

*

'Jones – let me in, Jones.' He raps insistently with his knuckles on the steel roof.

'Guv – I'm here!'

Skelgill, having found his Sergeant's car locked, swings around to see DS Jones's head and shoulders silhouetted in the silvery light above the stone wall. She brandishes an angular object, which she tosses cautiously onto the road. It lands with a metallic clang.

'What's that?'

'A wheel brace, Guv.'

'Are you allowed to have one of them on duty?'

'I'm definitely off duty, Guv. Catch.'

Now she raises a bundle of material – an unzipped sleeping bag that Skelgill duly intercepts – before clambering nimbly over and dropping down at his side.

'Were you changing a tyre or putting up a tent?'

'Guv – I felt like a sitting duck in the car. I was facing the wrong way and I couldn't really hear much, even with the windows down. I figured if I waited in the field it would be better – except it was freezing – but I keep the sleeping bag in the boot in case of a breakdown.'

She unlocks the vehicle with her remote and opens the trunk. Skelgill tosses his bundle inside and slams the lid. His gaze follows DS Jones as she skirts the back of the car. She's wearing ripped denim hotpants over black tights, with a skin-tight black crop top that reveals her midriff.

'You're well organised, Jones – if not exactly dressed for the occasion.'

'That depends on the occasion, Guv.' Flashing an impish smile, she looks across the top of the car at Skelgill then ducks inside.

Skelgill loads himself into the passenger seat. He pulls the door to, and is suddenly gripped by an involuntary shiver.

'You're right, Jones – it is cold – it's crept up on me. Clear sky – could be a ground frost tonight. Let's get that heater on.'

DS Jones turns the ignition key. 'What do you want to do, Guv?'

Skelgill is still shaking – perhaps his physiology is disrupted by adrenalin following his somewhat unearthly encounter. However, he unzips his jacket and pulls out the large envelope. He taps it distractedly against his chest.

'Maybe just drive a bit.'

DS Jones looks at him inquisitively, perhaps trying to divine his intentions. Then she puts the car into first gear and moves away slowly, obliged now to concentrate upon the improbably narrow thoroughfare. Skelgill is still and silent, and even when they reach the T-junction, where DS Jones balances the car against a slight incline, he seems unaware of their location.

'Keswick, Guv?'

'Sorry?' He looks across at her, blinking as if he has just woken.

'Will we head back to your car?'

'Er... no, no – turn left. Try Grasmere.'

The picturesque village and its eponymous lake lie ten miles to the south, and DS Jones accelerates purposefully along the deserted road. For the first few minutes Skelgill remains distracted, although when he does speak his opening remark must strike DS Jones as coming from left of field.

'Did your English degree extend to the Celtic alphabet?'

DS Jones keeps her eyes on the road, squinting into the headlamps of an oncoming vehicle. 'Not that I recall, Guv – why?'

'I was just wondering about the letter *'d'*.'

'You could Google it, Guv.'

'Suppose so.'

'Actually – isn't it similar to a Greek delta – without the extra squiggle?'

'Could it look like a six, backwards?'

'Er... yeah – that would be right.'

Skelgill nods, seemingly satisfied with this outcome.

'Why, Guv?'

'Well – to cut a long story short – there's a cabal that secretly controls the school through the Board of Trustees. They're drawn from the old families that rescued it from going bust in eighteen something or other. I reckon they get first pick of the university places, and thereafter capitalise on the old boys' network. Meanwhile it sounds like Goodman is leading a charge for the new money – and we probably know why.'

'Wow.' DS Jones's eyes are shining. 'But where does the 'd' come in?'

'They call themselves the *Derwen* – it's Celtic for oaks. Think Derwentwater. I've noticed a d-shaped emblem elsewhere. The guy had it on the sleeve of his cloak.'

'And who was he, Guv?'

Skelgill shakes his head slowly. 'He kept his face hidden the whole time – it was the first thing he said – he wanted to remain anonymous. Seemed to think I'd recognise him if I saw him.'

'And you've no idea, Guv?'

'If I had to guess, I'd say one of the aristocracy.'

'Are you kidding?'

'Either that, or Snyder, or the Chief's other half, or Gandalf.'

'That's quite a range of possible suspects, Guv.'

Skelgill claps his hands in a gesture of hopeless frustration. 'I simply have no idea, Jones. My first impression was of Snyder – because of his height. But the accent wasn't right – Snyder sounds like he could originally be from Eastern Europe. Then I considered it being Cholmondeley senior – who else would be more motivated to break the oath of silence and let us in on the secret? But a parent – a parent would be frantic – he was more concerned with losing control of the Board of Trustees.'

'Stiff upper lip, Guv?'

Skelgill lets out an exasperated gasp. 'It's possible, Jones – but hard to get your head round.'

'What was he like?'

'As I say, tall, posh accent, kept using military expressions.'

'So we can rule out Gandalf, Guv?'

Skelgill chuckles. 'Aye, I guess so – though I did let him know I thought he could be a fraud.'

'How did he react?'

'Convincingly – I'd say he's genuine.'

'What about the boy, then, Guv?' DS Jones's voice takes on a note of concern.

Skelgill watches the moon as they crest a ridge. He shakes his head. 'Nothing about him directly. But he's connected, I feel sure – though the guy refuted that. And it turns out that Querrell was right in the thick of it.'

'In what way, Guv?'

'He described him as their Grand Master.'

Despite her limited knowledge of the bigger picture, DS Jones quickly joins the dots. 'So he'd be a target, Guv? Surely this is what prompted the Chief to get us involved in the first place.'

Skelgill raises his hands as if to signal 'not so fast'.

'Let's say it lends some explanation to the lack of motive surrounding his death – whether by foul play or his own hand.'

DS Jones ponders for a second. 'You mean he might have fallen on his sword, Guv?'

Skelgill shrugs. 'We have to consider that possibility. Oakthwaite was his calling. Probably all he lived for. If he felt he was failing his colleagues or 'brothers' or whatever they call themselves.'

DS Jones seems agitated. 'But it doesn't change the situation, Guv – I mean about the boy. Provided he's not had an accident – it means we're still looking for somebody.'

'Correct. We are.'

'Is that where we're going now?'

'What?' Skelgill looks alarmed. 'No way – we're going for supper. I could eat a horse.'

DS Jones chuckles and shakes her head, then casually but skilfully swerves around a badger that is dawdling in the road ahead.

'Nice one, Em.'

She flicks a surprised glance at Skelgill as he uses her Christian name. After a minute she says, 'I keep a cuddly badger on my pillow, Guv – had it since I was tiny – I'd never be able to look at it again if I killed one.'

Skelgill makes a scoffing noise. 'Watch what you say at the station about badgers and pillows.'

The interior of the car is warm, and perhaps the heat combined with the late hour lulls them into a relaxed silence. Only when they pass the Grasmere sign does Skelgill jerk into life.

'There – take the right turn – carry on over the river and past the Co-op.'

DS Jones obliges, and soon they are cruising slowly along the narrow and winding village street.

'Get a shift on – this is like the opposite of driving with Leyton.'

'Guv – it's a twenty limit.'

'If we get stopped I'll deal with it.'

No sooner has DS Jones begun to speed up, than Skelgill suddenly announces, 'There – turn left.'

'Guv – it's a no entry.'

Despite her protest, with a squeal of tyres, she does his bidding.

'Now – into the car park and drive round the back of the building.'

They have arrived at one of Grasmere's larger though still relatively modest hotels. Skelgill's directions bring them to the service entrance, where a white emergency exit hangs partially ajar, and a sliver of yellow light stripes the gravel.

'Back in three minutes. In the meantime, read this.' He slaps the envelope into her hands and hops out of the car. Then, without formalities, he disappears into the building.

Almost as good as his word, he reappears shortly bearing a tray of provisions and steaming drinks, while a young woman, her blonde hair piled beneath a chef's toque, peers smiling around the door. She waves him farewell, making – gauging by Skelgill's reaction – some saucy remark that is inaudible to DS Jones. Her eyes linger upon his driver, although it's doubtful her vision can penetrate the darkened interior.

'You're obviously well connected, Guv.' DS Jones sounds perhaps a little piqued as Skelgill backs carefully into the passenger side of the vehicle.

'Jones, didn't I ever tell you – on my patch you're never more than ten minutes from the nearest bacon roll.' He turns and grins contentedly. 'Didn't you notice the resemblance? That was my cousin. Big noses run in our family?'

'I wasn't really looking, Guv.' She holds up the thick sheaf of papers. 'I've read this stuff – it's a list of names and dates going back exactly a hundred years – I'd say Oakthwaite old boys, and the year in which they left the school. Three Cholmondeleys in this period.'

'Miss Marple strikes again.' Holding the tray aloft, Skelgill gingerly swings his legs into the footwell. 'For that, you deserve your cocoa.'

'And the rest, Guv.'

Her tone is ambiguous, and Skelgill throws her a quizzical glance.

She places the sheaf of papers on the dashboard and presses the spread fingers of both hands to her breastbone. 'Taxi service. Lookout. Getaway driver.' She turns her palms towards him entreatingly. 'Pleasant company?'

Skelgill grins again. 'Well – I can't argue with that.' Still balancing the tray, he innocently appraises her figure. 'Leyton has his strengths – but mainly in the squashing of uncooperative villains department. Can I set you some homework?'

'I could be persuaded.'

'Leyton would also be first to admit he's not the sharpest knife in the drawer when it comes to analysis – and you know what I'm like with admin. Take the list – there must be a clue in there – interrogate your aunt. Call me as soon as you've got anything.'

'Guv – there must be five thousand names.' She shakes her head wearily. 'I'm just a soft touch.'

'No comment.'

30. OAKTHWAITE SCHOOL

'You look cream-crackered, Guv.'

'Didn't sleep well, Leyton – I think I was having nightmares about your cavemen and their stone axes.'

Indeed, Skelgill, whose day yesterday began in the small hours with a pike fishing expedition, was awake almost around the clock before finally snatching a few hours' uneasy sleep post Grasmere. Now he has rendezvoused with DS Leyton for a ten a.m. breakfast at the convenient point of intersection provided by the A66 burger van.

The detective Sergeant studies the last dregs of his tea like a fortune teller. 'Maybe that's a premonition Guv – perhaps Cholmondeley's holed up somewhere in the hills.' He says it with an engineered optimism that lacks much conviction.

Skelgill shakes his head, at the same time worrying a leathery roll with his teeth. 'There's no mines on Skiddaw, Leyton.'

'Don't mention it to the Chief, Guv – I told her that's where you were this morning.'

Skelgill has missed an operational review meeting at headquarters, much to the apparent chagrin of their commanding officer. Fortunately, DS Leyton was able to step into the breach and chair the session, and to suggest a sufficiently convincing alibi – suspecting, or at least hoping, that Skelgill's absence was due in some obscure way to the case, and that he wasn't actually telling lies on behalf of his immediate boss. The main gist of the news he has borne is that, despite a voluble response to the media coverage, there have emerged no substantive clues to the lost boy's whereabouts, and that the search continues.

Skelgill gives Leyton a cursory thumbs-up sign, but otherwise masticates in brooding silence. He may be pondering the likelihood of the Chief knowing what he was up to last night, and hence the probable cause of his tardiness this morning. Such information, of course, is presumably in the gift of the stranger he met at Castlerigg. Meanwhile, as is Skelgill's wont, it appears that he will not be troubling DS Leyton with details of his late-night assignation. Instead he chooses to continue to hear the debrief.

'We've extended the search area this morning, Guv – and we're inspecting all farm buildings and vacant holiday properties within five miles of the school. There's a checkpoint on the lane, like we discussed – nothing much yet, though, Guv.'

'Either side of twelve's the key time.'

'That's what I said at the meeting, Guv – we're looking for someone who regularly uses the route around midday.' DS Leyton watches a brown-and-gold-liveried package van sweep past them at well over the speed limit. He points a finger at its diminishing form. 'That reminds me, Guv – we're checking with all the delivery and supermarket firms – in case one of their couriers was out Oakthwaite way. Taxi companies, too. They should all have records.'

'Sensible.' Skelgill sucks his teeth. 'What about the tail?'

DS Leyton shakes his head and sighs. 'Not good news, Guv.' He pauses, as if expecting Skelgill to berate him, but no such complaint is forthcoming. 'DI Smart's got all the available teams tied up. They've been staking out some big drugs deal for a week and he reckons they're about to make the drop. Seems he kicked up a big fuss.'

Skelgill scowls. 'Generous of him.'

'Thing is, Guv – for a tail to avoid being spotted we'd need at least two cars – and then what if another of the staff left a few minutes later? We'd be really snookered.'

'What did the Chief say?'

'She wasn't too sold on the idea of chasing schoolmasters, Guv. She's putting what resources we've got into the public appeal. There's a mountain of desk work piling up.'

DS Leyton wipes his brow with the sheet of kitchen towel that accompanied his burger. 'She's looking pretty rough, beneath the brave face.'

'She's a tough cookie, Leyton. Let's just hope young Chum is, too.'

DS Leyton nods, and is silent for a moment. Then he ventures, 'I did have an idea, though, Guv – with regards to the tail.'

'Aha?'

'PC Dodd – on the gate – I've told him to ask everyone he lets through where they've been or where they're going.'

Skelgill inhales suddenly, as though he is about to reprimand his Sergeant for his stupidity, but he holds back while DS Leyton quickly elaborates.

'I figured, Guv – if anyone was up to no good – just say they knew where the boy was – they'd be thinking we're on their tracks – it might stop them doing anything... well, anything bad, Guv.'

'What, like feeding him?'

DS Leyton stares ahead and turns out his bottom lip, in the manner of a schoolboy in line to receive the cane. It is actually just a habit of his, but perhaps it engenders some reflex of sympathy in Skelgill – rather as a dog rolling over disarms its canine adversary – and it seems to make him reconsider his harsh retort.

'Look – Leyton – on balance – probably not a bad plan. I know you're not as stupid as you're cabbage-looking.'

'Right, Guv.'

'Just make sure Dodd calls you the minute anyone important leaves.'

DS Leyton perks up. 'Wilco, Guv.'

Now Skelgill frowns. 'So, what about these possible sightings?'

'Bit of a can of worms, if you ask me, Guv. Turns out it was a Scottish Bank Holiday. Seems like half the population of Glasgow went to Blackpool – or failing that, Alton Towers – for the long weekend. There were ginger-haired kids running amok at every motorway service station north of Stoke. It's a needle in a haystack job, Guv.'

'Without the needle.'

DS Leyton can usually detect when his boss teeters on the edge of one of his blacker moods. He averts his eyes and wipes his hands vigorously on the kitchen paper. 'Shall I drive, Guv – to the school?'

Skelgill nods. 'What about the press? Have they found out who he is, yet?'

DS Leyton's eyes widen and he shakes his head. He concentrates for a moment as he uses his mirrors to exit the layby and join the main carriageway. 'Seem to be toeing the line, Guv – you must have put the fear of God into them at the media conference.'

'Miracles never cease.'

'There was one internet piece the Chief was complaining about, Guv – trying to suggest that the police must have something to hide.'

'Such as?'

'It's just speculation, Guv – that we've let some local nutter go free who we should have locked up – and now we suspect him of being responsible.'

Skelgill raises an eyebrow but does not respond. While the entire school population has been briefed that there should be no conversations on the subject via social media, and the main channels of external communication have been temporarily jammed on Dr Snyder's orders, it has to be considered just a matter of time before the anonymous missing boy is identified and connected with Oakthwaite, and in turn with Cumbria Constabulary. This outcome should not unduly concern Skelgill as regards compromising the investigation, but it will land him in hot water when the blame unfairly but inexorably attaches itself to him. Meanwhile, the Chief's continued fortitude in resisting the urge to 'go public', though puzzling, has at least been placed into some understandable context by such edification as enjoyed by Skelgill at the standing stones.

Perhaps DS Leyton finds the silence a little uncomfortable, for he breaks it by recourse to the good old British fall-back of the weather.

'It's a nice day, Guv – I might even get my grass done tonight.'

Skelgill yawns and stretches, and seems to regain a modicum of enthusiasm. As a seasoned outdoorsman he is always ready to pontificate on the subject of the climate.

'Pressure's been building since that cold front came through yesterday. Might get a few days' sunshine. He cranes his neck and stares for ten seconds or so at the skyline above the fells, watching the slow drift of the scattered white cumulus. 'Wind's gone round to the south-east. It's going to be spot on for pike once the levels drop.'

But with this remark must come the realisation that he has little prospect of a proper fishing trip while the boy's disappearance remains unresolved, and he sags down into the passenger seat and leans against the headrest. He closes his eyes.

DS Leyton, driving more judiciously than usual, conducts them deeper into the leafy lanes that lead to Oakthwaite School. Skelgill to all intents and purposes might be asleep, but his Sergeant seems to know different, and as they near the gates of the institution he says, 'Penny for 'em, Guv?'

Skelgill opens one eye. 'You what, Leyton?'

'Penny for your thoughts, Guv.'

Skelgill makes a scoffing sound. 'Leyton, I'd willingly tell you – if only I could read my own mind.'

DS Leyton nods dutifully. 'Right, Guv.'

As they reach the gates and DS Leyton decelerates, Skelgill begins to unfasten the passenger door. 'Drop me here, Leyton.'

'Really, Guv?' DS Leyton sounds disappointed.

'Aye – I need to have a mooch around. Think a bit.'

DS Leyton complies. 'Sure, Guv. Only thing is – I was going to take you through the plans for the day. I've requested the use of Greig's office – as a base to coordinate the various search teams. I figured with it being away from the main school it would keep us clear of little noses poking in at the window. There's plenty of room and good views – plus all those maps of the Lakes.'

Skelgill purses his lips and nods approvingly. 'Fair enough – I'll catch up with you there. Good luck with Greig – I can't imagine he'll be a happy bunny.'

Skelgill acknowledges PC Dodd and has a brief chat with him before heading across to the gatehouse. The weather is indeed shaping up to deliver a magnificent day and the clearing resonates with birdsong as woodpigeons, wrens and willow warblers combine with others in a lively avian jazz ensemble. In the wings of this natural auditorium the morning air is still cool in thrilling contrast to the bruising heat of the sun at its centre. Swathed all around, lush vegetation shocks the eye, a luminescent lemony late-spring-green blur of chlorophyll.

He stands for a few moments facing the cottage. The runic symbol – what he now knows to be the sign of the *Derwen* – must seem to shine out from above the front door like a beacon, though it is but an innocuous lichen-encrusted smudge upon the lintel. He steps over to the garden seat; on such a day, and sleep-deprived, it could be tempting to recline like *Flaming June*. He slips from his jacket, but then only drapes it over the back of the bench before turning to approach the property.

The downstairs living area is largely unchanged from his first visit – the antique typewriter in the window, the outmoded desktop pc in the corner, the threadbare chair before the fireplace – only some unwashed mugs and a half-eaten packet of digestives testify to PC Dodd's occupation. The hearthrug is gone, but that must be connected with the unfortunate incident concerning Hodgson.

Briefly, Skelgill visits the upstairs room, though he does not linger – indeed it is the antiquarian *Wainwright* that most attracts his attention when he returns to the ground floor. He quickly locates the precious book, homing in directly upon the point in the shelves where he had previously returned it. Number five in the seven-volume series, it features the Northern Fells, a quarter of its pages given over to Skiddaw and Blencathra. He thumbs through until he locates the section on the former, introduced in the author's inimitably abrupt style with the defiant and perplexing sentence, *'Make no mistake about Skiddaw.'*

Skelgill begins to read, and after a minute shuffles across to Querrell's old armchair and lowers himself down, his eyes still fixed upon the extraordinarily legible script. Methodically, he works his way through the dense handwritten copy, chuckling here and there as the author's recalcitrant humour bites, dealing short shrift to Skiddaw's critics.

After a while it appears he has ceased to read and has drifted into reverie, for he dwells over-long on a particular spread. Whether it is something in the text that has distracted him, or the act of concentration that has allowed his subconscious to assume control, it is impossible to tell. While the mountain no doubt looms large in his thoughts, his present location must equally call to mind the unexplained facts of his nocturnal escapade: when two anonymous males were present, one of whom had a key, one of whom might not have left alive.

The clang of the heavy metal gates jolts him from his musings. PC Dodd must have admitted a vehicle, for now it slides past in a glimpse of blue metal and black diesel fumes – some kind of delivery van, whose driver disdains the speed limit. Reluctantly, it seems, Skelgill replaces the *Wainwright* in the shelf. Then he casually helps himself to a handful of biscuits, which he pockets upon retrieving his jacket. With a wave to PC Dodd, he rounds the cottage and picks up the running track as it passes the rear of the property. At a leisurely pace, he ambles into the woods.

While the songbirds aloft press on allegretto, beneath the canopy the still ether is striped with dank woodland smells. Skelgill has not gone far before he baulks at the sudden hot stink of fox, a musky marijuana blast that marks reynard's recent passage. Next his progress is ambushed by honeysuckle draped above the path, which leaks invisible molecules of sweet sickly scent upon him. And shortly he stoops, arrested by another unmistakable aroma, the cloying reek of carrion, to admire an immodest stinkhorn thrusting from the leaf litter, its glistening cap a sticky-bun breakfast bar for bluebottles.

As he is about to stand there's an onrushing patter of feet, and almost before he can react their owner is upon him, licking lavishly at his ear: Cleopatra.

'Down girl, down! My apologies, Inspector.'

Skelgill rises and the muscular piebald dog turns its attention to snuffling for the digestives concealed in his jacket. Meanwhile its master, Dr Jacobson, who has followed his canine charge around a twist in the path, makes uncertain progress with a walking stick at his side. The pyjama-like trousers are back on display, with open-toed sandals; his upper half is clad in an oversized white collarless shirt and an unbuttoned floral waistcoat, of the sort that was in fashion during their nineties' heyday.

'Good morning to you, Inspector – you appear to have developed an affinity with Cleopatra – she is rarely so affable.'

'Perhaps it's just folk with biscuits, sir.' Skelgill draws out one such sweetmeat from his pocket. 'May I?'

'Oh, she will be forever in your debt, Inspector.'

The dog wastes no time in despatching the treat, but then her ears prick up and she trots determinedly into the undergrowth.

Dr Jacobson makes an affected cough. 'Inspector, I owe you an apology.'

'Sir?'

'On Friday – when I made that flippant remark about London buses – I rather feel I tempted fate, what with the unfortunate disappearance of young Cholmondeley.'

Skelgill shrugs. 'In my job, sir, these coincidences happen all the time.'

'Well, nevertheless, it was a little gauche of me. And just now I thought Cleopatra must have interrupted you looking for clues – rather like Sherlock Holmes, with his nose to the ground.'

Skelgill grins self-consciously. 'No, sir – I was distracted, by an unusual toadstool – I'm on my way to the cricket pavilion – our temporary HQ.'

'Of course, Inspector. You have chosen the scenic route.'

At this moment Cleopatra bursts from the bushes, her legs and lower abdomen now wet and mud-encrusted.

'Oh dear, Cleopatra – you found a pond.'

Skelgill takes a step backwards as she shakes her coat. 'Give her a wash off in the lake, sir.'

'I am sure she would love that, Inspector, but I keep her well away – she is so headstrong, heaven knows what could happen. And isn't it always the owners that drown trying to rescue their dogs?'

Skelgill nods ruefully. 'I've certainly had cases where a dog walker falls through ice – and the pet eventually gets itself out. Animal survival instinct kicks in.'

Dr Jacobson affects a shudder. 'It doesn't bear thinking about, Inspector. In my condition I could not even risk a paddle.' He shakes the stick at his side. 'And how is your burden, Inspector?'

'I'm sorry, sir?'

'The investigation – any news of the boy?'

'Ah, well, sir...' Skelgill gives the impression that he is about to trot out the standard platitude about lines of enquiry, but then he relents and says, 'We've had a good number of reported sightings – we're just in the process of following them up – I'm hoping my Sergeant will have some news for me shortly. We're optimistic, sir.'

'Excellent, Inspector.' Dr Jacobson grins in his forced clownish manner. 'I had better not detain you from your business any longer. And please do let me know if I can be of any assistance. Even if it is only to offer you a decent cup of tea.'

'Thank you, sir. Good luck with the dog's bath.'

Dr Jacobson makes a gurning face and hobbles away, calling reprimandingly after Cleopatra, who seems to have disappeared again.

Skelgill watches him for a few moments, before turning and striding out at a much brisker pace than before.

It takes him about ten minutes to reach the boathouse, and upon arrival he makes immediately for the landing stage. Ever the alert angler, he treads cautiously upon the weathered planks.

However, if there are any fish stirring, their presence is concealed by a light but persistent ripple.

There is a small raft of duck out on the silvery water, but their colourless silhouettes at such a distance make them unidentifiable without binoculars. Then a large dark species he does know beats purposefully past, and he raises an angry fist like an irate farmer plagued by crows – it is a cormorant, pelagic scourge of inland fisheries.

Still watching the lake, he munches his way reflectively through a couple of biscuits, before he turns and retraces his steps to the boathouse, where Querrell's tired craft lies chained. Then he makes what appears to be a cursory inspection of the shoreline and the short grass close to the dilapidated building.

Perhaps satisfied that the water level is indeed falling, he consults his wristwatch. Then he surveys the rising ground ahead of him: the pavilion and the school sit upon the same azimuth, though neither edifice is visible owing to successive barriers of shrub and tree. He selects an apparently random route into a patch of willows, but emerges in due course from the thicket correctly moving in parallel to the low ridge of ground that he had noted from Sale Fell. Passing through another brake of springy ash saplings he reaches the perimeter of the first eleven cricket oval, with the pavilion not far ahead.

As he pauses to take stock, he espies a short tracksuited figure push what looks like a large hosepipe-reel out from behind the building. It is Mike Greig, and the mechanical device is a boundary-rope wheel. Skelgill stares intently, although on this occasion it is probably not the luxury item of cricket equipment that makes his eyes widen, but the rifle that is slung over Greig's shoulder.

Oakthwaite's Director of Sport has his head down as he gets to grips with the contraption – two hundred and forty yards of one-inch diameter rope weighs in at about the same a typical fourth-former – but at any moment he will look up and find Skelgill standing in his direct line of sight. Skelgill has just a second or two to make up his mind what to do – retreat, to hide and observe, or step out and reveal himself as a casual passer-by.

In the event he chooses the latter course, and hops quickly onto the short-cropped outfield to assume a casual gait towards the approaching sports master. In due course Greig glances ahead and, while he seems surprised to see the oncoming detective, he betrays no sign of concern as regards being caught in possession of a firearm.

'Howzit, Inspector?

'Expecting trouble, Mike?'

Greig grins in his laid-back way. 'Nah, Inspector, vermin – another one of my new duties – we've had jack rabbits sabotaging the square – their urine kills the grass – I'm on the warpath, ja?'

Skelgill tilts his head briefly to one side and puckers his lips, acknowledging the validity of this explanation. 'What is it, a point-two-two?'

Greig lets go of the rope wheel and slings the gun around, keeping the barrel pointed at the ground. He hands it stock first to Skelgill. It is an ominous-looking weapon, with a telescopic sight and a long matt-black silencer. Skelgill gives it a once-over – he checks that the safety catch is engaged, and breaks the barrel to satisfy himself that it is indeed an airgun. Then he holds it up and weighs it, before sighting on a rook that rests in a treetop in the direction of the lake.

'I could have done with this a few minutes ago.'

'Inspector?'

'A cormorant – one of my main competitors.'

Greig nods. 'Let me tell you this, Inspector, these things are just pea-shooters compared to what I grew up with. I take it I'm legal, ja?'

Skelgill hands back the air rifle. 'As long as you're over eighteen you can walk into a gun shop and buy one. To use it, you need to be on private land, at least fifty feet from the centre of the public highway.'

'Sounds like I'm fine, then?'

Skelgill nods. 'It is yours, Mike?'

Greig shakes his head. 'I found it in Hodgson's equipment store – tucked away behind a stack of marker poles. I've seen him creeping about with it in the past, so I had an idea it would still be there.'

Skelgill gestures towards the boundary-rope winder. 'You've got a match today?'

'Nah – all the external fixtures have been put on hold. I'm just running an inter-house twenty-twenty tournament this week to keep the boys occupied, ja?'

Skelgill glances across at the pavilion. 'It appears we've commandeered your office.'

Greig shrugs. 'You're welcome, Inspector – anything I can do to help. Anyway – I wouldn't like to get into an argument with your Sergeant.'

Skelgill grimaces apologetically. 'I believe the office was originally Mr Querrell's – before you came?'

Greig's expression is blank. He rubs a palm absently over his short ginger hair. 'Not that I know of, Inspector. He occasionally borrowed it after school hours – for his outward-bound briefings, ja?'

Skelgill seems satisfied with this reply, and in fact relatively disinterested. He casts about the cricket oval, as though he's trying to spot the telltale signs of rabbit damage. His eyes settle instead upon a couple of fresh peaty molehills that might be at deep square leg. He shrugs, then he begins to move away.

'Mike, I'd better let you get on with your work. If you're serious about the rabbits, you need to come out at night with a spotlight – though I wouldn't recommend it at the moment.'

'You mean in case I'm mistaken for a kidnapper, ja?'

'Something like that.' Skelgill winks. 'We've got marksmen on all the rooftops.'

Greig looks momentarily flummoxed by the British irony, but then he grins, before switching to a more serious tone to ask, 'No news of the boy?'

'Nothing concrete.' Skelgill shakes his head slowly. 'At the moment you're still the last person to have set eyes upon him.'

Leaving Greig perhaps a little taken aback by this parting remark, Skelgill makes a beeline for the pavilion. However, when he arrives at the foot of the wide wooden steps, he seems to have a change of mind, and continues past the building, and on towards the main school.

Rather in the way that the general population never set foot inside one of HM's prisons, nor have any real notion of how such an institution looks and sounds and smells, so they are insulated from Britain's great public schools, which operate in oddly comparable bubbles of splendid isolation. As Skelgill approaches the grand neoclassical façade he must be struck by the incongruity that many a comprehensively educated pupil, past or present, would experience: that this imposing palace set amidst stately parklands could be where you actually went to school. But if he is accosted by this thought, he does not allow it to delay him, and when he crosses from the great lawn onto the expensive ornamental sandstone chippings of the curving driveway, he veers left and begins deliberately to make his way around the perimeter of the imposing construction.

The majority of its windows are too high to afford the opportunity to peer inside, but in any event this does not seem to be his object. Indeed, whether he has an object at all is uncertain, and perhaps he is just whiling away some time before rendezvousing with DS Leyton and dealing with the inevitable disappointment and frustration of the failure of the operation to produce any concrete leads. Clearly, it is apparent that Skelgill does not set great store by either of the main theories that propose to explain the disappearance of Cholmondeley junior: that he is lost in the fells, or has left the district, whether by his own volition or otherwise. However, the Inspector is unable to articulate either his doubts, or his certainties.

The conundrum with which he wrestles can perhaps best be compared to his method for angling, which ostensibly approximates to a process of divination. Setting out on any given day to fish Bassenthwaite Lake, many subtle factors impose themselves upon his senses. For instance, there are the water conditions – the level, flow, colour and temperature. There is the season and its concomitant effects – the breeding cycle and territorial or migrationary behaviour of his target species; the constantly changing food supply – a whole myriad of invertebrates that may be displaying, laying, hatching, moulting or emerging. There is the local weather – sunlight, cloud cover, precipitation, barometric pressure. The breeze alone creates eddies and wind lanes that gather and funnel food, enticing smaller fish which in turn attract bigger ones. There is the distressing presence of predators, like ospreys and otters, and disturbance from other less inconspicuous lake users than Skelgill.

Multifarious influences such as these, perhaps twenty or fifty or even a hundred at any one time, cannot logically be computed. That is simply not an option for the rational part of Skelgill's fishing brain – no matter how much he might later pontificate over a pint, celebrating his acumen or bemoaning his bad luck. Yet Skelgill consistently does succeed in tracking down big fish. If he were asked to explain this feat he might put it down to experience – although, a 'sixth sense' would be a more apt description. This is not some supernatural phenomenon, however, but simply the process of absorbing, consciously or otherwise, the many clues that pertain to that particular day's conditions, and then allowing his subconscious to combine these with stored memories and, in due course, to make the necessary connections between those factors which are relevant: factors that will deliver his boat to that precise mark below which lies his quarry. Thus Skelgill will 'find' himself fishing in a certain manner, at a certain specific point on the great bayou, bolstered by a strong sense that he is in the right place.

Understanding this of Skelgill – the method that in equal measure baffles and infuriates his workmates – means it can be viewed as something more than random fortune when he produces a positive outcome. And being drawn as he is to the vicinity of Oakthwaite should tell his colleagues that he at least 'feels' something. It is just that the 'feeling' has yet to become a 'knowing'. In the watery depths of his subconscious, a formidable hypothesis is still to coalesce as a red-herring-free shoal that can break the surface of conscious awareness. But it is hoped for the boy's sake that this leaping revelation will come soon.

And perhaps herein lies the explanation for Skelgill's curious wandering behaviour this morning. Could it be that he drifts, guided by intuition, anticipating such inspiration? As he saunters now around the building, he meets a high perpendicular wall of locally hewn stone. There is a low archway, of the kind that might once have been a cloistered window. Perhaps it is a relic of the more ancient edifice – the castle, even – that once existed upon the site. He ducks through, and finds himself in an extensive walled garden. It is well tended, although it seems for ornamental rather than culinary purposes. There are magnificent herbaceous borders on all sides, a kaleidoscopic delight of red crimson rose peonies, great armies of blue spiked delphiniums, and the waving heads of giant yellow scabious. He pauses to admire a collection of butterflies that feed upon an adjacent *Buddleia*, its white cascading racemes crowded with red admirals, peacocks and small tortoiseshells in roughly similar numbers. He is able to approach them literally within inches. Indeed, so determined are they to gorge upon the perfumed nectar drawn by the morning's damp heat, that the papery rustle of their wings is audible in the windless oasis.

Except suddenly there is a voice, and the answering murmur of another. Glancing across the garden, Skelgill sees immediately that he is not alone. Upon a stone bench beneath an arbour of climbing roses, and partially concealed by box topiary set in unglazed planters, sit the figures of Mr Goodman and Dr Snyder. Seen together they make a somewhat incongruous pairing: the former short, stiff and tense, the latter decidedly lanky and languid – in fact they could almost be mistaken for pupil and master. Their eyes are cast down, as if they are scrutinising a pattern in the slabs at their feet, though it is likely to be something of a more abstract nature with which they wrestle.

They have evidently not noticed Skelgill's sure-footed entry into the horticultural quadrangle and, as per his recent encounter with Greig, he is faced with a binary choice of actions. He could slip away, and perhaps even creep around to the far side and attempt to eavesdrop from behind the wall, or he could saunter in, and pretend that his exploration in some way pertains to the investigation. But at this juncture Mr Goodman lifts his head and his beady eyes uncannily fasten upon Skelgill, catching him in the act of observation. Now the detective has little option but to cross the manicured greensward that separates them. He must feel self-conscious as he approaches the silent and staring couple.

'Can I help you, Inspector?' Mr Goodman's hostile facial expression contrasts with the literal content of his question.

'Quite the secret garden you have here, sir.'

The innuendo in Skelgill's casually spoken statement suggests he is not about to be intimidated. He closes to within a yard, obliging his antagonists to squint upwards into the sun that beams over his shoulder.

Mr Goodman scowls. 'We use it for private garden parties – after speech days, and to welcome dignitaries.'

There is a clear implication in his choice of words that Skelgill is neither invited nor welcome, and is trespassing well above his station.

After a lengthy pause, Skelgill says, 'It was Dr Snyder I wanted to speak with, sir.'

Dr Snyder, who has been leaning forwards in an uneasy pose, resting his elbows on his thighs, with his large hands flapping loosely over his knees, now sits upright and straightens his jacket – although he does not speak. Of the two, it is he that exudes an impression of being concerned – perhaps that they were overheard.

'I'd just like to confirm, sir, who else had keys for Mr Querrell's property?'

Dr Snyder coughs, and then spreads his palms in a gesture of explanation. 'As I believe I mentioned previously, Inspector, Mr Querrell was the sole key-holder.'

Skelgill considers the reply for a moment. 'Isn't that a little odd, sir?'

'Inspector, when it comes to Querrell, nothing can be considered odd.'

This terse interjection emanates from Mr Goodman. Skelgill ignores him, and continues to stare at Dr Snyder. After a few moments Dr Snyder relents under this scrutiny, to the evident annoyance of his boss.

'Inspector, during my first term, when I was assessing the overall security of the school premises, I did ask Mr Querrell if he would like me to keep a spare key in case his ever became misplaced. He informed me that there was no such requirement, since he very rarely secured the property.'

Skelgill nods as though he accepts this statement, but then he says, 'Yet it was locked after his death and Mr Hodgson subsequently managed to gain access.'

Again the Head interjects, his tone becoming increasingly impatient. 'Perhaps he climbed through a window, Inspector. Given what we have learned about him since, I don't imagine a spot of housebreaking was beyond his scruples.'

It ought to be apparent to the two schoolmasters that it is only by happenstance that Skelgill has stumbled upon their tête-à-tête, and that he is thus operating on the hoof. Indeed, Mr Goodman seems to detect this probability, and moves to press home his advantage.

'Shouldn't be deploying your resources elsewhere, Inspector? The school has the air of a prison camp, with a sentry on the gate and guards patrolling around the building. My information is that the boy has been sighted in Cheshire. Just what is the problem?'

Skelgill, quite possibly wishing for an exit strategy, stares blankly at the Headmaster. 'The problem, sir? My information is that *the problem* is much closer to home.'

If this were a playground spat of old, Skelgill might have appended his retort with 'So put that in your pipe and smoke it.' Instead he allows the gravity of his assertion to sink in, before turning and stalking back whence he came. There is no utterance from behind him, as if the putative conspirators await his complete disappearance before resuming their conversation. As he clambers through the aperture in the wall, his mobile ringtone tells him DS Jones is calling.

'Guv – I might have something.'

'Morning, Jones.'

'Er, yeah – sorry, Guv – morning... afternoon, even. I've only got a minute – DI Smart's just about to pick me up – I've been with my uncle – my *great* uncle.'

'Come again?'

'My aunt who works at the school – it's her old dad – he used to be a gardener there – in the sixties and seventies.'

'That's going back some.'

'I know, Guv – and it's just a tenuous connection – he remembers there was an incident on the lake in the early seventies.'

'Bass Lake?'

'Aha. There was a drowning, and it involved a boy being expelled.'

'That's probably why they don't do swimming or boating activities.'

'The thing is, Guv – he couldn't remember any of the names. So I've crosschecked the list you gave me. And I got the current roll of students and staff, from my aunt.'

'And?'

'Well – there are some names that appear back then *and* now. That's maybe no surprise, given the generations thing, but you never know. And there are oddities – like three or four names from the early seventies that are in brackets – I'm not sure what that means.'

Skelgill scratches his head. 'Search me.'

'Guv – that's DI Smart approaching – I'm waiting on the pavement. I'd better go. I'll email you the names I've pulled out – just in case there's something. He won't know what I'm doing while he's driving.'

'Okay – send me a text later if you get a chance to speak.'

'I'll do my best, Guv. But DI Smart thinks it could be tonight that we bust the cartel.'

'Wish him good luck from me.'

Skelgill hangs up, but then immediately redials a number.

'Guv?'

'Leyton – I need the keys to Hodgson's flat.'

'Right, Guv – they're in my glove box. It's all locked up. Shall I come over to the car park?'

'Don't worry, Leyton – I'll soon sort that.'

31. COCKERMOUTH

Twelve and a half miles after exiting Bassenthwaite Lake, the River Derwent, *'river of oaks'*, is joined by its most important tributary, the River Cocker. At this confluence nestles the market town of Cockermouth. In common with the Derwent, the Cocker gets its name from a Celtic expression, *kukrā*, meaning *'the crooked one'*. This is perhaps apposite in the context of Skelgill's mission, since its rushing waters are overlooked by the property rented until recently by the disreputable Mr Hodgson. Indeed, as he casts an expert eye over the rippling surface, Skelgill might be assessing whether the crooked fellow ever dangled a poacher's line from the window of his flat.

After a minute or two Skelgill turns his attention to the interior of the first-floor apartment. Reached from the main street by a door at the side of a newsagent's, a narrow uncarpeted staircase leads to a surprisingly spacious suite of rooms. This, however, is where the estate agent's spiel would break down. The place, with its shabby décor and soiled furniture is reminiscent of a large live-in caravan abused by itinerant building workers. There are half-empty mugs and milk bottles gone rancid, crumpled newspapers and takeaway wrappers dropped and abandoned where they fell, and, adorning surfaces from window sills down to the floor, unwashed plates, overflowing ash-trays and unfinished cans of lager. It is less of a home and more of a squat.

There are no ornaments or photographs, no curtains, and no obvious repository for admin. DS Leyton had reported a lack of electrical equipment, and other more direct indications that debts had been run up, and indeed generally scattered around are screwed-up betting slips and unopened bills. After a cursory sweep of the premises, Skelgill conducts a more methodical search. He checks drawers and a wardrobe – these house a limited assortment of worn apparel of the hunting-shooting-fishing variety. He finds a broad-brimmed *Tilley* hat – a piece of kit of high repute – which he is unable to resist trying on in front of a cracked mirror, though he is probably forced to concede it is not his style. He looks behind the wardrobe, under the bed, and shifts all the mats to check for loose floorboards. Then he investigates the places where something might typically be hidden – beneath the kitchen sink, up the chimney in the living room, and in the toilet cistern (where he does discover a small packet of what looks like marijuana that has fallen into the water). There's an airing cupboard that is entirely empty except for a copper immersion heater, and a fuse box on the landing, in which the electricity supply has clearly had its meter bypassed.

If Skelgill is hoping for something specific, it does not appear to have materialised. His trip has merely replicated the findings provided by DS Leyton's earlier visit – unless, by dint of experiencing the special ambiance of Hodgson's flat, he has subliminally inched towards his uncertain goal.

He leaves the property and enters the newsagent's. He doesn't announce himself, and instead buys an *Angling Times* and two *Mars Bars* and a caffè latte from a new-fangled machine. He departs without further ado and, munching upon the first item of confectionery, saunters along a route he obviously knows well, that takes him down to the two rivers' meeting point. The pungent ozone-scented air is filled with the insistent buzz of sand martins as they skim for mayflies. There is an open grassy bank with bench seats, and he takes one with a view across the shimmering waters to the picturesque *Jennings* brewery. An outside observer would comment that there is a peculiar element of the hair shirt about this little pilgrimage. For Skelgill to put himself within spitting distance of rising grayling and brown trout, within sniffing distance of the home of his favourite ale, without leave to take advantage of either, is an act of the highest order of asceticism.

Nonetheless, he exhibits no sign of succumbing to temptation on either count (though he has a fly rod in his car, and money in his wallet). Ignoring the sibilant cries of a small boy, loosely in the charge of a young woman who additionally pushes a large pram, Skelgill settles down with his coffee and surviving chocolate bar to peruse the news of the water world. Meanwhile the woman takes a seat on the next bench to his. He doesn't pay her much attention, other than a smile and a nod of acknowledgement. The toddler seems preoccupied with skimming stones, while the infant inside the pram is evidently asleep.

After a few minutes' comparative silence the woman receives a message of some kind. Her loud alert is set to the identical tone as Skelgill's, and automatically he reaches for his phone. He must now be reminded that DS Jones was to send him an email, for he opens the notification and scrolls through its details. Then he leans back against the wooden spars of the bench and gazes out across the eddying confluence.

He is clearly deep in thought, for he watches without reaction as the toddler, in taking on a rock that is too big for his boots, lifts the stone above his head and forgets to let go, with the result that he falls face first into the water. The woman is still busy with her social network. Meanwhile, little limbs flail in the shallows.

Thankfully, for the child's sake, it is only a matter of perhaps ten seconds before Skelgill does respond, and then in a few great strides he splashes into the water to pluck the boy to safety. Only now, attracted by the greater hullabaloo, does the mother – or nanny – seem to notice.

'Oh my word – oh my word! What happened?'

Skelgill marches back up the bank, holding out the dripping and kicking and spluttering creature, which he plonks into her outstretched arms.

'He fell in, love.'

'Oh my word – thank you. Thank you.'

Skelgill probably would like to give her a lecture about the perils of small children, fast-flowing rivers and *Facebook* – but now he seems gripped by the urge to leave the scene.

'All in a day's work, love.'

As the woman mildly rebukes the sodden boy, albeit with a large lump in her throat, Skelgill returns to his bench to collect his belongings. He drops the newspaper and empty coffee cup into a litter bin, and then strides doggedly away.

Retracing his steps to the location of Hodgson's flat, instead of immediately entering, he backs out into the road until his angle of sight gives him a clear view of the sloping slate-tiled roof. Like most properties in the street, the building has shallow gables and what looks like minimal clearance in the loft – indeed it is not unknown for this type of construction to have no usable loft space at all, and therefore no built-in access. However, if this is what Skelgill is checking for – and his deliberate nod suggests it is – then the small rooflight that he has observed provides the information he requires.

Back inside, however, a survey of the ceilings leaves Skelgill scratching his head. There is no obvious trapdoor in any of the rooms, nor even an indication that one has been plastered or boarded over. He loiters on the landing – the most common location for this sort of thing. He is clearly reluctant to depart and, perhaps as a last resort, he opens the airing cupboard. And there it is – a small square hatch just visible up in the shadows.

On one side of the cupboard are three shelves constructed from timber slats, with gaps between them designed to maximise airflow. Skelgill braces his weight against the doorjamb and uses the first shelf as a foothold. He levers himself up and is immediately able to reach the lid. He pushes against it and it lifts easily – in fact it is of the unhinged variety, cut slightly larger than the frame upon which it rests. He straightens his leg and raises the hatch with the flat of his palm, perhaps intending to flip it over into the loft space. But this action transfers most of his weight to his standing leg, and with a sharp crack the shelf gives way beneath him.

He falls awkwardly, tumbling backwards out of the confined space onto the landing. His rear hits the floorboards with a painful-sounding clump, and he just manages to prevent the back of his head following suit. His position might be undignified, but in fact it now saves him from further injury. Almost by reflex he rolls to one side as the hatch – dislodged by his actions and thus enabled to slip into free fall – bounces down off the copper and strikes him a glancing blow across the temple.

Swearing profusely he scrambles to his feet. He swings an angry boot at the hot-water cylinder, and is about to follow it up with a karate-style kick at the sagging timbers of the broken shelf when he notices that the supporting cross-member has been partially sawn-through from below: a booby trap.

He checks the other two shelves, and sees they have been subjected to the same treatment. And now he looks he finds sawdust on the floor beneath. Somebody – presumably Hodgson – didn't want anybody using this route. To climb safely into the loft will now require a ladder – or a stool, at least – and Skelgill is about to go in search of a suitable item when the trapdoor catches his eye. It is lying on the bare floorboards with its inside facing upwards. Held fast upon the square of plywood by a strip of torn masking tape is a folded *Racing Post*.

He kneels, and unpicks the tape and carefully detaches the newspaper – just a single sheet that comprises the front and back covers, with their corresponding inside pages. As he opens it a charred strip of white paper flutters out and settles beside him. It is a fragment of an A4 page – itself a photocopy of an old press clipping. Most of the content has been destroyed, but the header is legible: a date from the nineteen seventies, and the title *The Westmorland Gazette*. There's the beginning of a headline – the words 'Twin Tragedy' – but other than that nothing of the article has survived combustion.

Skelgill checks the front of the *Racing Post*. It was printed just twelve days ago – on the day that Querrell's body was discovered floating in Bassenthwaite Lake.

He rolls from his knees onto his backside, and rests against the distempered wall of the landing. He tilts back his head, with more of a bump than he probably intends, and then absently feels the point on his forehead where the hatch has left its mark. He folds his arms and stares for a minute or two into the void of the opposite wall. Then he locates his mobile and types out a text to DS Jones:

'Need you tonight. Serious. Screw Smart. Bring Leyton. Await further instructions.'

He transmits the message and watches the handset until the display tells him it has been delivered, and then read. Then he scrolls through his contacts until he locates Oakthwaite School. He taps on the telephone icon and raises the handset to his ear. Quite promptly, his call is answered. He speaks with careful enunciation.

'Good afternoon. This is Detective Inspector Skelgill of Cumbria Police. Could you put me through to the Headmaster, please.'

After about a minute – a delay that may be accounted for by pride and insouciance – the Head comes on the line with a perfunctory, 'Yes, Inspector?'

'Mr Goodman. Regarding our conversation earlier. Just to confirm that we are withdrawing the patrolling officers and the constable from the gate. You can inform your staff and pupils that we're satisfied there is no threat to their safety in the school and its grounds. Thank you. Goodbye, sir.'

Skelgill ends the call without waiting for what he might reasonably have anticipated to be a gloating response.

32. BASSENTHWAITE LAKE

As the midsummer sun dips behind Sale Fell Skelgill's boat slips from its mooring at Peel Wyke and slides out into the calm reaches of Bassenthwaite Lake. As far as the eye can see the surface is pooled with rises as fish of all kinds cash in on the abundant spinners returning to deposit their eggs in the surface film. For the second time today, Skelgill's passion beckons enticingly.

He rows at a steady four knots, making a beeline from west to east, covering the seven hundred or so yards in about five minutes. He is an accomplished sculler, and down the years has surprised many a fellow boatman by leaving their more streamlined craft trailing in his wake. Right now his aim seems to be the speediest crossing, as he takes the shortest route across the open water. Once within reach of the eastern shoreline he feathers his oars and allows the boat to drift some twenty feet from the wooded bank.

From here he gradually paddles southwards towards Oakthwaite. In due course he rounds a promontory from which – if he were to push out into the lake – he would be able to see the small pier and boathouse, tucked away some two hundred yards further into the bay. Instead, however, he prefers the cover of the overhanging alders, and indeed he winds his painter into a clove hitch around a sturdy branch above his head. Soon his boat finds a stationary berth, and the ripples that radiate from his leafy retreat gradually subside.

Skelgill's rowing seat is fashioned from a plastic chair 'borrowed' from the police canteen, its metal legs removed and the remaining shell bolted to the thwart. While this peculiar arrangement is a classic example of a Skelgill 'mackle', it does at least afford a comfortable sitting position for long periods, when a backrest is most appreciated. Thus Skelgill pulls on a midge-hat, fastens his cuffs, smears *Citronella* oil on the back of his hands, and settles down as if he is anticipating a prolonged vigil. After a couple of minutes, however, he reaches into the knapsack at his side, and pulls out his flask and one of several hurriedly assembled packs of jam butties.

Gradually, darkness begins to creep across the lake. Initially, however, there is a kind of false dawning – as the sun sinks lower beyond the north-west horizon its refracted orange rays strike a scaled underbelly of scattered stratus and these reflect upon the scene, sky and matching mirrored lake aflame with the day's rekindled embers. And then, as these fires subside, there is a quickening in the dusk, and pink fades to turquoise and blues blacken to showcase the stars and the rising moon. Soon it is only possible to see vague shapes and indistinct silhouettes, as the short but velvety night settles upon the Lakeland dale.

Time passes and Skelgill eats three portions of sandwiches. He is very diligent, silently unwrapping the cling-film, and placing his tin mug with great care. Sounds carry unimpeded and indeed amplified over still water, and even distant rises and plops seem just yards away. Beyond the far bank there is the occasional rumble of a truck on the A66, or the monotonous vrooming of a car, but as midnight comes and goes the traffic dwindles virtually to nothing. All else that reaches Skelgill's ears is of natural origin: the protracted hoot of a tawny owl, the strained cry of a dog fox, and the regular splishing and chirping of *Daubenton's* bats as they hawk for caddis flies.

Dunk. Unmistakably, through the resonant air, from the vicinity of the landing stage, emanates the distinctive hollow thud of an object striking the hull of a boat.

Skelgill is frozen, barely breathing, as he listens. Now there are more sounds of the same nature, lasting for perhaps half a minute. Then a moment or two of silence is followed by the clink and rattle of a chain. Next there is the clash of wood on wood, and the dipping of oars. Someone is propelling Querrell's boat from the boathouse.

As the splash of the oars becomes more intense, a sporadic doglike whining comes and goes, in two different tones, one high-pitched, one less so.

Gingerly, Skelgill rises to his feet and unties the painter. The oarsman is making heavy weather of his task, but Skelgill still takes great pains not to betray his presence. Carefully he retrieves a long black flashlight from his rucksack. He rummages for his mobile phone and, holding it inside the bag to mask its glow, he sends a two-word text message. Then he closes the drawstring and places the rucksack in the bow. Finally, he takes up the oars, and slowly but firmly begins to pull towards the sounds from across the water.

He endeavours to time his strokes to match the other rower, although this is not easy for the latter behaves like a novice; his strokes are irregular and lopsided, with frequent clunks and great splatters.

Then the commotion ceases.

Skelgill immediately rests his oars. Under cover of darkness he has closed to within about two hundred feet, and his boat glides nearer still under its own momentum.

From the direction of Querrell's dinghy comes the grating of metal followed by a *kerplunk*. It is an anchor being lowered.

Now the animal whimpering starts up again – and Skelgill realises it too has its origin in the boat ahead of him. It is the slightly lower tone, urgent and pleading, and curiously it is answered by the higher pitched whine from the bank.

There is something in this plaintive hooning that makes up Skelgill's mind. Perhaps at this moment he finally understands what is about to happen. Without further ado he flicks on his torch and directs it at the boat.

'Police! Stay where you are! Do not move!'

The shadowy figure in Querrell's old craft has his face obscured by a balaclava or some such garment. Notwithstanding, he ducks his head from the bright beam, and immediately sets about rowing away. The dinghy has swung around one hundred and eighty degrees, and initially he begins to make frenzied progress whence he came. The whining becomes ever more insistent.

Skelgill is forced to relinquish his torch. But without trace of panic he takes up his oars and sets an interception course. Not only must he know that he has the better of his opponent in this race – his opponent has forgotten about the anchor.

Within thirty seconds Skelgill has closed in sufficiently for him to see the dinghy in the gloom, and now he increases his stroke rate to ramming speed.

At fifteen feet he gives up his oars and clambers to the front of his own craft. He perches on the forward thwart and gunwale and makes ready to board the other boat.

Six feet before they collide the masked rower jettisons his oars – and then, incredibly it seems, follows them overboard. He disappears beneath the black inky waters with a well-executed swallow-dive.

Skelgill's boat crashes into its target with an almighty clunk and he is catapulted into its stern section.

He struggles unsteadily to his feet. Ahead there is a swirl of phosphorescence as the departing swimmer surfaces and begins with quick clean strokes to make good his escape.

But Skelgill – competent swimmer that he is – does not follow suit. Lying angled across the centre of the hull is a dark form – a long black bundle wrapped in what appear to be dustbin liners. It wriggles. And it whines.

Skelgill cautiously but urgently pats at the shape in the darkness, then he tears open a slit in the thick plastic.

Glinting in the moonlight, two frightened blue eyes stare up at him.

Skelgill inhales involuntarily, choking back a sob.

He sets his jaw. 'It's okay, son – you're safe now. The cops are here.'

Carefully he checks the tape that covers the boy's mouth – it is wound several times around the back of his head and will not be easy to remove in the darkness.

'Can you breathe okay?'

The tousled ginger mop nods.

'We'll get you to the shore – take it off there, alright?'

The bright eyes signal in the affirmative.

Skelgill swiftly takes stock of his situation. The boat has no oars. Already it has drifted away from his own, invisible somewhere in the darkness. He scans the faint horizon: with his knowledge of the fells he can calculate the lie of the land, and the location of the landing stage. In any event, he can hear the swimmer, each stroke becoming fainter, who seems to be taking the same bearing.

Furiously, Skelgill hauls in the anchor and dumps it carefully in the stern, clear of the boy. Then he reaches over the bow and feels for the painter. He gives it a sharp tug to check it is secure, and feeds it through his belt at the small of his back and ties it off in a double half-hitch.

Then, like the fugitive a minute before him, he kicks off his shoes and dives from the bow into his beloved Bassenthwaite Lake.

Strong swimmer or not, it takes him a good three minutes to tow the craft to the landing stage, and he is nearing exhaustion, treading water and gasping for air, when he feels the rocky bottom with his flailing toes. He takes a few more strokes, until the level is about chest deep, and then plants his feet and begins to haul the boat, lurching backwards, the last few yards.

Suddenly he must become aware of a presence, for he half-turns and glances up. Towering over him in the darkness, silhouetted against the turquoise star-studded sky, is the unmistakable tall, gaunt figure of Dr Snyder. Above his head he wields a boat hook. As Skelgill instinctively dives to one side, Snyder brings it crashing down. It misses Skelgill, but he has nowhere to go. The water is now only waist deep and he is forced, spluttering and choking to come back to the surface. And he is tied to the boat.

Dr Snyder raises the boat hook a second time.

In a harsh voice, he calls, 'Grab it – you fool!'

Skelgill hesitates for a second – but this time the long stick comes towards him in a more controlled fashion – and he takes hold with both hands.

Now Skelgill braces his feet against one of the uprights, and Dr Snyder levers him with deceptive strength onto the rickety boardwalk. Pinned beneath the burden of a weighty oxygen debt, he is unable to rise, or even to speak. Then he glances past Dr Snyder into the blackness beyond the boathouse – for there are troubled shouts from not far away. From within the building the higher pitched whining starts up again – it can only be a dog.

But before Skelgill can react there is a clatter of feet, and onto the pontoon skids DS Jones. She points a flashlight, and stops just short of the pair. Seeing Skelgill on his knees, and the unfamiliar Dr Snyder grasping a boat hook, her posture tells she is ready to spring into the fight on the side of her colleague.

'It's okay, Jones,' Skelgill gasps, 'He's with us.'

DS Jones seems momentarily unconvinced, and keeps her torch beam full in the recoiling Dr Snyder's face. Skelgill, meanwhile, rises awkwardly and unties the painter from his belt. Then he pulls in the boat and adeptly moors it to a supporting beam through a gap in the boardwalk.

Now DS Jones's torch alights on the precious cargo. 'Wow, Guv.'

'Untie him – check he's okay.'

'Sure.' DS Jones knows this is not a moment to ask questions. She steps to the edge and with a hand down from Skelgill drops lightly into the small craft.

'Jones.'

'Guv?'

'Phone his mum.'

DS Jones nods and turns her attention to the captive.

And now there's a scream from the darkness inland, and a male voice shrieks, 'Unhand me, you oaf!'

Immediately there is an exclamation of 'Aargh!' followed in quick succession by a popular cockney expletive, a dull thud, and a long groan.

'Come on.' Skelgill beckons to Dr Snyder.

They jog in the direction of the ruckus, and after about seventy-five yards reach an illuminated torch discarded upon the grass. Skelgill directs it to reveal the substantial form of DS Leyton, pinning down his masked captive, a knee in the small of his back, and one arm twisted unnaturally around from the shoulder.

'Nice one, Leyton.'

'Bastard just bit me, Guv.'

'I heard.'

As DS Leyton is fastening handcuffs, Skelgill stoops and pulls off the balaclava.

'I am arresting you in connection with the abduction of Michael Cholmondeley, and on suspicion of the murders of Edmund Querrell and Royston Hodgson. The game is up, Dr Jacobson – or perhaps I should say Jacobs?'

*

'It was Snyder! – it was Snyder! – *I* rescued Cholmondeley! – you've got it all wrong!'

These cries fade, as Dr Jacobson is loaded into the police *Land Rover* that has bumped its way down across the school playing fields. DS Leyton accompanies the detainee, and the vehicle departs, its headlamp beams swinging erratically like wartime searchlights, picking out pink-eyed rabbits as they sabotage the cricket square. Almost simultaneously, the ambulance containing Cholmondeley – still clad in his running kit and apparently little the worse for his ordeal – falls into line with the police vehicle.

Dr Snyder, DS Jones and Skelgill – the latter holding the lead attached to Cleopatra, whom he released from her tether inside the boathouse – spectate as the convoy disappears. It is Dr Snyder who speaks first.

'What is this about *Jacobs*, Inspector?'

Skelgill does not respond immediately, his thoughts seemingly elsewhere. 'This will all become clear in due course, sir.' He is still panting, slowly recovering from his exertions. 'Funnily enough it was your certificates that tipped me off.'

'I can assure you mine are all genuine, Inspector – certificates and name.'

'I don't doubt it, sir.'

The quartet stands in silence for a moment. Even the dog seems a little subdued, shell-shocked by the events of a few explosive minutes. Then Skelgill says, in a neutral tone of voice, 'What were you doing down here, sir?'

Dr Snyder rubs his large hands together. 'I'm rather a night owl, Inspector. I needed to go out to my car – I had left a box of ring binders in the boot. It was the sound of the dog that attracted me. I imagined it had somehow escaped from Dr Jacobson's quarters.'

'So you came to investigate.'

'It all happened very quickly. I found the dog and realised the boat was gone. As I came out to look a figure burst from the water's edge and sprinted past me into the darkness. I could hear splashing sounds out on the lake, coming closer, so I waited on the landing stage. Then just before you reached the shore a commotion started up beyond the bushes as your colleagues apprehended Dr Jacobson.'

'Luckily they didn't pounce on you by mistake, sir.'

'That would have been unfortunate. Your Sergeant doesn't look like a chap to be trifled with.'

'I guess we would have sorted things out.'

'But you got your man, Inspector.'

In the gloom, Skelgill seems to shrug. He sighs with obvious relief. 'We got the boy.'

'Quite, Inspector – upon which note, if you have no objection, I shall go and report the good news to the Headmaster.'

'Sure.' Skelgill watches as he takes his leave, then calls after him, 'Dr Snyder?'

The tall figure halts in the gloom; with his long dangling arms and cadaverous head it could be a scene from a Mary Shelley adaptation.

'Do you by any chance know of the whereabouts of the ribbon from Mr Querrell's typewriter?'

Dr Snyder coughs. He clasps his hands and his gaunt silhouette takes on an air of discomfiture. 'Er, actually – yes, Inspector. I thought it might be prudent to place it in safe keeping.'

'Excellent, sir – we'll know where to find it. And please tell Mr Goodman the police will catch up with him in due course.'

'I shall convey that verbatim, Inspector.'

Dr Snyder bows deferentially and with great strides lopes away into the darkness.

As soon as he is out of earshot, DS Jones whispers in a low voice, 'What's the score with him, Guv?'

Skelgill begins to lead the dog towards the landing stage. Without turning his head, he says, 'He'll make a good witness. I think he's an insider.'

'How do you mean, Guv?'

'I reckon he's a plant – one of the *Derwen* – or at least connected. I think his CV was concocted and they managed to get him to the front of the queue for the Deputy Head's job.'

DS Jones now follows Skelgill, who continues right to the end of the creaky pontoon and lowers himself down, dangling his legs over the end. DS Jones takes a seat beside him, and then the dog casually inveigles itself between the pair of them.

'What was that about the certificates, Guv?'

Skelgill rubs his hands together as if to warm them – indeed he must be getting cold as the adrenalin in his bloodstream ebbs and the chill of the night air begins to penetrate his soaking clothes.

'I'd been looking at Snyder's qualifications, displayed on his wall – a little later I noticed Jacobson had the same kind of thing – but there was something not right about them. Then when your list came through – with the name Jacobs on it – alarm bells started to ring. I can't be certain, but I reckon he's added the extra letters – simple bit of forgery – Jacobs becomes Jacobson. Very clever – except it makes the name look off-centre.'

'But *two* Jacobs, Guv – what about that?'

'I'm not sure, Jones.'

'They were in brackets, Guv.'

Skelgill is silent. He shakes his head.

'How about the boy, then, Guv – where do you think he hid him?'

'Can't be far from here. A professor pal of mine told me about a tunnel that led from the old castle down to the lake. I've searched – there are signs in the landform. I'm sure we'll find the exit now we know what to look for. And I'll bet there's a hidden entrance in the school cellars. I reckon Querrell knew about it as well.'

'So how do you think he abducted him, Guv?'

'What's the best cover in the world if you want to hang around somewhere and not attract attention to yourself?'

'Er, dunno, Guv. Invisibility cloak?'

Skelgill ostentatiously pats the dog, which has obediently flattened itself, to lie with its snout between its extended front paws.

'Hint.'

'Oh – a dog.'

'Correct. On Saturday it was pouring with rain. None of the boys wanted to take this little lady for a walk. That suited him. The Skiddaw Challenge course runs right past this spot. Jacobson was Cholmondeley's housemaster. He probably ordered the kid over – maybe dragged him into the tunnel. I noticed traces of the dog down here – the obvious signs in the grass, you know? Then this morning he made a point of telling me the opposite. Plus he was acting like he was disabled – hobbling with a stick. He looked perfectly fit when I interviewed him in his rooms.'

'But why abduct the Chief's boy in the first place, Guv? Surely it was asking for trouble – he must have expected that all hell would break loose.'

'The boy must know something – presumably connected with Querrell. He'd overheard an argument while he was waiting outside Jacobson's quarters. Or maybe Jacobson just *thought* he knew something. It probably didn't help that we interviewed him. I imagine Jacobson found out and assumed we were onto him.'

'Thankfully he didn't drown him straightaway, Guv.'

Skelgill remains quiet for a few moments, perhaps counting his blessings. Several times in the past ten days he has sailed perilously close to the wind. 'I know, Jones. I've been asking myself why he didn't try at the weekend. Maybe, as you say, he was expecting a big hue and cry – intended to wait until it died down. He didn't bargain for Cholmondeley not being missed until Monday. Then of course we had officers on site. Until I stood them down this afternoon.'

'Was that deliberate, Guv?'

'Once I started to put two and two together, I figured maybe the fox would venture out if we called the hunt away.'

'You did well to suspect Jacobson, Guv.'

Skelgill rubs his fingers through his damp hair. 'All through this business he's given me the feeling of something not being quite right. A bit too accommodating. Quick to cast aspersions. Keen to hear how we were getting on. Trouble is, we've had this red herring of Goodman and the billionaires – despite there being something in that – which Jacobson took pains to point out.'

'I did wonder how come you were so confident about this stakeout, Guv.' Perhaps Skelgill's success frees her to admit to her erstwhile trepidation.

'To be honest Jones, your list of names was probably the trigger – even if I didn't know it at the time. There I was, staring at the word 'Jacobs', and right in front of my eyes this little kid fell into the Cocker.'

'Really, Guv?'

Skelgill nods ruefully. 'Aye – it was just by the bank – but he still could have drowned. Even then I can't say the penny dropped. I was acting on autopilot when I went back to Hodgson's flat. But the hidden press cutting – suddenly there was a connection. Once I felt sure Hodgson was part of the bigger picture, I got some sense of what it actually might be. That was probably the key piece of the jigsaw. Then lots of others started to fall into place.'

'And the *Derwen*, Guv – where exactly do they fit into all this?'

'Pass.'

They sit in silence for a while; perhaps contemplating that there is yet much to be understood about this case. DS Jones absently plays her torch beam over the calm surface of the lake.

'What about your boat, Guv? I don't see it.'

Skelgill laughs ironically. 'Trying calling my mobile – and listen carefully.'

'It might drift down the Derwent, Guv.'

Skelgill shakes his head. 'Don't worry, I thought of that. I dropped the anchor when I jumped out. She'll come to rest soon enough. The underwater search crew can bring her back for me in the morning. I reckon we've saved them a job.'

Without warning he reaches across and closes his fingers around DS Jones's wrist.

'What's that?'

'What, Guv?'

'Out there – move the beam back to the left. About there.'

DS Jones, guided by Skelgill, does as requested. After a few trial attempts, Skelgill holds her arm still. The spotlight hovers on a point about thirty feet from the shoreline.

'There, look.'

'It's just a bubble, Guv.'

'It's a bubble *float*.'

'A what...?'

'I noticed the rig was gone from Querrell's rod – and who else would fish here?'

Skelgill slides off the landing stage into the water. The dog leaps to attention and DS Jones has to scrabble for the leash to prevent the canine from following her new best friend. Meanwhile Skelgill has struck out for the almost-invisible item of tackle.

'Keep the beam on it!' He yells this as he lifts his head to breathe.

DS Jones complies as best she can – Skelgill's waves are already reaching the point where the transparent plastic float bobbles. But he seems to know where he is going. As he reaches the pool of torchlight he stretches out and grabs something. Then, treading water, he appears to tug at what must be a line. After a few moments of spluttering and splashing, he suddenly flips over and dives from sight. Twenty seconds later he surfaces like a seal, taking a great gasp of air and holding what looks like a black cylinder in one hand. Then, hampered by his prize, he rather awkwardly paddles back to the pontoon. Here he passes up a small metal flask to DS Jones. The dog bounces around, grateful for Skelgill's return, and now licks him prodigiously as he hauls himself onto the landing stage.

'Feels warm in there now. You should try it.'

'You're crazy, Guv.' DS Jones shakes the flask – it rattles. 'What is this?'

'Let's see.'

Skelgill twists off the cup and then unscrews the sealing cap. Out from the flask he tips into his palm a small shiny padlock key.

He nods several times. 'I reckon I've just worked out how Querrell met his fate.'

'Guv?'

'He was hiding this key. Maybe he was worried about it being stolen from his cottage – or even from his person. The float would act like an invisible marker buoy. He couldn't swim. So he used his boat. Crept out at night. Perhaps he'd even been lying awake thinking about it – he had no socks on. Except he was followed. All you'd have to do was tip him out. Then dress it up to look like suicide.'

'And Jacobson's a good swimmer.'

'Despite his protestations.' Skelgill points a confirmatory finger skywards. 'You know – he's got a display of swimming trophies in his study. I assumed they were prizes Blencathra House had won. I bet they're his. Now I recall, he tried to distract me when he noticed I was looking at them.'

'What do you think the key is for, Guv?'

'I've got a pretty good idea.' Skelgill nods slowly. 'Did you manage to come in your car, or do I need to hotwire the Head's Merc?'

'Unfortunately mine, Guv – nothing so exotic.'

'It'll do – at least we know the heater works.'

DS Jones reaches across and takes a grip of Skelgill's shirt. 'You're going to take some drying out, Guv.'

'We've got a forty-minute drive – I'll hang my kecks out of the window.'

DS Jones chuckles. 'What about the dog, Guv?'

'I guess she comes, too.'

33. WASDALE HEAD

'This little beauty had better fit.'

Skelgill is shivering. Despite its quick-drying properties, his outdoor clothing is still damp. DS Jones patiently holds the flashlight until he eventually manages to fiddle the key into the lock.

'Yes.'

His triumphant tone tells of success, even before the padlock snaps open. He slips it off the hasp, and pulls the door of the bothy towards them. DS Jones leans forward to illuminate the interior. The walls are of bare stone, with pew-like bench seats around two-and-a-half sides. There are a couple of low tables, an old bureau and, at one end, a log burning stove and stack of neatly chopped firewood.

'Look, Guv – oil lamps.'

Hanging from beams are two traditional hurricane lanterns. Skelgill lifts them down and gives each a shake to test for paraffin. There's a box of matches on top of the stove, and in a short time a homely glow suffuses the little cabin.

'Guv – this could be what we're looking for.'

Using her torch, DS Jones has been examining the bureau. She has folded down the lid to reveal a stack of papers of various kinds held in a manila cover. The first item is a press cutting from *The Westmorland Gazette*.

Skelgill is investigating the stove, perhaps with a view to getting it going and warming up the place.

'Guv – listen to this, from nineteen seventy-three. Twin Tragedy At Top Lakeland School.'

At the first two familiar words Skelgill's ears prick up. He freezes in a kneeling pose with his fingers wrapped around a batch of kindling. DS Jones continues to read aloud.

'Disaster struck during Oakthwaite School's annual Bassenthwaite Challenge, when a promising swimmer drowned. A P Jacobs, aged fourteen, was disputing the lead with his younger twin brother, G W Jacobs, when he got into trouble. Westmorland Police believe that the unfortunate pupil struck some underwater obstacle, such as part of a tree washed into Bassenthwaite Lake following the recent storms. Both brothers had achieved representative swimming honours at county level. Oakthwaite staff were unavailable for comment, although it is understood that the surviving twin, G W Jacobs, has been withdrawn from the school.'

Skelgill, holding his breath, now exhales audibly.

'Two boys called Jacobs.'

'Looks like you were dead right about the name change, Guv.'

'Well – he didn't deny it.'

'And the brackets – that could indicate pupils who left before their final year.'

Skelgill nods slowly. DS Jones carefully turns over the newspaper clipping, to reveal another beneath it. This one is from the *Eastern Daily Press*. A small article has been outlined in blue biro. Again she reads.

'Fakenham Preparatory School have announced the immediate departure of a schoolmaster following an incident in which another member of staff narrowly escaped drowning. The accident occurred during an outward-bound weekend on the Norfolk Broads. Dr D W Jacobs, the master supervising the trip, was apparently unable to assist his colleague, Deputy Head Graham Parker, who had fallen overboard. A police investigation revealed that the life-jacket worn by Mr Parker was defective, and had failed to inflate. The school declined to make any further comment.'

'What year was that?'

DS Jones squints at the small print in the light of her torch. 'Nineteen ninety, Guv.'

'Jacobson joined Oakthwaite in ninety-one.'

'Guv.'

'Aha?'

DS Jones holds up the sheet of newsprint. 'Do you think Querrell was blackmailing him?'

Skelgill turns his attention to the stove, and begins to feed kindling into the grate. He shakes his head.

'I think Hodgson was blackmailing him.'

He strikes a match and holds it in place until a splinter takes light. Then carefully he adds more pieces, and soon flames begin to percolate up through the little lattice that he has built. After watching for a few moments he delicately slides one of the thinner logs into position, so that the burgeoning fire licks around it.

'Hodgson was sent to find Querrell on the morning they realised he was missing. He looked first in the gatehouse. I reckon he caught Jacobson in the act of destroying evidence. The computer had been wiped, and there were paper ashes in the grate. But not everything was completely incinerated – such as the photocopy I found in Hodgson's flat.'

'That wouldn't be sufficient, though, would it, Guv? It doesn't tell you much.'

'It worked for Hodgson. He didn't have to know the story. He finds Jacobson burning a pile of papers – he'd be cute enough to work out there was something to hide. And no need to tell Jacobson exactly what he'd salvaged from the ashes. He must have thought he'd struck gold.'

'So there was a clear motive for murder, Guv.'

Skelgill adds another log, and peers critically into the stove. 'They agreed to meet at the gatehouse. It was common knowledge that Hodgson liked a drink. Jacobson took a bottle of whisky – I noticed the one on his dresser had been replaced. He gets Hodgson blind drunk. *Bang.*'

'But how did Jacobson get the gun, Guv?'

'I think we'll find he's got keys to every lock in the school. Remember, after Querrell, he was by far the longest serving master. He's had well over twenty years to look for opportunities to make copies.'

The fire is now crackling reassuringly, and Skelgill lowers himself into the most adjacent pew. Just then there is the barking of the dog – still inside DS Jones's car – followed by a polite knock on the wooden door. The pale face of a tall man peers through the opening.

'Inspector Skelgill.'

'Correct.'

Although Skelgill answers, the man in fact was making an introduction.

'We've met before, of course. I'm Copeland – from the inn.' He steps inside and holds out a hand. Skelgill remains seated. Then he turns to address DS Jones. 'Sergeant Jones. Very pleased to meet you.'

'How can we help you, sir?' Skelgill sounds a little nonplussed. This man knows their names.

'I saw the smoke, Inspector.' He studies Skelgill's still-damp attire. 'It appears that you have been somewhat tested. Rather than try to keep warm in here, may I suggest that when you have finished you come over to us? There's a log fire in the snug, and we have a night porter. He does an excellent line in hot steak sandwiches, cocoa... something stronger – be our guests.'

Skelgill turns to DS Jones. She has her lips slightly parted, and an unfamiliar look of mild awe in her eyes. 'Okay with you, Sergeant?'

'Er – sure, that would be great.'

'That's settled then, Inspector. I shall leave the front door on the latch – just ring the bell at reception when you are ready.'

And with that the man nods discreetly and backs out, closing the door carefully behind him. Skelgill and DS Jones exchange glances, as if each is waiting for the other to speak first.

After a moment, DS Jones says, in hushed tones, 'Guv – you know who that was?'

'Copeland, he said.'

DS Jones nods in an exaggerated manner. 'Guv – *Lord* Copeland. He's the biggest landowner in Cumbria. Top of the local rich list.'

Skelgill shrugs his shoulders. 'People are all the same to me.'

DS Jones shakes her head in exasperation. 'And how did he get our names?'

'He must know the Chief. She could have phoned ahead of us.'

'Strange though, Guv.'

Skelgill grins. 'Still – gift horse and all that. Let's take these papers down the road. And we'd better feed blooming Cleopatra.'

'Guv?'

'Aha?'

'*Cleopatra*?'

'That's what she's called. Jacobson's a history teacher. Daft name for a dog, I know.'

'It's not that, Guv – I studied the Ancient Egyptians for A-level. You know how Cleopatra came to power?'

'Poison?'

'Drowning, Guv. Her brother the pharaoh drowned in the Nile.'

*

'Decent ale this, Jones.'

'It's alright for some, Guv.'

'Aye, well – one of us has to keep our wits about us.'

'I could murder a glass of Chardonnay.'

'Let your hair down – we can kip in the bothy – it'll be cosy in there now. You can have the sleeping bag.'

'Ha-ha, Guv – oh, look – here comes the food.'

Skelgill sits back in anticipation while DS Jones gathers together the haul of paperwork rescued from Querrell's climbing hut. Cleopatra has been obediently lying at their feet beneath the low table, but now the scent of grilled steak proves irresistible, and she springs to attention. Fortunately she has been catered for, and the avuncular night porter makes a great fuss of presenting an expensive-looking selection of meaty offcuts. They congratulate him for his sterling efforts, and spend the next few minutes eating in contented silence. DS Jones finishes half of her portion, and slides the remainder to Skelgill, who raises an approving eyebrow as he tucks into the last of his own sandwiches.

'Guv – it's quite a pattern – now we know the history of Dr Jacobson. These drowning-related incidents.'

'His favoured M.O.'

'But his own brother, Guv? And aged fourteen.' DS Jones shakes her head disbelievingly.

Skelgill seems preoccupied with his second helping.

DS Jones frowns pensively. Then she reaches for her attaché case and retrieves the Oakthwaite leavers list. Adeptly she works her way through the pages, folding a corner here and there. When she finishes, she looks questioningly at Skelgill.

'Guv – his male line could be *Derwen.*'

'How come?'

'Look at this.' She holds out the stapled papers and flicks through to the pages she has marked. 'Our Jacobs left in nineteen seventy-three. Then there was one in nineteen fifty-one, and the last before the list ends left Oakthwaite in nineteen twenty.'

'We don't know they're all the same family.'

'Still, Guv – it's not a common name. And the time intervals are about right.'

Skelgill nods, pursing his lips. 'So what are you suggesting – he committed good old-fashioned fratricide?'

DS Jones opens her palms in exhortation. 'He was the younger twin, Guv. Wouldn't the family place on the *Derwen's* council have gone to his brother?'

'That assumes he knew about it. The guy I met at Castlerigg said they don't tell the next generation until they come of age.'

'It's by no means unlikely, though, Guv. And what about that school in Norfolk – the Deputy Head – what if that were all about ambition? Say he wanted his job.'

Skelgill has a twinkle in his eye. He is clearly impressed by the deductions his Sergeant has made. 'Okay – so take it a step further – say he wanted Querrell's job.'

'Exactly, Guv.'

'I mean among the *Derwen.* What if he were after the position of Grand Master? There's a motive for murder. At the rate Querrell was going, he was likely to outlive him.'

But now DS Jones bites her lower lip. 'Thing is, though, Guv – wouldn't the others have been wise to him?'

Skelgill is undeterred by this possibility. He shakes his head. 'Not necessarily. I think had they known, they would have acted. Snyder is obviously in the dark – whatever his connection. And Querrell might only have *suspected* that Dr Jacobson was Jacobs the schoolboy – even if he'd known him as a young teacher. Maybe he recognised him – maybe not. People can change a lot between their early teens and adulthood. I was a right ugly little squirt.'

'Now you're fishing for compliments, Guv.'

Skelgill affects diffidence, and declines to reply.

'That might have been what the argument was about, Guv.'

Skelgill nods. 'Perhaps Jacobson was pushing Querrell to stand aside. If Querrell refused to cooperate – told Jacobson he'd expose him as a fraud – he wouldn't have appreciated the danger he was in.'

'The boy may have overheard Jacobson threaten Querrell, Guv.'

Skelgill nods.

'Guv, it would explain why Querrell decided to hide the original materials and the key.'

'Pity he didn't get a chance to tell anyone. It might have saved Hodgson's bacon.'

DS Jones sighs. 'At least he had the presence of mind to do it.'

Skelgill puts his hands behind his head and stretches his back, a pensive glaze clouding his eyes. 'Just think – with those cuttings destroyed and Querrell gone, Jacobson could have laundered his past. The boy Jacobs left over forty years ago. He's history – his name's off the radar. And the school has no records – Snyder told us the archives were destroyed in a fire in the early nineties.'

'Could that have been Jacobson, Guv?'

'If I were a betting man, I'd say odds on. And once he'd got control of Querrell's alumni files, the Jacobs family would have become the Jacobsons. The *Derwen* are in turmoil as it stands. He'd be just the man they need – hails from *Derwen* stock, favours the old-school traditions, eyes and ears on the ground. They'd probably have welcomed him with open arms.'

'He's played a long hand, Guv. I wonder if he had his sights on the Head's job?'

Skelgill nods. 'We're talking a serial killer, here. Causes the death of his brother. Makes an attempt to drown one rival and succeeds with another. Blasts a blackmailer. Abducts the boy with intent to murder him.'

'It's going to be some size of court action, Guv.'

Skelgill groans. 'And I thought we were just investigating a bent Headmaster.'

DS Jones grins sympathetically. 'What of him, Guv?'

Skelgill shrugs. 'I think we'll leave that one up to the Board of Trustees. I suspect he's nearing the end of his shift in Cumbria. If they want to report him, we have a file ready.'

DS Jones nods. 'So the Chief was right to be suspicious about Querrell's death, Guv – but for the wrong reasons.'

'I think we'll find all the answers we need in here.' Skelgill reaches out and taps the manila file that lies on the table. 'But that's tomorrow's job.'

'Inspector, it *is* tomorrow.'

The voice is that of Lord Copeland, and he has silently approached bearing a tray with two filled liqueur glasses and a small decanter. He smiles benignly at DS Jones, for she is unable to stifle a sudden yawn that comes upon her.

'Since it is three a.m. I thought you might both appreciate a nightcap, Inspector. This is our secret family recipe sloe gin – guaranteed to give a good night's sleep, of which I am sure you are in need.'

DS Jones, as the designated driver, begins to hold up protesting palms, but Lord Copeland continues.

'We are fully booked, as we tend to be at this time of year. However, we keep a VIP suite – the Derwent Room. You are welcome to use it – perhaps to snatch a few hours' sleep. It has a large double, and a very comfortable chaise longue. I shan't press you – but if you decide to avail yourselves, here is the key.'

He places the small tray carefully on the table. A key with an ornate oak fob lies between the two glasses of ruby liqueur.

'And now I bid you goodnight, officers – if and when you do leave, if you would kindly pull the main door closed behind you?'

He bows courteously and turns away, a satisfied smile creasing the corners of his mouth.

Skelgill leans forwards and casually hands a glass to DS Jones. She appears to be daydreaming, her eyes fixed upon the table, but then she reaches out and picks up the key. She lifts it to eye level, dangling the fob.

'Look at this, Guv.'

Skelgill blinks several times, as if with the pendulous motion she is succeeding in hypnotising him. Then he realises what she is showing him: the wooden carving has the shape of a Celtic letter 'd'.

'Well, that explains a thing or two.'

'He's one of them?'

Skelgill shrugs, and then laughs, as DS Jones suddenly downs her drink in one.

'Guv – you know in your text – the one where you said '*Screw Smart*'...?'

'Aye – cancel that.'

'I did delete it, in case he saw it.'

'How did you get away in the end?'

'The operation got pulled. The Chief wasn't happy with the evidence.'

Skelgill tastes the liqueur and smacks his lips approvingly. 'Shame for Smart.'

DS Jones suddenly raises her hand to cover her mouth.

'Oh, Guv – I've just thought.'

'Aha?'

'What will we do with Cleopatra?'

'She can have the sofa-bed.'

***

Next in the series...

THE TIES THAT BIND

When a man is found strangled by a climbing rope beneath the lake district's notorious sharp edge, it is assumed he is the victim of a tragic accident.

But Detective Inspector Skelgill suspects otherwise, and his fears are borne out when a second corpse is discovered close to Striding Edge. Soon it appears that a ritualistic serial killer stalks Cumbria's fells.

As the body count increases, Skelgill must determine the connection between the seemingly randomly selected targets – for it is the only hope of ending the reign of terror and unmasking the perpetrator.

'Murder on the Edge' by Bruce Beckham is available from Amazon

Made in the USA
Monee, IL
22 December 2020